Queerceañera

ALEX CRESPO

HARPER TEEN
An Imprint of HarperCollinsPublishers

HarperTeen is an imprint of HarperCollins Publishers.

Queerceañera
Copyright © 2024 by HarperCollins Publishers
All rights reserved. Printed in the United States of America.
No part of this book may be used or reproduced in any manner whatsoever
without written permission except in the case of brief quotations embodied
in critical articles and reviews. For information, address HarperCollins
Children's Books, a division of HarperCollins Publishers, 195 Broadway,
New York, NY 10007.
www.epicreads.com

Library of Congress Control Number: 2023943319
ISBN 978-0-06-325740-5

Typography by Julia Feingold
24 25 26 27 28 LBC 5 4 3 2 1

First Edition

Chapter One

THE TEXAS HEAT clings to my skin like burrs, but the droplet of sweat tracing its way down the length of my spine has less to do with our janky AC and more to do with the Instagram post that's pulled up on my phone. My screen dims for the fourth time since I got out of the shower, and I tap it again so I can reread the caption.

Here's the thing: staring into space is not normally a part of my morning routine. So far, every morning this summer has been a race against time for me to get in the shower before my sister, grab a plate of whatever breakfast my dad has cooked up before it gets cold, and meet up with my best friend, April. If I spend any time on Instagram at all, it's to post whatever I've been working on to my art account and exit the app before I get the chance to start obsessing over like counts and comments.

But today, it's my personal account that's open on my phone. I've been perched on the edge of my bed for long enough that my hair is halfway dry, but I can't seem to pry myself away. The smell of a sharp and savory breakfast is drifting up the stairs, and "Baila Esta Cumbia" is blasting on the other side of the wall I share with Carmen. Both are clear signs I should already be downstairs or out the door, but right now, I need a little extra time to compose myself more than anything else.

Of course, I don't get to compose myself at all, because if I don't go down willingly, the party comes to me instead. Selena's crooning enters the hallway, and my door flings open before I can jump up and lock it.

"I think when a certain someone gets released from Mountain View, we should take a little road trip and pay her a visit," says Carmen, music still blasting from the phone in her pocket.

"Dude, it's way too early for this," I say, watching as she hurriedly sweeps her hair into a topknot. She's got the same dark curls as me, but none of my consideration for personal privacy and volume control. "You've gotta stop trying to make me an accomplice to your crimes before 10:00 a.m."

"First of all, my pitch last week to reclaim all the stolen artifacts from the British Museum and give them back to their original owners wouldn't be a crime, it would be justice. Second, this is literally what siblings are for."

"You might want to consult Dad on that one. I'm pretty sure he said sibling relationships are about unconditional love and support, not felonies and misdemeanors," I sigh, scooping up the T-shirt I abandoned after my shower and pulling it over my head.

For the wallflowers and the ones
who have to go it alone.
You deserve to be celebrated too.

"I'm shocked and disappointed. How can you call yourself gay if you're not willing to put your life on the line to avenge Selena?"

I shoot her a tired look as I grab my phone and sketchbook off my bed. "The LGBT community is not a monolith, Carmen."

"You're so right. Thank you for showing me that some of you are painfully boring," she replies cheerily. Normally we'd play-argue back and forth like this for a while, y'know, as part of the morning routine. But my heart isn't fully in it, and I know she can tell.

When I scoot past her to head downstairs, she follows close behind me. "Hey, hold up. Why are you being all quiet? Did you get another weird comment on one of your art posts? Because some people wouldn't know good art if it reached out and slapped them in the face."

Ugh. It drives me crazy when she does the creepy sibling telepathy thing. With everyone else, I feel like I can fly under the radar when I'm upset. Carmen can always see right through me, and she never hesitates to call me on my shit when she does. But she doesn't know the real reason I'm holding onto my phone for dear life, and I'd like to keep it that way for as long as possible.

"It wasn't that," I reply as I hurry down the stairs.

"So why aren't you more entertained by my sparkling commentary on the intersection of pop culture and queerness?"

"I dunno, have you considered that maybe you're not as funny as you think?"

"Nah, that can't be it. You look . . ." She takes a moment to search for the perfect word. "Constipated. Like, emotionally."

We reach the bottom of the stairs, and I turn so she can fully see the disgusted look on my face. "You're nasty. I liked it better when you were at college."

"Oh please, we both know that's a lie," she says, and I hate that she's right. "Your life would be boring as hell without me."

Carmen and I round the corner and find Tío Gael at the kitchen island, chopping up papaya and chatting with Dad as he moves between four different saucepans on the stove. Tío claps a hand on my shoulder and plants a kiss on my cheek before I fully register he's there. That's the thing about our house, there's always someone over who's technically not supposed to be.

"There's our boy," he says warmly before turning to greet my sister.

"Ah, Joaquin!" Dad booms, arms thrown wide and eyes crinkling at the corners when I move over to the stove. Everything smells amazing—one of the perks of having a pro chef for a dad. "I didn't know if you were awake yet, chaparro."

"How could I not be? I'm the only person in this family who values peace and quiet, apparently," I grumble, but when he throws an arm around my shoulders and gives them a squeeze, it's hard not to smile.

"Yes, yes, you are," he replies with a laugh that fills what little

4

quiet space is left in the room. "I need to finish prepping for the quince I'm catering later, but there's still time for breakfast."

Dad rarely takes on catering gigs now that he's become a bigger name in the Austin food scene. But he has a soft spot for quinceañeras—something about celebrating girls' transitions into adulthood with all their friends and family pulls on his heartstrings. When a friend of a friend mentioned his daughter's caterer backed out at the last minute, Dad jumped at the opportunity to save the day. He always likes helping people who are in a bind. That, and he can't resist a good party, even if it's for someone who he barely even knows.

"Shit, I forgot that was today. Do you need an extra set of hands?" I ask, but Dad shakes his head, pointing to Carmen and Tío Gael.

"Don't worry about it. I've got these two and a few temp staff who I know I can rely on," he says. Dad pushes an empty plate into my hands, taking my phone and sketchbook and placing them on the kitchen counter. "We're having chilaquiles con huevos, and I added extra guajillo just for you. Serve yourself before it gets cold."

Carmen slides up behind us before I can grab my phone again, and anxiety spikes in my chest. "Dad, doesn't Joaquin look constipated?"

He gives her the same appalled look I did on the stairs. "Mija, please. We're about to eat; no seas asquerosa."

"I don't mean it literally. I'm saying he looks upset."

"I don't have time to eat," I interject, trying my best to ignore Carmen as I hand the plate back to Dad. "April is picking me up any minute."

Dad's hand goes to his chest like I've committed some grave crime, and Tío Gael pipes up, "There's no way you can skip breakfast—not if you're going to be out in this heat."

I'm about to open my mouth to argue when out of the corner of my eye I see Carmen freeze. She's staring at my phone, and I can tell by the way her brows draw together in shock that this is the first time she's seeing the Instagram post I've been staring at for the better part of the morning.

At first glance, it looks like a pretty run-of-the-mill post from my mom. In the photo, she's standing with her new husband, Josh, and two young stepkids, Olivia and Aaron, on the boardwalk. Mom is wrapped in a pashmina, dark curls loose around her face as she smiles at the camera. Josh towers over her and has his arm around her shoulders, leaning down to press his cheek against the top of her head. Olivia clings to her dad's leg, Aaron holds onto Mom's arm, and a rainbow stretches over the Austin city skyline in the background. But then there's the caption: A rainbow is a promise of God, not a symbol for pride. Blessed to have a God-fearing family that understands.

Mom has posted stuff like that before, but this is definitely the most obvious one yet. Carmen doesn't need to read between the lines to get the jab at me, and frankly, it makes me feel like hot garbage. Not only because of the stab in the back from my mom, but also because I knew Carmen and Dad would feel awful and try to cheer me up. Again.

"You've got to be kidding me," Carmen says under her breath, and I can tell she's working herself up to either cuss our mom out, give me a pep talk, or both.

Dad and Tío Gael glance between the two of us, unsure of exactly what happened to tank the mood so quickly, and I want more than anything to avoid the inevitable looks of well-meaning pity they'll shoot my way when they read the caption for themselves. So when April honks her car horn outside, I take it as my cue to make my escape, swiping my phone and sketchbook off the counter.

"This has been great and all, but I gotta run."

"Wait, are you sure you're—?" Carmen starts.

"I'm good," I cut her off hastily. When she starts to follow me out of the kitchen, I add, "Seriously, don't worry about it."

In the front entryway, my mask of composure finally slips away, and the too-familiar feeling of shame heats up my face as I wrestle on an old pair of Converse. I'm about to grab my longboard when I hear the frozen scene in the kitchen start to come back to life. And same as I did when Mom and Dad used to fight, I can't help but pause at the edge of the hallway and listen.

Carmen is telling them about the caption, and Dad is swearing loudly in response, because of course he is. He's usually pretty lev-elheaded, but not when it comes to backhanded comments on my sexuality. I love him for caring enough to get pissed off on my behalf, I really do. But I also feel guilty for dragging him into this thing with Mom all over again.

"She knew he would see that, and she posted it anyway," he fumes, and I can perfectly imagine the way he's gesturing as he paces around the kitchen. His voice is as sharp as it used to be when he and Mom argued, and it sends a biting jab of panic into my chest. "How can she act this way with her own son? He's done nothing wrong. Nothing."

"The only perk of her living close by is that I can drive over and tell her off myself," Carmen says bitterly. I know she's bluffing because Carmen has barely spoken to our mom since the divorce. But still, knowing my sister has my back makes the lump in my throat a little easier to swallow.

When I leave the house, the sight of April's Jeep waiting for me in the driveway gets me the rest of the way there. She waves at me through the windshield, her bright smile flashing against russet skin deepened by a summer tan. No matter what's been going on in my life, for the last five years, April has always been the calm at the center of the storm. When I slide into the passenger seat, the silence inside the car feels like an oasis. Before she even says hello, April hands me the aux cord.

"No music," I groan, plopping my head against the headrest.

"Drive me to the nearest sensory deprivation chamber and throw me inside, okay?"

"Another peaceful morning at the Zoida household?" she asks wryly as backs her way down our driveway.

"You have no idea."

Chapter Two

EVER SINCE THE graffiti park on Castle Hill closed down, April and I started hanging out south of the river to skate. Cruising around Zilker instead of a skate park has some serious drawbacks, though. For one, I haven't memorized the cracks in the sidewalk well enough to avoid completely wiping out and making an ass of myself, especially when my thoughts are a million miles away.

April keeps her mouth shut when I bail once, twice, or even a third time. She only says something the fourth time, when my board flies away from me and I almost stumble headfirst into oncoming traffic.

"Are you going to tell me what's on your mind, or should I let you get run over?" April asks, offering a hand to help me up. "Whoever was driving that Prius was ready to take you out."

"If I get run over by anyone, it's going to be by a tech bro in a Tesla. I'm getting that sweet, sweet lawsuit money," I muse, ducking down to scoop my longboard up from where it had clattered down the curb and onto the street.

"You're deflecting."

"It's what I do best."

April tries to suppress her smile, but she doesn't quite manage it. When we get going again, April sets our pace a little slower so we can talk without having to shout over the sound of our wheels clacking on the pavement or worrying about taking out any slow-walking tourists.

"If you're done trying to commit insurance fraud, can we please figure out what we're doing for your birthday?"

"Summer literally just started, and I feel like you're giving me homework," I sigh. "That's cruel, you know that?"

"Hey! I'm not cruel, I'm proactive."

"What if I said I don't want to make plans?"

"Denied. We have to do something fun," April replies with a smile, shifting her weight to hop over a particularly nasty crack in the sidewalk. "Perfect summers don't plan themselves."

I'd heard her say some iteration of the same thing approximately forty-five times in the last couple of months. April is dead set on us having the most eventful, memorable summer possible. According to her, everyone waits until the summer after senior year to have their last hurrah, and she doesn't want to leave making all our best memories until the last minute.

Translation? She's freaked about senior year. And honestly, I don't blame her. The only problem is that April is a social butter-fly and insists on making me one by proxy.

"If you're not going to give me a straight answer, can we at least figure out what we're doing next weekend? Cami's parents are going to be out of town," April says, coasting beside me, and the grin on her face already tells me everything I need to know.

"Oh, cool. So she's going to have some nice, quiet alone time? Good for her," I deadpan, pushing a few times to haul myself up a hill. April squawks somewhere behind me but catches up quickly.

"It's not going to be a big party, I swear," she says, already in full begging mode. "But everyone's going to be there."

"Those are two completely contradictory statements."

"You know what I mean," she sighs, and I shoot her a question-ing look as we split apart to avoid a group of pedestrians. When we rejoin in the middle, she adds, "Everyone, like, everyone we care about. Bryce, Savannah, and Jaz already said they'd go."

"Aren't we all going to a concert in a few weeks anyways? I'll see them then."

"Well, yeah, but it's not like there's a limit on how often you can hang out with your friends," April says. "I know they'd be psyched if you came."

I mull it over as we come up on a crosswalk, letting my momen-tum taper off so I roll to a stop. It's not that I don't believe her, not really. But "our friends" have always felt more like April's friends who happen to hang out with me by extension. Just thinking of walking into a party where I only know a handful of people makes me start sweating—that is, more than I already am, since it's a million degrees outside.

"I'll think about it," I say finally. By the looks of it, April knows that's code for *no*, but she doesn't argue. Instead, she pops her skateboard up into her open hand, lime green deck littered with stickers flashing in the sun, and turns to squint down the street.

"I need to get in some AC before I melt," she says, holding her box braids away from her neck with her free hand. "The record shop is a few blocks down, want to come with?"

The sun beats down on us as we wander over, so even though the store is close by, we're both overheating by the time we duck inside. The blast of cool air that hits us as we step across the threshold feels like an actual gift from god. The owner greets April by name—both of her moms are well-known local musicians, so in places like this, she's practically royalty.

April's family is laid back in a way I used to envy when I first met her in seventh grade. We would spend hours hanging out in their at-home studio after school, and the energy was so chill that it almost felt like an alternate universe to mine. It's no surprise that April wants to follow in her moms' footsteps, or that she's set her sights on Berklee College of Music for college. As I watch her start to sift lovingly through albums, I have no doubt she's going to take the place by storm and make them proud.

And damn, suddenly my mom pops back into my head, along

with the post that I almost managed to forget while we were skating. It's not fair to compare April's moms with mine, but it's hard not to. Something pinches in my chest, not as sharp as jealousy but not as dull as real anguish. I'm in the middle of trying to parse how I feel when I turn to round a corner and run smack into a guy I hadn't even noticed was standing next to me.

"Jesus, I'm so sorry," I wheeze, positive I clipped his elbow with my board. "Are you okay?"

"You managed to get me right in the funny bone—good aim," he says with a good-natured laugh.

He's probably around my age if I had to guess. He's broader and taller than me by a long shot, not that it's a huge feat or anything. His straight, jet-black hair is pulled back into a messy ponytail, and the shorter pieces in front almost cover his eyes, but not quite enough for me to miss the way he's staring at me. He gives me a once-over while he rubs some feeling back into his arm, and the attention makes me shrink a bit.

"I really am sorry," I say, hugging my board to my chest. "I was fully zoning out."

"No harm, no foul," he assures me. I fully expect him to turn away, but instead, he leans a little closer and tips his head to the side. "I think I've seen you here before."

"Oh, probably," I say, glancing at April, who suddenly seems weirdly invested in our conversation. "My friend and I are here pretty often."

"Yeah, I totally remember you," the guy says, but he doesn't look over at April at all. He keeps his eyes trained on me as he leans on the record stand next to us. "I think you might have bought the Streetlight Manifesto album I had my eye on."

My brow furrows. "Sorry?"

"Nah, don't apologize. I can't fault you for having good taste," he says easily. "I don't know a lot of people who are into them. When I saw you grab it, I was like, I have to say hi next time I see this guy."

"Oh, yeah. Hi, I guess," I say, and he smiles a little at that for some reason. I'm not really sure why the conversation has gone on for as long as it has, or what else there is to say, so I make a break for it. As I start to sidle past him, his expression falters. "I guess I'll see you around?"

"Oh," he says haltingly. I'm not really sure why he looks so disappointed. "Yeah. I guess so."

I manage to make my way to April without assaulting anyone else, but after a second of riffling through records, I notice she's staring at me like I've grown a second head.

"What?"

"That was incredible," April says, voice low. "I've never seen anyone so completely clueless that they're getting hit on."

It takes me a second to put two and two together, but when I do, I can feel my face heat up. "All the fan fiction you read is making you delusional."

"Dude, he basically said, 'Hey, come here often?'" April says in what I can only assume is her best impression of a sultry man's voice. "You're oblivious."

"I'm not oblivious," I reply, turning back to the records. "I'm just . . . distracted."

"Oh, so you finally admit it?" April asks, but she doesn't press me on it. It's one of the things I love about her—she knows me well enough to understand I'll come to her with whatever is stressing me out eventually when I'm ready.

Truth is, April and I got close back in middle school because we were dating. The relationship was catastrophic, to say the least, equal parts April trying to convince herself she wasn't aro ace and me trying to convince myself I was bi instead of gay. I was desperate to stay in the closet as long as I could, and she kept my secret until I was ready to come out at the beginning of my junior year. She was there for all of it, so I know that if anyone could understand how frustrated I'm feeling about my mom, it's April.

She doesn't seem surprised when I finally start explaining how the morning unfolded in all its chaotic glory. We're hovering in front of "punk bands A–D" when I start venting, and we end up at "punk bands Q–T" by the time I finish.

"I can't believe her. I mean, I can, because of course she'd say something like that, but it's still seriously messed up," April says, waving the Limp Wrist album she picked up somewhere in the middle of my vent session. "*A god-fearing family*, ugh, please. I'll give her something to fear."

With April coming in at a whopping five foot nothing, it isn't exactly the weightiest threat in the world, but I appreciate it anyway.

"I still don't think she means it the way it comes off," I say, not sure if I know exactly how to make her understand. "You know she's . . . opinionated. She always speaks her mind, that's how she's been forever. But she said everything was fine when I came out, so maybe this isn't directed at me, right?"

April nods slowly, though she still looks doubtful.

This is how things had been for the last seven months. Mom has pretty traditional Catholic beliefs, but when I came out to her, she seemed okay with it. And for a while, I was really happy that our relationship felt the same as it always had. She made time to grab lunch with me and meet up with Dad at parent-teacher conferences. She came to Carmen's birthday party and cried when she hugged her goodbye at the end of the night. There were subtle, critical remarks here and there, Mom needling Carmen about her future, or hinting that I should be trying harder in school. It stung, but things felt normal.

It wasn't until later, after she got remarried, that the judgmental comments started to ramp up. She shared vague posts about "traditional family values" on Facebook, corny quotes reposted so many times you could count the number of pixels that made up every letter. I started to doubt if I could talk about being gay around her. Pretty soon, our lunches went from being full of real conversations to idle small talk. She would invite me to cookouts and days out with her stepkids, and I would say I'd try to go, but we both knew I wouldn't.

A rift formed between her and Carmen that only seemed to get wider since she was away at college, and then deepened when Mom's social media posts seemed to get more and more pointed. I'd try to put on a brave face, and Dad and Carmen and April would try to make it up to me somehow.

April pauses her search through the records to peer over at me as if she's read my mind and says, "I know it seemed innocent enough before, but things have gotten worse."

"I know. I'm just not sure where to go from here," I say as April continues to rummage through the records. "I wish I knew what was going through her head."

"At the end of the day, does it really matter? Whether she meant to or not, she's hurting you and making you doubt yourself. It's, like, intent versus impact or whatever."

I give April a sidelong glance, and she pauses. "You sound exactly like Carmen when she's doing that post-divorce thing where she acts like she's my mom now."

"She might have fed me that line the last time I was at your house for dinner, sue me," April says with a shrug, and I finally let out a genuine laugh. "Girl's gotta put every dollar of that psych degree to work. If we're not fully healed and self-actualized by the time she graduates, she should get a refund."

I chew my lip, ruminating on what April said. "I mean, I can see what you mean."

"About free therapy?"

"No. I mean, sure, that too. But about the intent versus impact thing," I say, shuffling through record after record of jazz musicians I've never heard of. "If I think about it that way, it makes a lot of sense why Carmen barely talks to her now."

"Wait, have they still not seen each other at all since Carmen came home?"

I shake my head. The last time Carmen and Mom were in the same room was in January when I won a Gold Key at the Scholastic Awards for one of my paintings. Mom seemed really proud of me, and I was riding a high all day until she made a comment about how art was a fine hobby, but not a realistic choice for a career. Carmen saw the way it put a damper on the entire day for me, and after that, I'm not sure if they've even exchanged texts let alone seen each other in passing.

"That's got to be rough," April says quietly.

"It is, even if they won't admit it. And you wanna know how Mom is overcompensating?" I ask as we move deeper into the store. "Felix. She posted the other day that he's staying with her this summer. According to all her gushing on social media, he's attending this fancy coding boot camp in Austin for the next few months."

"Felix?" she asks, hand pausing over the albums before the recognition dawns on her. "Oh, oh my god. That's her godson, right? The one she's always going on about? Isn't that the guy who—?"

"No, no, no, we are not taking a trip down memory lane. If you love me, you will not tease me right now."

"You're so dramatic."

"Well, I do hate him."

"That's funny, that's not how I remember it," she says with a laugh that turns into a cackle when my face heats up.

"Okay, yes. We used to be close when we were kids, really close, but he moved away and took up a permanent position being my mom's ahijado consentido instead. Apparently, he can do no wrong in her eyes. He's allowed to be gay without a single comment about it, but god forbid I am. Literally."

"Do you think you'll see each other at all while he's here?"

"God, I hope not," I say, trailing behind April as she moves to the front of the store to pay for her album. "I don't need to see her fawning over him only to have her turn around and criticize me."

April buys us some bottled water at the register, and we sink down onto the curb outside the shop to gulp it down. Even in the shade, the heat feels like it's trying to suffocate me.

"You're right to be mad, you know. She's being a total hypocrite."

"I know," I say, fiddling with the cap on my water bottle. "Even though I know she's the one in the wrong, it still hurts. The divorce was hard enough on its own, but coming out on top of that made it feel like everything about our relationship changed overnight. I just wish she'd talk to me."

"And then what?" April says, not unkindly, and it catches me a little off guard.

"I don't know, maybe I could get her to understand," I murmur. I can feel April's gaze on my face even though my eyes are glued to the stained laces of my sneakers. "If I could show her I'm happy, that I'm proud of myself, then it might make her more comfortable with the idea that I'm gay."

"Maybe. Or maybe you can just be happy and proud without having to change anyone's mind," she says. When I don't reply right away, she bumps her shoulder gently against mine. "I don't want you to feel like you have to shrink yourself down for small-minded people, even your own mom. You deserve to take up all the space you want."

I'm not exactly sure what to say in response, so I drop my head onto her shoulder, and she presses a warm hand to my curls. As I feel the sun thawing out the last stretch of cool skin chilled by the AC, I have a hard time picturing myself taking up any space at all in a life that feels so cramped.

Chapter Three

APRIL AND I end up staying downtown well into the evening. We post up at a little family-owned cafe, and she tells me about her most anticipated album releases as I doodle people in the sketchbook I drag around with me everywhere I go. Drawing is my biggest stress reliever, and at this point, I need all the help I can get. We only pack up and head back to her car when the light is too dim for me to see my own pencil strokes.

By the time she drops me off at home, lightning bugs are hovering over the lawn, and the neighborhood is quiet. Like morning routines in our house, nightly routines are super predictable. There's a soft glow coming from Carmen's window on the second floor, and I'd bet anything she's on her nightly FaceTime call with her longtime boyfriend, Ryan. And when I head inside, I'm not surprised when I find my dad reading *Food & Wine* on the sofa, illuminated in the warm lamp light. He has an interview with them next week on the history of Tex-Mex cuisine, and with the way he always dazzles the press, I know he's going to nail it.

"Hey," I say, dropping my keys into a little bowl on the side table. "You know you don't have to stay up and wait for me, right?"

Dad looks up from his reading with a smile. His reading glasses are perched on the end of his nose, and his gray-streaked hair is still wet from his evening shower. "I know, I know. But I can't sleep until you're home safe."

I've heard him say this a hundred times, but after the day I've had, that simple statement is enough to make me well up. Dad must have seen some emotion cross my face, because he pats the spot next to him on the couch.

When I sit, he doesn't launch into a goofy story about work or fill me in on family chisme like he normally does when it's just the two of us. Instead, he puts his magazine aside and places his reading glasses on top of the glossy cover.

"So, did you have a good day?"

It seems like a simple enough question, but we've had the same version of this conversation a dozen times now, and I think I know what he's really asking. "Dad, I'm fine. You don't have to worry about me."

"It's my job to worry about you, mijo," he says firmly, but it doesn't make me feel any less guilty. "Carmen told me about that caption, and I know you like to deal with things on your own but—"

"I talked about it with April, and I got my frustration out here," I say, rapping my knuckles against the sketchbook in my lap. "I'm good, I promise."

"I'm glad to hear that," he says. In the dim light of the living room, his expressive face is creased with concern. "I've let the relationship between you and your mom stay between you two, because I know that's what you want. But if you ever need me to step in, you say the word, okay? Carmen and I will always be here for you."

I nod, but I still want to kick myself for making them worry about me. And at the same time, I'm not sure if their concern is enough to soothe the sting of rejection I'm still feeling from Mom. Which feels silly, because when I came out Dad and Carmen weren't just accepting, they were actually excited for me. Carmen came home for Thanksgiving break with her laptop covered in Pride stickers and a never-ending list of advice on dating boys. Dad made me a three-tier coming-out cake, and I practically had to beg him not to decorate the house with rainbow streamers. He still sends me every positive news article he sees about LGBT rights, and he's more amped about my first Pride Month out of the closet than he was about Christmas.

But all that love from them doesn't fully erase the fact I want to feel accepted by Mom. It feels selfish and ridiculous to feel this way, but it's where I'm at right now. I don't know how to explain any of it to Dad, but even without vocalizing it, I think on some level he understands.

"Do you remember when we first signed you up for art lessons?" he asks suddenly, though I'm not sure exactly what prompted it or the smile spreading across his face. "You must have only been around six years old."

"I guess. Why?"

"There was a class we took you to where the teacher was always trying to 'fix' your drawings," he says. "Then we transferred you to another class, and the new teacher said they had never seen someone so young develop their own personal style like you had."

"Well, yeah. Art is subjective."

"Life is subjective," Dad says warmly. "What one person thinks is a problem could be your greatest gift. That's the kind of thing that makes you special. And, for the record, I always thought you were brilliant."

"I think you're a little biased in that department," I say, stifling a laugh.

"You bet I am," he says, patting my knee and getting to his feet. "You've always had so much to offer, and if someone isn't able to see that, it doesn't make it any less true. I want you to remember that."

"Yeah, I guess," I murmur. I understand what he means, but I'm not sure if I can really believe it.

I fiddle with the edge of my sketchbook as he tucks his magazine under his arm. But as he leaves, he pauses at the doorframe. When I look up at him, I can't quite parse the expression on his face.

"I am so proud of you, Joaquin. I can't say for sure if your mom will really understand, but if I have to be proud of you for the both of us, then I will."

I sit in the quiet of the living room a little longer, savoring the silence and contemplating what Dad said before I eventually flick off the lights and head upstairs too. I only make it up one step when I trip over something in the dark, and I don't even need to look to know it's a pair of Carmen's shoes, tossed haphazardly in the way they always were before she moved out of the house and into the dorms.

Rolling my eyes, I scoop them up and stalk up the stairs, but pause before I reach her room. Carmen's door is halfway open, the blue glow from her LED lights spilling into the hallway. I can hear her saying goodnight to Ryan on the phone, as I peek inside. She's sprawled out on the ground, in a makeshift nest of notes and textbooks from the summer class she's taking at the local community college.

I had teased her when she told me she wasn't taking the summer off, calling her a nerd for wanting to get her gen eds out of the way so she could get into lectures that genuinely interested her in the fall. But honestly, I love how much she loves school. It's one of the things that makes it hard for me to blame her for needing space from Mom, since she only ever had negative things to say about Carmen's choice to study psychology.

She was always saying little things to suggest Carmen should choose something more "useful" or "lucrative" to study. It was odd, because she would still brag about Carmen's full-ride scholarship and perfect GPA to anyone who would listen. But at the same time, it seemed like she wanted to micromanage her life, and Carmen wouldn't have any part of it. Mom's not-so-silent judgment of her relationship with Ryan, claiming that Carmen was "wasting her time" with him despite his constant doting, was another nail in the coffin for their mother-daughter relationship.

As Carmen finally hangs up and tosses her phone to the side with a content sigh, I wonder what Mom would think if she could see her now. If she could see how happy Carmen is when she's allowed to just exist, would that change her mind? I'm not really sure.

Carmen jumps a little when I shoulder her door open, and then squeaks when I toss her shoes at her.

"Stop leaving your shoes on the stairs. I almost tripped and died," I say, dodging a half-hearted slap from Carmen to join her on the floor.

"Good, you deserve it," she replies lightly. "There are a bunch of leftovers in the fridge from the quince if you want them."

"Already ate with April," I say, avoiding Carmen's notes as I lay down on the plush carpet. "She already forced me to talk about my feelings, and so did Dad. If you say anything even remotely shrink-like, I'm putting Nair in your shampoo."

"Wow, I'm sensing a lot of healthy anger here," Carmen says, slipping into a faux-agreeable tone that drives me nuts. "Where do you feel that emotion in your body?"

"*Dude.*"

"All right, I'm done. I swear," Carmen says, grinning.

"Whatever. How was catering duty?"

"Fun but exhausting," she says, stretching her arms over her head. "This girl's chambelán was late and she almost had a meltdown. It was fine, but I was low-key having war flashbacks about my own quince."

"It wasn't that bad," I say, and Carmen frowns. Her quince was beautifully organized and so fun, but it wasn't without its own drama. "It's kind of weird to think we probably won't go to one for a while. Like, for years, probably."

Elisa, our youngest cousin on our dad's side, had her quince last year. Dad catered it, and the whole thing was bubblegum pink and boisterous and so *her* that it makes me smile just thinking about it. But Carmen and I are the babies of the family on our mom's side, with the rest of our cousins in their 30s and starting families of their own. Most of our family friends are on the older side, so the odds of us getting invited to any quinces in the coming years are slim.

"Huh, I guess you're right," Carmen says. "I hadn't thought of that before. It's kind of a bummer, isn't it?"

"Yeah, I guess it is," I say with a sigh. "It was nice knowing we'd be able to see the whole family in one place. And seeing everyone so focused on celebrating that one person and making them feel special is always sweet."

I stare up at the lights shifting on the ceiling and think back to when we went to quinces multiple times a year, back to when things between Mom and Dad were still good. We would all get ready together, the house brimming with music and laughter. There was this tangible excitement and joy in the air that was hard to replicate outside of events like those.

Dad helped me knot my tie until I learned to do it myself, and when he spritzed me with his cologne, I felt so grown up. Mom always helped Carmen do her hair and makeup, and the memory of them giggling together over the bathroom vanity feels so close and distant at the same time.

"It really is sweet," Carmen says, and when I glance over at her, she seems deep in thought. She looks over at me, brows pulled together, and I almost ask what she's thinking. But suddenly she laughs and says, "I guess we are getting old. Next, we're going to start getting invites to weddings and baby showers, huh?"

"Ew, stop, that makes me feel ancient. I don't want to think about it," I say with a grimace, and Carmen laughs again.

"See, right when I start thinking you're all grown up, you say something that proves you're still a baby. When Ryan and I get married, we won't invite you."

"Good. If I have to listen to you two talk about how much you love each other for hours, I'll hurl," I say matter-of-factly. Carmen reaches out a hand to shove my face, and *ugh*, she absolutely smells like she was in the kitchen all day. "Dude, you reek. Get your oniony hands off me."

Carmen sits up, looking horrified. "Shut up, I'm about to take a shower."

"Hell no. I was out sweating in the sun all day. I'm taking mine first!"

We both glare at each other for a second and then scramble toward the hallway. Carmen tries to yank me back by the collar of my shirt, but I've had years of practice dodging her. She swears at me when I shut the bathroom door in her face, and I cackle as Dad calls out from the other end of the house begging us not to kill each other. It's stupid and ridiculous, but it's the kind of familiar chaos that makes me feel like things aren't so bad after all. As steam fills the bathroom, I let the hot water wash the rest of my worries down the drain.

Chapter Four

THE NEXT MORNING, I sleep in for way longer than I have in years. I'm disoriented when I check my phone and see the time, and it takes a second for me to realize why. There isn't the smell of food wafting up from the kitchen, and there isn't any music playing on the other side of my wall. The whole house is dead silent.

The first thing I think is that everyone has been wiped off the face of the Earth overnight, and I'm the only one left, *I Am Legend*-style. But when I go downstairs, I can hear Dad and Carmen talking in hushed tones in the kitchen. Well, as hushed as two very loud people can manage. They're hunched over Dad's laptop at the kitchen table, backs turned to me.

"What's wrong?" I ask from the doorway, and they both almost jump out of their skin. "Did someone die?"

"What? No," Carmen says, ushering me into the room. She's got the same look on her face as she did in fifth grade when she decided to steal my diary and do a dramatic reading at the dinner table. "Come sit."

"I'd rather stand," I mumble, glancing between the two of them. "You're kind of freaking me out."

"Carmen and I were talking a little bit this morning," Dad says, eyes twinkling. He's all earnest, watching my expression with barely contained glee. "We know it's been a tough year, and we wanted to find some way to celebrate."

"Celebrate what?"

"You," Carmen says, like it's the most obvious thing in the world. "Do you know about queer prom? I guess they're getting pretty popular, from what I read online. Apparently, they even had one downtown last year."

I nod along, but I can't imagine what they're getting at. It's always made me happy that events like that exist, but it's not the kind of thing I'd feel confident going to myself. I've never even gone to homecoming, despite April trying to drag me with her every year.

"Well, we were reading all about it, and we thought it would be wonderful to do something like that for you. And then our conversation last night got me thinking, and it hit us," she says, clapping her hands together. "We can throw you a—Dad, what did you call it?"

He finally steps aside so I can see what's on the laptop screen, and when my eyes land on the brightly colored images they have pulled up, my heart falls into my ass.

"A queerceañera," he says, smiling from ear to ear. "Like a queer quinceañera. Get it?"

I look between the two of them in utter disbelief. "You're kidding, right?"

"Not at all," he replies cheerily, and unfortunately, I can tell he's dead serious. "Doesn't it sound incredible?"

"That's—" *Impossible*, I think. *Ridiculous. Completely out of the question.* "I'm seventeen years old. And I'm a boy."

"Details, details," Carmen says, planting her hands on my shoulders and steering me in front of the laptop. When I see they've already started a mood board with theme concepts, I start to wonder if this whole conversation is an elaborate nightmare. "It would still hold the same meaning. It's to celebrate your coming of age and into your identity."

"Oh! And it's perfect because your birthday falls during Pride Month," Dad adds, clearly pleased with himself that he's made the connection.

They're both looking at me like I'm going to throw my arms around them and thank them for the fabulous idea, but I feel like a deer caught in headlights. There are a thousand reasons this won't work, most of which start and end with the fact our entire family would have to be invited. I haven't seen most of them since before I came out and facing them all at once feels like a disaster waiting to happen.

"It would cost a lot of money," I blurt out. "I don't want you to spend anything on me, especially not when we're saving up for college. I'm not—"

"We would have spent a little on your eighteenth birthday anyway," Dad interrupts, squeezing my shoulder eagerly. "And I talked to your Tía Fernanda—you know she does party planning now, yes? She can handle all the flowers and the rental services for free."

I feel the blood drain out of my face. "You already told her about this?"

"And she loved it," he says, beaming at me. "Let me get my phone. She sent me some ideas in the family chat on WhatsApp."

My jaw is practically on the floor, and not in a good way. The second he leaves the room I turn on Carmen.

"Oh my god, you let him put it on WhatsApp without asking me first?" I hiss at her, and she rolls her eyes like they hadn't just committed one of the cardinal immigrant family sins. "What's next? Are you going to rent a billboard? No, better yet, hire a sky-writer so everyone can see it from Mexico."

"Okay, so I'm getting the vibe you're not thrilled about this."

I suck in a deep breath and finally sink into the chair in front of the laptop. I'm not mad at them. I don't have it in me to be angry when they're both so excited. It sounds fun in theory, but this isn't *me*. I don't like attention or fanfare, especially not if it revolves around my coming out.

"I appreciate what you're trying to do here, but this is way too much," I say with a sigh. "Is this about Mom? Because I told you, I'm fine."

"It's not. I mean, not entirely," she says, pulling out the chair next to me. "I talked to Dad last night, and when I mentioned what you said about how we probably wouldn't be going to any more quinces, he really fixated on that. And the more he talked about it, the more I understood what he was getting at."

"Really? Because I'm still lost."

"You said it yourself. Seeing everyone rally around one person is really sweet. And it's not just the event itself—it's everything leading up to it," she says, and for a second, I *do* get it.

Carmen's quince was five years ago, but I still remember the party planning like it was yesterday. The way everyone on both sides of our family pitched in, the pride on our parents' faces when Carmen showed them the dress she'd picked out. It felt good that everyone was working toward the same goal. It felt special.

"Think about it for a sec," she says, pressing on. "You're going to be off to college next year, and who knows if we'll ever have time to pull something like this off again. It's something we can all do together, something to remind you that you have a support system."

"But can't y'all support me in private? Like, in a low-key way?" I ask, laughing a little at the sheer absurdity of the situation, and Carmen joins in.

"You and I both know low-key is not a part of our vocabulary," she says, scrunching her nose. "We really want to do this for you. And I'm not saying you should do it for me or for Dad. I'm saying you should do it for you. This could be a really good thing."

"I guess, I don't think—I'm not sure if I deserve all this attention."

"You do deserve this," Dad says behind us. "And we're not the only one who thinks so."

Dad hands me his phone, and the messages flooding the family group chat are not what I was expecting. There are questions, many of them the same as the ones I've been asking myself. But there's also my cousins who I haven't seen in years who are figuring out when they can book their tickets to fly to Austin. There's Tía Regina asking if I'd need help with my hair, and there's Tío Gael offering to get me a custom suit for the special day.

I can hardly believe it, but they really seem like they're on board. And for the first time in ages, I feel like maybe, just maybe, other people are going to be as proud of me as I am of myself.

"What if someone gets offended? I know Abuelo can be pretty uptight. I don't want to make him uncomfortable," I say, but I instantly feel sheepish as the words leave my mouth.

"Screw 'em," Carmen says with a grin, echoing my thoughts. "We've got your back."

"I couldn't have said it better myself," Dad adds, placing a steady hand on my shoulder.

I'm not sure if it's the extra sleep that's gone to my head, or if Dad and Carmen have been working overtime to perfect their pep talk routine, but I'm considering saying yes. I'm sitting there chewing the inside of my cheek when April's words come back to me from the day before. *You deserve to take up all the space you want.* And suddenly, I don't feel like this queerceañera thing is the worst idea in the world. I'm not sure if I'm ready for any of it, but I think I could be.

"Okay," I say after a deep breath. "Let's do it."

Chapter Five

IT ONLY TAKES about twenty-four hours for me to start doubting my decision.

Honestly, Dad and Carmen are driving me insane. Under any other circumstances, a quince would take six months or more to plan out in its entirety. But since my birthday is in less than a month, they both jump into party-planning mode the second I say yes, which is mostly them bombarding me with dozens of questions I don't know how to answer.

"I already told them there's no way I'm going to have a traditional quince court," I say, trailing behind April as she heads down the stairs. I ended up staying at her place the night before, but we both know I can only hide out and be melodramatic with her for so long before having to face reality. "And there's no way I'm inviting any of our friends to this."

"Wait, why not?"

"You know exactly why not. I'm not going to subject them to the absolute chaos that is my extended family. They probably wouldn't want to come anyways," I say, and April looks like she's about to argue, but I keep talking. "Carmen wasn't happy with that either. And she said if I don't have a formal court, then I at least have to find a chambelán. And to do it as soon as humanly possible."

"The chambelán is like your escort, right? Or like your date?" she asks, heading into the kitchen.

"Yeah. How am I supposed to find a chambelán in a week if I haven't been able to find a boyfriend in seventeen years? I told her that forcing me to find a date was upholding outdated and patriarchal social norms about companionship."

"Could be really compelling commentary if you weren't just saying it to be avoidant."

"That's what she said too. But there are a hundred other things I don't want to deal with. I'm going to have to sign off on a venue, approve the guest list, and hire a photographer," I sigh as April rummages through the pantry. "I still can't believe they tricked me into saying yes."

April laughs, only because she knows I'm not even taking myself seriously at this point, and I don't expect her to either. "Tricked you with what—their genuine love and support?"

"I was swept up in the moment! It was psychological entrapment, April. I'm a victim."

"Unless you plan on suing them for emotional damages, you're going to have to face them eventually," she says. "Pancakes or cereal?"

"I'm not sure I can eat," I reply, but she slides me a bowl and spoon for cereal anyway.

I slide my phone onto the island counter and slump down into the seat next to her. I know avoiding the problem won't make it disappear. Muting my notifications so that I haven't had to see the constant stream of WhatsApp messages from my family certainly feels like it could, but April is right.

"I never know how to talk to my dad when he's like this, and Carmen is all invested too," I say as she fills our bowls with cereal. "How am I supposed to tell them that I might want to call the whole thing off?"

"Is that what you're leaning toward?" she asks, and I'm surprised that my knee-jerk reaction is to say no, I don't want to cancel the event. But then I think about it for another two seconds, and I change my mind again.

"I don't know," I groan, burying my head in my hands. "My brain automatically goes to the worst-case scenario. What if this whole thing is, like, misrepresenting gay people to my extended family or something? What if it leaves a bad taste in everyone's mouth?"

"You shouldn't have to be the ambassador for the entire LGBT community," April says, and even though she's pointing out the obvious, it feels nice to hear it from someone else. "Plus, you already identified the main issue. You said you're focusing on the worst-case scenario, but have you thought about the good things that could come out of this?"

"Like what?"

"This is a good opportunity to push yourself out of your comfort zone. And who knows, there might be a silver lining to all this that you don't even realize yet," she says, nudging my phone toward me. "Maybe the first step is checking your messages."

"I hate it when you make sense, you know that?" I say, already typing in my password.

"Totally, I'm the worst."

When I look at my notifications, a good chunk of them are from the family group chat. There are a dozen texts from Dad and Tía Fernanda asking for my opinion on vendors, and another handful from Carmen threatening to kick my ass if I don't come home and help them out. But there's one text that's not from either of them—it's from my mom.

I heard about the party you're planning, the text reads. We haven't had lunch together in a while. Maybe we can get together and talk about it then. How's Friday?

And as if that weren't enough, there's another text right below it, time-stamped a few minutes after the first: Felix would like to come too.

April leans over to take a peek and freezes.

"Uhhh, maybe you were right to avoid reading your texts," she says, eyes flitting between the screen and my bewildered expression. "What do you think it means?"

"I literally have no idea," I say, still processing as my eyes scan the screen again. "She's right though, we haven't seen each other in a bit. I'm surprised this is what made her want to reach out."

"I wonder what she wants to talk about," April says, brows pulled together.

"She was super involved when Carmen was planning her quince. Maybe she doesn't want to be left out," I say. It takes a second, but then something clicks. "Wait, what if this is the silver lining you were talking about?"

"Huh?"

"For the queerceañera. I mean, planning Carmen's quince was the last time I really remember us feeling like a family. Mom was so invested in it going well. Maybe this can be a sort of reminder of that."

"I guess I didn't think you were going to get her involved."

"Neither did I. But I don't know—maybe this is our opportunity to find some common ground," I reply.

It's a long shot for sure, and part of me wants to skirt around her invite to lunch and avoid the topic altogether. But I can't remember the last time I had an opening like this to make some progress with Mom.

"Yeah, maybe," April says softly, though I can't quite read her face. "But what about Felix?"

My eyes scan the text and land on Felix's stupid name again. "He's irrelevant."

"Oh, please," April says, instantly seeing through my bullshit. "You told me ages ago that Felix was your first kiss, and you clam up every time I've asked you to tell me more. That's highly relevant if you ask me."

"Okay, yes, we kissed one time. But it's way more complicated than that. Felix and I were—" *Inseparable,* my brain supplies. *Best friends. More than that.* "He was my person. Felix is the son of my mom's best friend, so we were basically attached at the hip since birth. I was obsessed with him, and I thought he felt the same about me. He was, like, my gay awakening before I knew what being gay even meant."

April hits me with puppy dog eyes. "Oh my god, so he was your first love?"

"I'm not sure if you can really be in love at eleven years old," I reply, but I'd be lying if I said I hadn't thought the same thing for years.

Felix was whip-smart, unbelievably funny, and confident as hell. We went to different elementary schools, but he came to our house after classes were over more often than not. In the summers, we were with each other almost 24-7, and it felt almost inevitable that I'd fall for him as hard as I did. I was captivated by him, but it wasn't that he was the sun and I was in his orbit. He always made me feel special too. He made me feel like *me.*

I shake my head like I can physically shake those useless,

too-soft ideas out of my brain. "It doesn't matter either way, because he moved across the state at the end of sixth grade. We promised we'd talk every day, but all of a sudden, he stopped picking up the phone when I called. We haven't spoken to each other since."

"Ouch, that's cold. Even I would be pissed if someone did that to me," April says, and I ignore the not-so-subtle implication that I tend to be a little overdramatic at times. "Why do you think he's tagging along for lunch after y'all haven't talked for so long?"

"Curiosity, maybe? Or he wants to make himself feel better about ghosting me, I don't know. Like I said, he's irrelevant," I say firmly, because it might be the only thing I'm absolutely sure of at the moment.

April watches as I unlock my phone one more time. Nervousness about the queerceañera is still sitting heavy in the pit of my stomach as I reread the text from Mom, and I can't tell if getting her involved would help it ease up or make it worse. Instead, I switch to the chat where Tía Fernanda has been sending vendor options. It's flooded with questions, links to small businesses, and messages littered with dozens of exclamation marks. I can't help but smile a little at her enthusiasm. Before I make a decision about any of this, I should at least see what she has in mind.

Chapter Six

PREDICTABLY, TÍA FERNANDA is over the moon when I agree to go to her place and look at her initial ideas for the queer-ceañera. She clears her afternoon, and I head straight there from April's house.

I'm still trying to avoid going home like the plague, and now my mom's text about lunch is swimming around my head too. But as I pull up to my tía's apartment complex, a little sense of peace washes over me. This isn't the first time I've sought her out instead of heading home and dealing with whatever I have going on in my life, and I'm sure it won't be the last.

When Carmen and I were younger, we had a phase where we fought like crazy from the moment we woke up to the second we went to bed. One day, I threatened to run away if she wouldn't leave me alone. I have no idea how Tía Fernanda even found out about it, but she picked me up from school every day for the rest of that week and let me hang out at her apartment until I cooled down.

Then there was the divorce, when our house felt too tense and suffocating to focus on schoolwork. When Mom was moving out, Carmen and I slept over at Tía Fernanda's place almost every night for a month. We couldn't be around the boxes and packing peanuts and tape, so Tía kept us busy making vegan cinnamon rolls and solving puzzles instead. It gave me breathing room to figure out how I felt about everything, and now I'm hoping I can do the same.

I park in a guest spot and follow the hedges and carefully manicured flower beds into the lobby. The building itself is sleek and minimalist, all sharp angles and shiny finishes, and my ears pop on the way up to the seventeenth floor. I only have to knock on the apartment door one time before it flings open.

"Come in, come in!" Tía Fernanda says, planting a kiss on my cheek and ushering me inside. She's wearing a linen dress embroidered with flowers and tangling vines that falls all the way to the floor. Her short-cropped hair is perfectly coifed as ever, curls arranged in carefully gelled finger waves. "How's my favorite ahijado?"

"I'm your only godson. I shouldn't win that title by default."

"Of course you should, don't be silly. If I can't be biased about you, then who can?" she asks, and my thoughts flit to Felix. Except no, hold on, I am not thinking about him. Nope, absolutely not. "You didn't answer the question though, mi cielo."

"Oh, I'm fine," I reply when my brain catches up. Tía's brows pull together at the lackluster answer, and god, sometimes she's so much like Dad it freaks me out. I quickly correct myself, saying, "I mean, not just fine. I'm good. Really good."

"Excellent. Now come, make yourself comfortable," she says, shooing me toward the sun-drenched living room. I almost trip over her cat, Luna, on the way, a pure white puffball who's always loved me or loves the attention I give her. "You want something to eat? Drink? I have homemade kombucha if you want some."

"Water would be good," I say, sinking into her plush couch. The second Luna sees my lap is open real estate, she jumps up and makes herself at home.

As I run a hand through her cloud-soft fur, I do feel a little of the tension I've been carrying dissipate. The apartment could feel sterile and modern with its massive windows and stark white walls if that's what Tía Fernanda wanted. But it's easy to feel at home here—she's filled it to the brim with tropical plants, crystals, and books about healing. There are even some prints of my art hanging on the walls, anatomy studies and small portraits from life drawing classes, which she insisted on paying for even though I would have gladly given them to her for free.

"I'm so glad you stopped by. It feels like it's been ages," Tía Fernanda calls out from the kitchen, and I can hear the smile in her voice. We see each other in passing all the time, because like Tío Gael, she pops in and out of our house without much warning. But she's always happy to get one-on-one time with me, and the feeling is mutual. "Now that Carmen is back for the summer, I insist we do something fun together. Without your dad, though. We don't need him cramping our style. How about a little yoga retreat? Oh, or a relaxing beach day?"

"I'd love that, and so would Carmen," I call back, and Luna meows up at me from my lap like she wants in on the plans too. "We haven't been able to do much lately since Carmen is busy with class."

"And that cute boyfriend, I hear," Tía Fernanda says, breezing back into the room. She's holding ice water with what I have to assume are edible flowers floating on top in one hand, and a plate loaded with carefully cut veggies, olives, and crackers in the other. "What about you?"

I reach up to help place the snacks on the table, careful not to jostle Luna too much. "What about me?"

"Is there anyone special in your life?" Tía Fernanda asks with a wry smile, and I laugh a little.

Unlike the entire rest of my extended family, I know she's not asking to be nosy or report back to everyone else about my love life. She was one of the only people who didn't press me on why I didn't seem interested in dating when I was growing up. I have no idea if she suspected I was gay and kept quiet on purpose, or if she was just respecting my privacy. Either way, I'll always be grateful for the space she gave me back then.

Since I came out, she does ask me about boys a little, but never in a prying way. She brings it up as casually as if she were talking to Carmen or any of my cousins about their love lives, like the fact that I'm gay is no big deal, and it feels really nice. Still, it's not like I have anything interesting to report back.

"I'm not seeing anyone. If I were, you'd probably be the first to know," I reply honestly, taking a sip of my water.

"You know, I heard Grindr—" she starts earnestly, and I almost do a spit take. "What? You don't use dating apps?"

"I mean, no, but I wouldn't exactly call it a dating app," I say once the danger of choking has passed, but then decide against going down that rabbit hole for the time being. "How do you even know about stuff like that?"

"I'm a very worldly person," she says, leaning down to scratch Luna behind her ear. "I may be getting older, but I'm not going to end up like your dad, scrolling on Facebook every day."

"Please do not talk to my dad about the intricacies of Grindr."

"If you insist," she replies lightly.

"How's work been?" I ask, hoping to redirect her attention, and it works like a charm.

"Oh, it's been amazing," Tía Fernanda says warmly, turning away to rummage through a bookcase on the far wall. "I've gotten to meet so many new people through this and seeing them so happy never gets old. It's more time-intensive than I thought, but I don't think that's a bad thing. You know I like to stay busy."

I hum in agreement as she pushes some pothos vines out of the way to thumb through an array of colorful binders. Event planning is a new endeavor for her, but from what I've heard, she's already got a massive client list. Before that, she was a Reiki healer for a while, and before that, a freelance astrologer.

She's been traveling and doing odd jobs ever since my tío passed away. Dad said becoming a widow changed her perspective on life, but I've never known her to be anything other than the free spirit of the family. I've always thought it was cool that she does whatever she wants, moving on when her latest fascination no longer interests her. Abuelo still seems a little perplexed by it, but Dad thinks it's a brilliant way to live.

"Ah, here you are," she says, tugging a purple binder off the shelf that looks way, way too full to make any kind of sense.

"That's not for the queerceañera, is it?" I ask. There's no way she got that far into planning, right? It's only been a day.

"It is!" she says with a warm smile and my heart plummets. "I might have gotten a little carried away."

"None of it is set in stone, is it?" I ask, barely managing to keep the panic out of my voice.

"Well, there are some vendors that I'll leave up to you, but some I have to insist we go with," she says, flipping the binder open and thumbing through some of the tabs. "Caterer is easy, keeping it in the family and all. There's a florist at a nursery in Round Rock that charges criminally low for centerpieces, so I already know we're going with them—"

She keeps flipping through options, pointing out the ones she thinks are easy yeses, but I'm not fully listening. I knew that Dad and Carmen were going to get ahead of themselves, but this? This is on a whole other level. A cold bead of water from the glass in my hand drips onto my finger, icy against my skin as my stomach twists with guilt.

"I . . . didn't realize that you'd done so much work already," I say when Tía Fernanda pauses for a moment.

"It's not as much as it seems. That's the fun thing about this job, I'm pulling from a list of vendors I already have relationships with, so—" She stops suddenly when she catches my eye, hands still on the pages. "Oh, that's not a good look. What's wrong?"

"I'm not sure this is the best idea. Not about you planning it. You obviously know what you're talking about. It's just . . . the whole thing. I'm a little worried that it's too much," I say, and the way her expression softens makes me feel worse somehow. She abandons the binder and sits back on the couch, turning to face me fully.

"I didn't know that. I thought you were excited."

"I was, for a minute," I reply. "But then I started, you know, thinking."

"That's never a good thing," she says wryly, managing to get a little laugh out of me. Still, the pressure on my chest hasn't eased up. "What is it that you're worried about?"

"Well, for one, I haven't seen most of the family since I came out."

The one perk of having a big chunk of my family in a whole other country was that I didn't have to come out to them face-to-face. We could have done a group call, but the thought of it alone made me break out in a cold sweat. So I went about it another way—I had Dad talk to Abuelo one-on-one first and then wrote my family a letter that I shared on our WhatsApp family chat.

Even with that layer of separation, it was still the most terrifying thing I'd ever done. I couldn't bring myself to check my notifications until Carmen gave me the all clear to look, promising me that everyone was being supportive.

"But everyone was so happy for you when you came out," Tía Fernanda says, and the sincerity in her voice makes me want to believe her so, so bad. "And they're excited for you now too! You've read the group chat, no?"

"I have, but what if they're just saying that? What if they're uncomfortable and don't want to say it to my face?"

Her brows go up for a second, her expression half surprised and half crestfallen, and I feel like she can see right through me. She knows I'm talking about Mom even if I don't say it out loud. She probably knows about Mom's latest Instagram post too. If Dad didn't tell her, then Tío Gael must have, since he was there when Dad and Carmen were discussing it in the kitchen.

That's how our family works, for better or worse. Either way, it's not like Carmen and my issues with our mom, or anything about the divorce, is some big secret. Our relatives don't bring up the divorce, not directly at least, but they know it's been hard on us. They know things aren't the way we want them to be.

"I understand why you might think people are only telling you what you want to hear," she says carefully. "I can't speak for everyone, but as for me? I would never lie to you. When I say I support you no matter what, that I want to celebrate you, I mean it."

She rests her hand on my cheek, warm and sincere, and I honestly do believe her. I believe she wants this to be a good experience for me and can almost believe everyone else does too.

I take a deep breath. "I want to be excited. I just don't know why this all feels so . . . scary."

"Because it *is* scary. It's scary to let people in," she says, and then points to one of my prints hanging on the wall. "I remember when you didn't want to show anyone your art."

"Posting it on social media still freaks me out sometimes," I reply.

"But you do it anyways, right? Sometimes, you have to put yourself out there to see what comes back," she says. "People can't meet you halfway unless you let them. So if you're up for it, give us a chance, okay? Let us show up for you."

I nod, eyes flicking back to the prints on the wall as I consider what she's said. "I'm still not sure why I let you pay for those."

"It's simple. I had to be your first paying customer. That way when you get famous, I can resell them and make a fortune," she says, smile spreading into a grin as I start laughing.

But beyond the silly joke, something has finally settled in my chest that's felt restless and uneasy since yesterday morning. I finally feel like I've fully settled on my decision, and I want to go ahead with the queerceañera. I want to put myself out there and see what comes back.

Even so, Tía Fernanda doesn't push me to make any decisions about the queerceañera for the rest of the afternoon. We chat about my art, and she helps me weigh the pros and cons of opening commissions even though I'm not sure I'll have time for it when school starts again. I tell her about April's mission to craft the perfect summer, and she suggests a road trip to Tijuana. I can't tell if it's a serious suggestion or not.

But in the back of my head, what she said stuck with me. I turn her words over in my head as I drive back to my house, spacing out at stoplights and wondering if letting people show up for me includes giving Mom the same chance.

By the time I pull into my driveway, I know the answer. Before I head inside, I pull out my phone, open my texts, and agree to meet up with her on Friday.

Chapter Seven

I MAKE TWO huge mistakes when I show up for lunch.

My first mistake is getting there fifteen minutes early, which means I have fifteen extra minutes to make myself even more nervous than I already am. I stayed up half the night trying to imagine what Mom is going to say to me, and then spent the other half wondering why on earth Felix has to be there to witness it.

Talking about him with April must have broken some dam inside my brain, because even when I get to the restaurant, I can't seem to stop thinking about him. It's stupid. For all I know, he could be a totally different person than the kid I remember. I don't know if he's going to be the same boy who carried me home on his back when I skinned my knee, or picked wildflowers from my backyard and wove them into my curls. There's no guarantee he's the same boy who stood at the end of my driveway the day he moved away, wiping the tears that were streaking down my face.

This kind of brings me to my second mistake, which is letting the hostess seat me outside. It seemed like a good idea in theory, but I'm so on edge that I tense up every time a dark-haired woman or a guy my age walks by. And I'm only, like, 80 percent sure I know what Felix looks like now. Every time Mom has posted a photo of him on Instagram, I've scrolled past it as fast as I could. I don't think he could have changed that much—I doubt that he outgrew his dimples that always made him look younger than he really was, or suddenly gained the ability to tan without burning first, a curse passed down from his Irish dad. But another part of me panics that he might walk right by without me even noticing I wonder if I'd recognize him even if I looked him right in the eye. But it turns out I don't have to worry. Because when I'm nervously checking my phone for the four hundredth time, I hear someone call out from the opposite side of the patio.

"Jay," he says, voice octaves deeper than the last time I heard it. I don't need to look to know it's him, because there's only one person in the world who's ever called me by that nickname.

Felix is somehow exactly the same as he is in my memories and totally different at the same time. He's got the same slim build as when we were kids, and his deep brown eyes still look like resin when they're in the sun. But his hair is grown out, light brown pieces of it falling around his face and curling against his neck, and the full cheeks that gave him a baby face for years are long gone.

My heart clenches suddenly, and I realize I feel hurt that he grew up and I wasn't there to see it. But I don't have time to dwell on it, because Felix closes the gap between us in three long strides and pulls me into a bone-crushing hug.

It knocks the wind out of me, half from force and half from shock. Last time I checked, we were basically strangers, so I'm not entirely sure what he's doing. But damn, he's *tall*. We used to be eye to eye, but now he's towering over me by half a foot. And he's got biceps, and a killer jawline, and—

"You have a nose ring," I say stupidly, and when he grins down at me, it makes me want to burst into flames. He looks good, really good, and I kind of hate him for it.

"Oh god, yeah," he says, lifting a hand to his face like he forgot it was there. "My friend and I got matching ones on a whim, it was dumb."

It's not dumb, I think before I can stop myself. *It's cute.*

When Mom clears her throat behind me, I almost jump out of my skin. Her curls are pulled back from her face in a loose twist, and I recognize her sundress as one Carmen bought her for Mother's Day a few years back. Mom looks bronzed and glowy like she always does in the summers, but her expression is a little pinched. I don't understand why until she glances between me and Felix, and my face heats up when I realize I'm still standing very, very close to him. Too close for her liking, apparently.

"Joaquin," she says quietly. "People are looking."

I step back from Felix and greet her, leaning in to give her a quick kiss on the cheek, and glance at the neighboring tables. Nobody is paying any attention to us at all. I want to point it out or tell her that two guys hugging really shouldn't be a big deal, but I don't say anything. I slip into my chair, and they settle in across from me. Felix looks a bit deflated too, but Mom didn't say his name, did she?

We order our food quickly, but once the menus are taken away, I feel weirdly exposed. Am I supposed to start talking first? I don't even know exactly why we're here.

Felix clears his throat. "You, uh, look older. I mean, of course you do, you literally are older. Not in a bad way though. You look fine. I mean, you look good."

"Um, thanks?" I reply, but it comes out sounding more like a question than anything else. Is he making fun of me? We haven't seen each other in six years, and that's all he has to say?

"You do look well. And your hair is so much longer," Mom says. She reaches out to brush a stray curl out of my eyes, and it's one of those moments where I feel like a little kid again. It's the kind of gesture that has always been so normal between us, fingers brushing my forehead to check for a fever or comfort me after a bad day at school. It's the kind that I've really missed. "How have you been?"

"I've been good," I start to reply, but I'm not exactly sure how to elaborate. Is it too soon to bring up the queerceañera? Would it make her feel awkward if I mentioned Tía Fernanda? Finally, I settle on saying, "Things at home have been good."

"I'm glad. What about school? Are you still getting good grades?"

I nod eagerly. "Finishing junior year was tough, but I did okay. I'm set to take some AP classes next year, which is kind of intimidating."

"Are you worried you won't be able to handle them?" she asks, brows drawn together. "Felix already started taking AP courses last year, but he is on the honor roll."

"It's really not that big a deal," Felix interjects, but Mom waves him off.

"Don't be silly. You should be proud of yourself. Taking AP Calculus and AP Computer Science at the same time is incredible," she says, and then turns her attention back to me. "Which course will you be taking first?"

"AP Art," I reply, and my mom pauses.

"Oh, well," she says lightly, "that's not a real AP course, is it?"

And there it is, the exact type of comment from Mom that makes me feel like I've shrunk five inches in a second flat. I don't think she means it to sound so judgmental, but how else am I supposed to take it? And to make matters worse, Felix is looking at me with this horrible pity in his eyes like he expects me to burst into tears any second. But I don't want to let it get to me, so I try to rally.

"It is. It'll be pretty time-intensive," I say, sounding a lot more confident than I actually feel. "I'll be in it for the whole year, and I'm probably taking AP English in the spring too, so I'm worried about the overlap. But Carmen promised she would help me study, so . . ."

I realize halfway through my rambling that I probably shouldn't mention Carmen when she and Mom are hardly speaking, so I end up trailing off clumsily. Mom shifts uncomfortably in her seat, and Felix looks back and forth between us as the silence stretches into catastrophically awkward territory. *Shit.*

"Man, I haven't seen Carmen in a million years," Felix blurts out, leaning across the table. I'm not sure if I feel grateful for his obvious attempt to dispel the awkwardness, or annoyed that he's possibly making it worse. "She must be in college now, huh?"

"Yeah, she just finished her sophomore year so she's home for the summer. I don't love sharing my bathroom with her again, but other than that, it's been fun."

"I didn't realize she was back in Austin," Mom says quietly. I almost expect her to say something else, to ask about Carmen like she clearly wants to, but her attention is suddenly glued to her ice water. Looking away doesn't do anything to hide the pain in her eyes, though.

"I'd love to see Carmen while I'm in town. It's been ages," Felix says, somehow continuing the conversation he's mostly having with himself at this point. "I mean, obviously I want to see you too. That's a given."

I glance back at him, and I'm surprised at how sincere he looks. Why does it feel like we're on two completely different planets right now? Since when does he want anything to do with me?

"Well, we're going to be pretty busy planning my queerceañera," I hedge, and miraculously, Mom suddenly checks back into the conversation.

"Yes, about that," she says, leaning forward. "Don't you think it's a little . . . much?"

Even though I had been thinking the exact same thing a few days ago, my stomach drops. "Sorry?"

"You're turning eighteen, and a young man at that. It's a bit silly to be playing dress-up like this, no?"

Every word that leaves her mouth makes me want to fold in on myself and disappear. This is exactly what I was afraid to hear from my extended family, but coming from her, it hurts even more than I'd expected.

"Well, it's unconventional, but that's the whole point," I say, but I can tell she's not really listening.

"None of the traditions will make sense if you change them that much," she replies, smoothing the cloth napkin on her lap. There isn't any malice in her tone. She's just saying what she believes. "At least that means you won't have to explain a chambelán to the family."

Our waiter returns with our food, but I'm frozen in place as he sets my plate in front of me. Felix's eyes are boring a hole in the side of my head, and I can't tell if I'm closer to yelling at someone or shutting down completely.

"I was surprised when I heard about this whole thing in the first place. It doesn't sound like something you'd want to do," Mom says after the waiter leaves. "But then I got wind that it was really your father's idea and, well, I guess I shouldn't be surprised."

I open my mouth to reply, but Felix is the one who speaks first.

"I think the whole thing sounds amazing," he says evenly. He's smiling, but when my eyes meet his, I can tell he's mad. It's not a look I've seen on him many times, and it makes me nervous. "Jay is really putting himself out there, and I think we should support him."

Mom turns to him, confused. "Felix, this isn't about you."

"Since I'm the one escorting him, it kind of is."

I gape at Felix. The smile hasn't left his face, and I kind of want to kick him under the table, or maybe strangle him. Mom looks like she might be thinking the exact same thing.

"You're escorting him? Since when?" she asks, and it comes out a little louder than necessary. She clears her throat, then a little quieter adds, "You haven't said anything about this before."

"Well, I didn't want to speak too soon, but Jay and I have been texting about it," Felix says confidently, even though I can't imagine anything further from the truth.

Mom turns to me, and I manage to shut my mouth before she realizes my jaw is on the floor. I can't for the life of me understand why he's lying.

"Joaquin, is this true?"

And maybe it's that I can feel Felix's eyes on me again, or maybe I've totally gone off the deep end too, but my reply tumbles out of my mouth before I can stop it. "Yeah, yeah it is."

Mom glances over at Felix, who still looks completely unfazed, and back at me one more time. Her expression softens a bit.

"Well, I guess that does change things a bit," she says slowly, fiddling with her wedding ring.

Felix smiles. "Good. Jay deserves to be celebrated, don't you think?"

"He does," Mom replies, but it sounds tentative, more like a question than a heartfelt agreement. My throat feels tight as she looks down at the table, unable to meet my eyes. "I'm . . . I think I need to freshen up a bit. Please excuse me."

Felix and I both watch in silence as she pushes her chair back from the table, scoops up her purse, and heads inside the restaurant.

Felix turns to me with a pained smile. "So, that could've gone better."

"Are you insane?" I shoot back, glancing over his shoulder to make sure my mom is fully out of earshot. "What was that?"

"It was a little white lie."

"No, no it was not. It was a huge, massive lie," I snap. "Do you have any idea what you just did?"

"I'm sorry, okay?" Felix says, holding his hands up between us. "You looked upset, and she wouldn't stop. I had to say something."

"You really, *really* didn't," I reply, but Felix isn't listening. He reaches across the table and grabs my phone before I can stop him. "What are you doing?"

"I need to borrow your face for a second," he says, holding the screen up to my face until it unlocks with a click. "I'm giving you my number."

"I don't want your number. I want to go back in time to five minutes ago when you weren't ruining my life," I say, watching in disbelief as Felix swipes into my messages and starts typing.

"I'll make it up to you, I promise," Felix says, sliding my phone back to me. "We can figure this out together, okay?"

I want to tell him that *we* aren't going to do anything because we're not a "we" but then Mom reemerges from the restaurant and slips back into her seat before I get the chance. All I'm left with is Felix's phone number, a date to my party that I didn't even want, and a lie that's probably going to wreck my summer.

Chapter Eight

OKAY, SO MAYBE this doesn't have to be the end of the world. At least that's what I tell myself as I drive home, you know, so I don't run my car off the road. I can just call Felix and convince him to take back what he said. Then he can go to my mom and tell her that he was joking, and that will be the end of it. Simple.

As I park in my driveway, I'm actually feeling a bit optimistic. All I have to do is make sure nobody else finds out in the meantime, and—

"Chaparro, you didn't tell me you already found a chambelán!"

Oh, kill me now. Dad is beaming at me as he comes around the side of the house, donning the old pair of Levi's and UT Austin cutoff he always wears while doing yard work. He's got his gardening gloves in one hand and his cell phone in the other.

"Uh, what?"

"Getting a call from your mom was a little unexpected. But

hey, what great news!" he says, waving his phone at me. "For the record, I never thought you'd have any trouble getting a handsome novio one day. You did get your good looks from me, so—"

"Novio," I repeat numbly. *Who the hell said anything about a boyfriend?* "¿Qué novio?"

"Felix, obviamente! Your mom said you two were very cozy at lunch. I think the phrase 'all over each other' was used."

I think back to the look on her face when she saw me and Felix hugging, the way she was staring at us when Felix said we had been talking for weeks, and it takes every ounce of my willpower not to bang my head into the nearest wall. How did one date to a party turn into dating? If this is some sort of divine punishment for lying about being sick to get out of my First Communion, I'll have to start going back to church for real.

"I always thought you and el gringito would make a good couple," Dad says, rubbing his chin. Felix is half Mexican on his mom's side, but he never spoke Spanish as a kid, so the joking nickname "gringo" stuck all the same. I haven't heard it in ages, and if I had any say in the matter, it would stay in the past like Felix himself. "Wait until the family hears about this! You may have made some people a lot of money. You know they like making bets about this kind of thing."

My eyes widen. "You didn't happen to mention this to anyone, right?"

"Only your Tía Kristina," he replies, totally oblivious.

Tía Kristina is the biggest gossip in the entire family. Maybe in all of North America—I really wouldn't put it past her. If she knows something, it means everyone knows. It's too late to threaten Felix into taking back what he said. My life is officially over.

"I need to talk to Carmen," I say thinly, and thankfully, Dad doesn't seem to notice I'm dying inside.

"She's pulling weeds out back with Ryan."

That sounds very fake to me, but I head to the backyard anyway, thoughts still racing. Carmen is, in fact, not pulling weeds at all. She's spread out on a lounge chair, a magazine in one hand and a glass of lemonade in the other. Ryan is doing all the real work, black hair pushed back in a baseball cap, tan skin slick with sweat as he digs into a flower bed.

How Carmen managed to bag such an unbelievably nice guy is totally beyond me. Even his family is obsessed with her—the Nguyens invited her to celebrate Tết with them a few months back, and as far as I can tell, she hasn't scared them off yet.

"Joaquin, my man!" Ryan calls out when he sees me, getting up and extending a fist for me to bump. There's sweat dripping down his tan arms and dirt all over his hands, but I dutifully touch knuckles with him anyway. Still, he can tell right away that it's lacking its usual enthusiasm. "What's with the long face, dude?"

Right on cue, Carmen pops her head over the back of her chair.

"There you are, you little liar! I can't believe you found a chambelán and didn't tell me. And Felix of all people? You need to spill now."

"First of all, you have to dial it down a notch. I don't want Dad to hear," I say as I sink down onto the edge of her chair. "I don't have a chambelán. Felix was lying."

"That's weird," Ryan says, eyes narrowing. "Why would your boyfriend lie about something like that?"

"He's not my boyfriend either! God, this is such a shit show."

"Well, that's not what everyone in the group chat is saying," Carmen says, tapping her phone screen. "So what the hell happened?"

"For starters, I met up with Mom for lunch," I say, and Ryan's eyes flick to Carmen's carefully neutral expression. He knows as well as I do that they've barely spoken at all in the last few months. "I'm sorry I didn't mention I was going to see her. I wasn't sure if it would upset you."

"Hey, don't do that," she says, shaking her head. "You can always talk to me about stuff like this. You two have your own relationship. You can see her if you want to."

"Well, now I'm kind of wishing I hadn't," I sigh.

I launch into a summary of the disastrous lunch and Felix's bizarre behavior throughout the whole thing. Ryan joins me in perching on the edge of the lawn chair, as rapt as Carmen is by the whole story. I'm careful to leave out Mom's reaction, or non-reaction, to the news Carmen is back in town for summer. When I'm done explaining how it's all a lie, Carmen nods sagely.

"You know what? This makes a lot more sense," she says and quickly backtracks when I shoot her the withering look to end all withering looks. "It's not that I think you can't get a boyfriend, chill. I just figured you'd tell me if you did."

"Well, I didn't," I say, fishing my phone out of my pocket. "Which is exactly why I have to set this straight."

"Oh no you don't," she says, catching my wrist before I have the chance to unlock it.

"It's either that or fake my own death."

"Listen, smartass, don't you remember what happened with Francisco?" she asks, and it stops me in my tracks. Carmen's quince would have been picture-perfect if her boyfriend at the time, Francisco, hadn't had the audacity to break up with her a month before the event. "Every conversation that day started with '¡Qué pena!' and 'Pobrecita Carmen.' It was awful."

"I would never abandon you like that," Ryan chimes in, pressing a kiss to the top of Carmen's head. I resist the urge to roll my eyes at their PDA.

"I think I'd rather deal with that than deal with Felix for the next month."

"You don't get it," Carmen says. "People still bring him up and it's been five whole years. If the same thing happens with you and Felix, it's all anyone's going to talk about. You can either deal with

Felix for a month or hear about him dumping you until you're twenty-five. Your call."

I don't want to admit it, but Carmen is right. If everyone is expecting Felix to escort me, they're probably not going to believe it was all some big misunderstanding.

Plus, it's not lost on me that Mom's interest in this whole event might now hinge on what happens with our fake courtship. All her criticism stopped as soon as Felix mentioned he was involved. If I kick him to the curb, whatever chance I had of the queerceañera bringing me and her closer together, no matter how minuscule, could go with him.

"If Felix had kept his mouth shut, none of this would be happening." I sigh in resignation. "When I saw Tía Fernanda the other day, I told her I wasn't seeing anyone. How am I supposed to explain this to her?"

"Dude, I'm your own sister and I thought you were hiding this from me," Carmen points out. "People know you keep to yourself. It's fine."

"Okay, but I've also never even had a boyfriend before. How am I supposed to pretend to be in a relationship with Felix when I don't even know how dating works."

"It's not that hard. Men are simple creatures," Carmen replies and then turns to Ryan. "No offense, baby."

"None taken," Ryan says with a shrug. "I'm just happy to be here."

As much as I want to believe her, I seriously doubt anything having to do with Felix is going to be straightforward. Pretending to be my date to a party is one thing, but pretending to be in a full-on relationship? That's a whole different ball game, and I can't imagine anyone I'd want to be lumped together with less than him.

But April did point out I tend to focus on the negative, so as I pull up Felix's contact info, I try to put on a brave face. Maybe by the end of all this, I'll finally be able to put my past with Felix behind me. It feels impossible, but stranger things have happened, right?

Chapter Nine

FELIX IS TRUE to his word, and he happily agrees to meet up so we can figure out how to navigate his big, stupid lie. The snag is that the only day he's free this week is the same day Dad enlisted me, Carmen, and April to help perfect a tasting menu for his upcoming guest spot at a local restaurant. I want to get this thing with Felix under control as soon as possible, so I ask him to meet us there in the morning when we'll have the restaurant mostly to ourselves.

April offers to pick me and Carmen up, and I use our quick drive downtown to fill her in on the situation with Felix and my mom. Like Carmen, she ignores the fact that my life is in shambles and is instead charmed by the whole idea.

"This is my ideal dating scenario," April beams as she pulls off the highway. "You get romanced and I hear all the juicy details secondhand."

"Except we're not really dating, and I'm not going to get romanced. We hardly know each other now. We're just old friends."

"Yeah, that's what historians would say. But I'll call it what it really is: gay."

Carmen bursts out laughing in the back seat, and I flip her the bird in the rearview mirror as April turns onto South Congress.

"Go ahead and laugh all you want, but y'all are my only support system if this goes south," I say, rubbing the bridge of my nose between my fingers. I haven't even talked to Felix yet and I already have a headache.

After mulling it over a bit, I decided against telling Dad the truth about me and Felix. I love the guy to the moon and back, but I'm not sure if he can manage to keep a secret that big, and I don't need any more loose ends. But I'd be lying if his excitement about me and Felix reconnecting didn't play a small part in the decision too.

"You're such a drama queen. Felix was your best friend for years," Carmen says, reaching from the backseat to pinch my arm. "It was about time you two buried the hatchet."

I want to point out that it's Felix's fault we fell out of touch in the first place, but I don't get the chance because April gasps mid parallel park.

"Speaking of which, is that him?"

My hand drops away from my face, and it is him, leaning

against his bumper a few cars down from us. He looks exactly like he did yesterday—tall, confident, annoyingly handsome—but it still surprises me for some reason.

"Any reason you failed to mention that he's super hot?" April asks with a smirk as she cuts the engine.

"It's not important," I shoot back, but when Felix makes eye contact with me through the windshield, the way my heart jumps into my throat definitely means something. Something bad, probably, but something nonetheless.

"Felix Campbell-García," Carmen calls out, jumping out of the car first, "who gave you permission to grow up so fast?"

I can tell it takes a second for Felix to recognize her, but when he does, the smile that stretches across his face is dazzling. "I could ask you the same. Last time I saw you, you still had braces."

"Ew, please don't remind me," Carmen pouts, but she pulls him into a hug anyway.

"It's good to see you," he says warmly, then turns to April, who's joined us on the sidewalk. "And you are—?"

"April Ward," she replies. "I'm the best friend. Joaquin has told me all about you."

Felix raises a brow at her. "Has he now? That's interesting."

Oh, hell no. Before things get out of hand, I tug on Felix's sleeve. "Meet and greet is over. We have things to discuss. We'll catch up with y'all later, okay?"

"Take all the time you need," Carmen teases, waving us off along with a giggling April.

As I pull Felix to the side door of the restaurant, I catch them whispering furiously to each other. Whatever it is they're planning, I'm positive I don't want to know.

Dad got settled in the kitchen earlier that morning, and since I want to avoid him for the time being, I end up leading Felix through a maze of back halls. He follows me like a puppy past the freezers and into a pantry.

"We have a problem. I mean, bigger than the problem you already got us into," I say. When I stop and turn to Felix, he's looking down at me with bald curiosity. "Everyone thinks we're a couple."

He blinks at me, and I'm not entirely sure what to make of the expression that passes across his face. "Did you tell them we're dating?"

"Obviously not, I didn't even want to be in this situation in the first place," I sigh, leaning my back against one of the shelves. The cool metal feels good against my back—it's hot back here, and Felix standing so close isn't making it any better. "Somewhere between my mom calling my dad and my dad telling my tía who then preceded to tell everyone she knows on WhatsApp, something got lost in translation."

"Ah, the good old 'WhatsApp rumor' to 'full-blown family scandal' pipeline. I know it all too well."

"It's not funny," I say, even though I know it kind of is. Or at least it would be if it were happening to anyone other than me.

"You're right, I'm sorry," he replies sheepishly.

"You better not have been bluffing when you said you'd help me out," I say, "because the way I see it, you're going to have to play boyfriend of the year up until my queerceañera, or I'll never hear the end of it."

"I wasn't bluffing, I swear," he says. When the frown on my face doesn't budge, his tone softens. "I really am sorry, you know. I didn't mean to put you in such an awkward position."

"Why did you, though? Why did you have to lie?"

"I don't know," he says, rubbing a hand against the back of his neck. "I was excited to see you again, and the queerceañera sounded cool, so I thought lunch was going to be nice. I didn't expect it to go the way it did. I didn't feel comfortable with the way your mom was talking to you. I thought if she knew I was involved too, she might go easier on you."

The second the words leave his mouth, my temper flares. I wanted to give him the benefit of the doubt that it was all a stupid mistake, that his lack of filter got the best of him. But if this is Felix living out a weird savior complex where I'm his charity case, then I don't want any part of it.

"So, what?" I ask, pushing off the shelf and into Felix's space. I expect him to take a step back, but he doesn't. "Are you just doing this out of pity?"

"I don't pity you, Jay. I care about you, same as I always have."

I'm not sure if it's him using that damn nickname again or what, but my heart hiccups in my chest. A small, childish part of me wants to ask him how he has the nerve to show up and act like he cares about me after years of silence, but I can't quite get the words out. We stare at each other for three unflinching seconds, and then he looks away.

"Plus, you're not the only one who would get something out of this," he continues. "I went through a really messy breakup at the end of the school year, and my parents still don't believe me when I say I'm fine now."

"Messy how?"

"Messy enough that I had trouble getting out of bed for a while. My grades tanked. It was rough," Felix says, and even though his voice is steady, I can tell this has been weighing on him. "If we pretended we're dating, it would kill two birds with one stone. You get your family off your back, and I get my family off mine."

I'm surprised by how much that makes sense. I know that having Felix on my side will make my mom a little bit more open-minded about my queerceañera. And if there's something in it for Felix too, it'll be an extra layer of insurance that he'll pull his weight in making it seem realistic.

"If you agree to do this," I say carefully, "then you can't flake out on me, understand? And if we're going to sell this, we're going to need a story."

Felix perks up. "You got it. It'll be the best damn story they've ever heard."

And in a weird way, it kind of is. We decide to stick with what Felix said at lunch, that we'd been texting for a while before he came back to Austin. We'll have to make up for lost time and get to know the little details about our current lives to make it realistic, but it doesn't seem that daunting when all is said and done. Felix is surprisingly cool about the whole thing. Oddly enough, he almost seems excited.

When we finish outlining our plan, we both agree it would make sense for him to say hi to my dad on his way out—might as well rip that particular Band-Aid off. We're heading back through the hallway together when something else occurs to me.

"To be clear, you don't have to do anything other than say we're together," I add over my shoulder, and Felix quirks his head at me. "Like, we don't have to do PDA or stuff like that. You don't even have to help plan the party."

"I want to, though," he says eagerly, then immediately backtracks. "I mean, help with the planning, that is. It would be fun. Besides, what kind of boyfriend would I be if I let you fend for yourself?"

"A perfectly average one," I say, and Felix scoffs behind me.

"You've gotta raise your expectations. We're not aiming for average. We're aiming for spectacular," he deadpans, and it startles a laugh out of me. When I'm not in the middle of an existential crisis, Felix can be pretty charming. Not that I'm planning to tell him that, of course. "So April, Carmen, and Ryan are the only ones who know the truth, right?"

"Yeah, and I'm not planning to expand that circle. My dad can't know about any of this, okay?"

"Roger that," Felix says as we round a corner, and I can't help but feel a little bit guilty for almost biting his head off before. Sure, he's the one that got us into this mess, but he's also doing me a huge favor by going through with this whole charade.

"How are you so chill about this? Aren't you at least a little bit nervous we're going to get caught?" I ask, but when I glance over my shoulder again, Felix shrugs.

"Shouldn't be hard to make it seem like we're into each other. It's not like we haven't had practice," he replies, and for a second, I forget how to breathe.

Throughout this entire conversation, neither of us has brought up our history together. I figured it was because it was so far behind us that it wasn't worth mentioning, or maybe our kiss meant too little to him that he had already forgotten it. But now I know he's thinking the same thing as me. We've done this before, but back then, it was for real.

I don't get any time to process this revelation, because the instant we set foot in the kitchen, my dad descends on us like it's the second coming of Christ.

"Look at this, our boys are back together again! This is how things should be. I always knew you two would work things out. But my god, Felix, you're so grown up," Dad rattles off, setting aside the ceviche he's plating to wrap an arm around Felix's shoulders. Then he turns to me with a wink. "Qué guapo, ¿no?"

Felix looks down at me with barely concealed amusement, and I can tell Carmen and April are on the verge of losing their shit on the opposite end of the counter. The best I can do without combusting on the spot is half-reply with, "He does look pretty different."

"Well, you haven't changed one bit," Felix laughs, and I'm not entirely sure what he means by it.

"Isn't that a bad thing?"

"No, it's a good thing," he says, and the softness in his voice catches me off guard. "A very good thing."

Something dangerously close to butterflies tickles my stomach, and I have to look away for a second to regain my composure. He's a little bit too good at this.

"Oh wow, y'all are too sweet," Carmen says, pressing a hand to her heart. Her words are dripping in mock sincerity that Dad is too happy to pick up on. Next to her, April nods.

"The sweetest," she adds, and I have the distinct feeling they're about to gang up on me.

"You two are going to look so handsome together all dressed up," Dad chimes in.

"We were just saying that y'all need to get your outfits sorted

ASAP," Carmen coos. "You should ask Tío Gael and Tía Ximena if they can hook you both up with the custom suits they mentioned."

"Also, my moms know this amazing woman who has a dance studio on the East Side," April adds, and the smile spreading across her face is absolutely devious. Well, as devious as April can get, which isn't much. But still. "I'm sure she'd be happy to give you two lessons. There's a part where you'll have to do a waltz together, right?"

"There is, and dance lessons are a must. I'm sure you won't mind cozying up to each other for an afternoon, right?" Carmen asks, batting her lashes at me with a faux innocence that could annoy a saint.

I can tell they're trying to get me and Felix to spend time together, but it takes a special skill set to be this obvious about it. Between Carmen being biologically hardwired to push my buttons and April always wanting to play matchmaker, I probably should have seen this coming. I try to imagine what my life would look like if I weren't surrounded by full-time agents of chaos. I come up blank.

I turn my attention to Felix, sending him strong psychic signals that he doesn't have to say yes to any of this, but for whatever reason, he's eating it up.

"That sounds so fun! I would love to," he replies, turning to me. "You tell me when and where, and I'll be there."

"You sure? You really don't have to—"

"I'm positive," he reassures me with a smile.

"Are you two done flirting?" Carmen interjects, and I make a mental note to dunk her toothbrush in the toilet later. "Because if you are, we could use an extra set of hands."

And even though I assure him that he really doesn't have to, Felix stays for the rest of the morning to help us tweak the tasting menu. He asks Carmen all about college as we help prep ingredients, and he wins April over in record time by complimenting the Stray Kids T-shirt she's wearing under her apron. He tries every experimental dish we put in front of him, even the really weird stuff, which Dad is over the moon about it. And every once in a while, he glances over at me, sharing a smile that feels private in a way that's both surprising and painfully familiar.

I can't get over how bizarre it is that this boy who I thought had exited my life forever is standing elbow to elbow with me, dicing tomatoes like no time has passed at all. Part of me wants to take it at face value, but there's a voice in the back of my head telling me that I still haven't figured him out—or figured out where we stand. Felix may have miraculously walked back into my life, but I haven't forgotten how he walked out of it without warning too.

Chapter Ten

PLANNING A MASSIVE party in under a month has major drawbacks, but the biggest one is that I can't drag my feet about coordinating plans with Felix. I'm dreading the back-and-forth with him, still not sure how to shake the awkwardness I feel about getting to know him all over again. But it turns out I was worrying for nothing, because it ends up being out of my hands anyway. You know, like everything else in my life.

I'm drawing on the couch, headphones blasting the noisiest EDM possible to eliminate the possibility of forming cohesive thoughts, when Dad taps me on the shoulder. He beams at me as I turn the music down and pull the headphones off to hang them around my neck.

"Tío Gael and Tía Ximena agreed to create custom suits for you on short notice," he says, and my stomach swoops. "They're expecting you and Felix there tomorrow morning at 8:00 a.m. sharp."

"Wait, what?"

"I was chatting with them yesterday after your sister reminded us about their offer and they're so excited," he says, breezing into the kitchen. Carmen is picking through a bag of chips at the island, and Dad grabs a handful as he walks by. "The turnaround time is tight already. Might as well get it out of the way, no?"

"I mean, yeah, I guess," I reply, twisting to look over the back of the couch. "But Dad, you should've asked me first before setting that up."

Dad stops, chip halfway to his mouth, to look at me with genuine confusion. "Why? You weren't thinking of getting your suits somewhere else, right? I think if you did, Gael would cry himself to sleep."

"No, that's not—" I start, trying to think of how to say he's being too pushy without deflating his enthusiasm, but I'm at a loss. "Never mind, it doesn't matter."

Dad gives me a thumbs-up and happily carries his snack out of the kitchen, leaving me to glare at Carmen.

"He's right, you know. There's no point in putting it off," she says before I can think to complain. "If it helps, I already texted Felix. He said he'll meet you there."

"The hell, Carmen? When did you even get his number?"

"It would be weird for me not to have a direct line to my future brother-in-law, don't you think?" she asks with a grin, squeaking when I throw my pencil at her from across the room. "You have to get this done whether you like it or not. You two will be fine. Just don't be late!"

It seems simple enough, but later that night, I end up tossing and turning for hours. I keep going over the plan Felix and I landed on, imagining every way it could possibly go wrong.

Plus, I feel super weird about spending time with Felix in general. He's been totally friendly, too friendly even, but I'm not sure how to act around him. I'm at this odd intersection of knowing him too well and not knowing him at all.

So I end up doing what I do best, staying up way later than I should and drawing to relieve my stress. It works, enough for me to eventually get a few hours of fitful sleep. I wake up in the morning with eraser shavings littering my sheets, pages of my sketchbook full of new drawings, and a massive headache. But if Felix lost a single wink of sleep over the predicament we're in, he doesn't show it. He's somehow at the tailor shop earlier than me, perched on the hood of his car, bright-eyed and bushy-tailed. When I pull into the spot next to him, he waves at me cheerily.

"How are you so awake right now?" I ask, dragging myself out of the driver's seat and hauling my backpack with me.

"Lots of coffee. Maybe a little too much," he replies. "But I didn't want to show up half-asleep. Gotta make a good impression when you're meeting the family, right?"

"Right," I say, though it's a bit funny to me that Felix would ever worry about first impressions. He seems to win over everyone he meets without even trying.

I text Tío Gael that we're here, and he buzzes us into the shop. When we step inside, the smell of warm cotton and lavender fills my nose. The space is small but homey. Clear morning light streams through the windows, illuminating the walls filled with bolts of colorful fabrics, design sketches, and rows of neatly organized sewing tools.

I have a lot of fond memories of hanging out here as a kid when both my parents had to work. Tío Gael and Tía Ximena would let me lay on the floor and draw for hours. My cousins Valentina and Elisa snuck me little snacks and kept me company, and I always felt safe and doted on here. But now, the usual sense of calm that washes over me whenever I'm here is mixed with pinpricks of anxiety.

Neither my tío nor tía has met Felix before, and he becomes the main attraction the second we step through the door.

"So, this is the mysterious boyfriend, then," Tío Gael says, squeezing Felix's hand in a firm handshake. By the look on Felix's face, maybe "crushing" would be a more accurate description.

"That's me," Felix says with none of his usual bravado. Tío Gael finally releases his grip on Felix's hand, but he's still sizing him up.

"Valentina and Elisa were dying to meet you too, but they both had plans. I guess I'll just have to report back to them myself,"

Tía Ximena says, looking Felix up and down like she's assessing a particularly interesting swatch of fabric rather than a real human being. "Hmm, very cute. You're taller than I'd expected."

"Oh yeah, I get that from my dad," Felix says with a smile. "I'm six foot even."

Tía Ximena gives me a conspiratorial look. "Is this your type, then? Tall boys?"

"The last time I saw him in person, he wasn't even five feet tall," I reply dryly. "The height is new to me, so I'm still undecided."

She raises a brow, and I swear at myself internally. Not even five seconds in and I already sound like the shittiest boyfriend in the world—awesome. At least Felix doesn't seem to mind. He laughs a little, though he also shoots me a look like he doesn't know if he should be pleased or offended.

"You've always been my type, and I'm not afraid to admit it," Felix replies, and I resist the urge to roll my eyes at him. It feels like he's laying it on a little thick, and Tío seems to agree, crossing his arms over his chest.

"Oh, so you're one of those types, huh?" Tío Gael asks, narrowing his eyes. "A smooth talker?"

Felix glances over at me, a little bewildered. "Um?"

"Valentina dated a boy like that once, didn't she?" Tía Ximena asks, turning to Tío Gael, who nods sternly.

"He was always making jokes, couldn't give a straight answer about anything," Tío Gael says. "I never trusted him."

They both turn to Felix again, who looks like a deer caught in headlights.

"You're not a playboy, are you?" Tía asks, and I balk at her.

"Hold on a second—"

"No way," Felix cuts in, shaking his head. "I'm a one-guy type of guy. I mean, I love monogamy. Huge fan. Can't get enough of it."

"Good, that's what I like to hear," Tía Ximena replies. "Joaquin is very sweet. He deserves someone loyal who will look after him."

"I will. I mean, I do!" Felix says, clearly frazzled.

"Guys, ease up a little, okay?" I say, glancing between my tío and tía. "You don't need to cross-examine him."

"We only want to make sure you're being treated right," Tío Gael says, arms still crossed over his chest.

"Especially since you're so private about your love life. We didn't even know you had a boyfriend until a few days ago," Tía Ximena adds. "How long have you two been dating anyways?"

"Two months," I say, exactly at the same time Felix decides to say, "Two weeks."

Tío Gael and Tía Ximena stare at us for a beat, and we stare at each other.

"It, uh, depends on when you start counting, I guess," I stammer.

"Right! Especially since it's been a bit of a whirlwind romance, totally unexpected," Felix says with a nervous smile. Technically he's not lying. It *was* unexpected. "But all the best things in life are, right?"

Tío Gael and Tía Ximena share a look as they lead us over to the back of the shop.

"He really is a smooth talker," Tía Ximena murmurs to Tío Gael. I elbow Felix behind their backs, and he looks at me with a wild expression that says *I have no idea why this isn't working.*

"I know it's hard to believe, but he's being genuine. He's always been a little over-the-top, but he's a good guy, and—" I take a breath, steeling myself for what I'm about to say next. "I really like him."

Tío Gael and Tía Ximena's expressions soften a fraction as we reach the fitting platform near the dressing rooms.

"Okay, okay. Enough introductions," Tía Ximena says, a small smile playing on her lips. "Let's get your measurements taken."

"Do you know what your main colors will be for the event?" Tío Gael asks as Felix steps onto the platform first. Maybe it's the nerves, but Felix decides to pipe up.

"Absolutely—"

I catch his eye and shake my head furiously from behind my tío's back, and Felix frowns.

"—not. No idea."

"I haven't picked them yet, but I do have a concept in mind for my suit," I say quickly, pulling my sketchbook from my backpack before Felix has the chance to put his foot in his mouth again."I know you usually do the opposite, but maybe we could start with the outfit and go from there."

"I like the way you think," Tío Gael says, leaning over to take a closer look.

I didn't want to show up that morning with no direction of my own, so during my anxiety-induced drawing session the night before, I started sketching different concepts so I could visualize what look I was going for.

Halfway through, I realized I want my suit to be more than an eye-catching outfit. I want it to have some symbolic significance too. I took inspiration from the last three colors of the original pride flag—turquoise for art, indigo for harmony, and violet for spirit—and built out my idea from there. As Felix gets his measurements taken, I point out the elements of my favorite options to Tío Gael.

"If you don't think it would look good, or if it's too complicated, please tell me," I say as he pores over the designs. "You obviously know best."

Tío Gael rubs his chin, and for a second, I'm scared he's going to say it's impossible to make my idea a reality. But then he nods, throwing an arm around my shoulders.

"I can picture this perfectly! It might be a little tricky to find a fabric to match this pattern, but I'll try my best. And we can take this darker color here," he says, pointing to one of the sketches, "and make Felix's suit to match."

"Do I get to see this masterpiece of fashion design too?" Felix says, hopping off the platform once Tía is done with him.

"Uh, the sketches are a little rough," I say. To be honest, the idea of showing Felix any of my drawings makes me want to break out in hives. It's way easier for me to share my art online, where nobody knows me. There's a certain distance there that makes it less intimidating. But showing it to someone I've known for years is so much more weighty.

Felix must notice my hesitation, because he reaches over and closes my sketchbook in one swift motion. "Now that I think about it, I want to be surprised on the day of. I trust your judgment and your fashion sense."

As I get my measurements taken, my tío and tía pepper Felix with questions. Thankfully, they're mostly about his summer plans and not about our relationship. But when we have to recount the fake story of how we got together, we stumble over ourselves again.

"Well, we started texting in April—" I start, and Felix's eyes immediately go wide.

"I think it was May," he says pointedly.

"Right, uh, I got your number in April, but we only started texting in May," I cover quickly. "And then, you know."

"Yep, sparks and butterflies and all that good stuff," Felix says.

Tío Gael and Tía Ximena exchange another weighty glance, and I feel like melting into the ground. Eventually, Tía Ximena is pulled away by another customer, and Tío Gael heads into the back to find some sample suits we can try on.

"I feel like I just got interrogated by the FBI," Felix says as I step off the platform, quiet enough that nobody will hear him.

"I didn't think they were going to grill you like that," I whisper back. "They're kind of overprotective with my cousins. I guess they went into bodyguard mode from force of habit."

"You can say that again," Felix says with a little snort. "It could've gone smoother, but we're not half bad, huh?"

"We almost got caught like fifteen times. I'd say that's very bad. Horrible, even."

"But you saved it. Great line, by the way. Glad to know you *really* like me," Felix says with a grin.

"Please stop talking."

"Given how little we know about each other's lives now, I think it could have gone worse," he says, and his optimism amazes and annoys me in equal parts. He settles down on one of the couches near the dressing room. "For the record, my ex and I broke up in April, so it would be better to say you and I started talking in May."

I nod, crossing the room to join him. Felix is right—there's a lot we don't know about each other. And, in turn, there are a lot of ways our story could fall apart without us even realizing it. Learning a bit more about his breakup seems like a good place to start, and I'd be lying if I said I wasn't a little bit curious. Sue me.

"What's your ex like?" I ask. Then, so I don't sound shamelessly nosy, I add, "It's probably something I should know, in case someone asks."

"Hmm, that's true," Felix says, looking away as he chooses his words carefully. "Caleb is pretty outgoing, kind of spontaneous. And I guess we have a lot of the same interests. He's the one who gave me the idea of enrolling in the program I'm doing this summer."

Maybe it's because of the comment he made earlier about me being his type, but I'm a little surprised that Caleb sounds like the polar opposite of me. And, though I kind of hate to admit it, it sounds like they were a good match.

I want to ask him why they split up, but Felix is picking at a loose thread on the edge of the couch, and it seems like even talking about Caleb in passing has stressed him out.

"Are you two at least on good terms?" I try. "I mean since things ended."

"I guess so, but it's kinda complicated. We have a lot of mutual friends, so I feel like we have to be on good terms—otherwise, we'd risk splitting up the group. I don't want any of them to have to take sides. And even though we broke up, I still care about him a lot, y'know?"

I nod, but I'm not entirely sure how he means it. After all, he said he cared about me too, didn't he? I wonder if he cares about Caleb the same way—like, they had a good run, but it's all over now. Or maybe for them, things aren't really over at all. It shouldn't matter, but it bugs me for some reason.

Tío Gael returns with four suits each, leaving us to try them on while he helps the other customers who are starting to filter in. Felix and I head into the changing room, and I'm grateful when he decides to change the subject.

"I'm really glad you're still doing art," he says, voice drifting over from the stall next to me. "I would've been so bummed if you stopped, you were amazing at it. You must have a massive portfolio by now, huh?"

"Yeah, it's kind of ridiculous. I have an art account on Instagram where I post my work, so that keeps me motivated to keep creating new stuff," I say, not mentioning that the like count and comments I get sometimes give me more anxiety than inspiration. Instead, I pull on a black shirt so I can try the double-breasted black pinstripe suit that caught my eye. It's kind of giving mafia vibes, but not in a bad way. "Art school is the plan. If they take me, that is."

"They'd be stupid not to," he says, and I'm glad he can't see how pleased I look as I slide on my suit jacket.

"What about you? Are you planning to do . . . computer stuff?" I ask, and Felix's laugh is loud enough that it echoes a little in the changing room. "I'm sorry, I really don't know that much about coding."

"I think the term you're looking for is software engineering, but computer stuff works too," he says with a smile in his voice. "I do think that's what I want to do. It would pay well, which is a big perk, but I genuinely love it. And not to sound like a douche, but I'm pretty good at it too."

"That's not douchey at all. It makes sense. You've always been brilliant."

The compliment rolls off my tongue before I can think to hold it in. It's nice hearing Felix talk like this. When we were kids, if he really loved something, he always gave it his all. I like knowing that part of him hasn't changed.

I head into the hallway to inspect myself in the full-length mirror, and I'm surprised that I kind of love what I see. I'm not used to seeing myself in a suit, and my hair would probably look better slicked back, but dressing up is pretty fun.

"You're doing wonders for my ego here," Felix replies, and I hear the latch to his stall slide open. "Most people are like, 'wow, that seems really boring' but I swear it's not. Fixing bugs is sort of like solving a puzzle. Nothing beats the feeling you get when the final piece clicks into place."

I'm about to reply, but when Felix steps into view, my brain completely short-circuits. He's wearing a sharply tailored maroon suit that brings out the warmth of his eyes. The white shirt underneath is unbuttoned a bit, and a black tie is hanging loose around his neck.

"Yeah," I manage haltingly. "I think I know what you mean."

"You do?" Felix asks, and maybe it's my imagination, but I feel like he's staring at me too.

"Sure. Problem-solving, puzzle pieces, all that jazz," I say, trying to organize my thoughts from before he came out looking like *that*. "Art isn't all about imagination and creativity. Sometimes it's about finding a solution. You can move a shadow or change the undertone of a color and a whole piece will click, like you said."

"Damn, you made that sound way more poetic than I did," he says, turning to inspect himself in the mirror. "You have a great brain. I mean it."

"Well, hopefully Pratt likes my brain as much as you do, because I'm gonna need a fat scholarship if I get accepted," I say, and Felix's brows shoot up.

"Wait, Pratt in New York?" he asks, and I nod. "No shit, Columbia is basically my dream school. What are the odds we end up living in the same city again after graduation?"

I don't know if it's Felix's infectious enthusiasm or the unexpected intimacy of the whole conversation, but I'm weirdly excited about it. There's no way of knowing if either of us will get into our top choices, but as Felix finishes knotting his tie, it doesn't feel that far-fetched.

"We clean up pretty nice, huh?" he asks, meeting my eyes in the mirror and flashing me a dimpled grin.

I take a second to appreciate our reflections as a pair, and I realize that side by side, it almost seems like we matched our suits on purpose. He's right, but it's not just that we look good—it's that we look good together.

"Who would've thought," I reply, and Felix's smile gets wider.

Chapter Eleven

MAYBE FELIX'S BLIND optimism about our situation had gotten to me, but after the suit fitting, I thought the not-so-great impression we left on my tío and tía could fly under the radar. That is, until Carmen called for an emergency meeting to discuss our "performance," choosing the morning Dad was off doing his *Food & Wine* interview to gather Felix, April, and me at the house.

We're spread around the back patio in various states of relaxation. April is sipping iced coffee and looking positively delighted to be included, and Felix is stretching his long limbs in the hammock hanging in the corner. And then there's me, not relaxed in the slightest, leaning against the cool siding of the house and debating if I want to make a run for it.

"I thought you two said you talked things out," Carmen says looking between me and Felix. "What happened?"

"What do you mean what happened? We went, we did our

little charade, and we got fitted for our suits," I reply, but Carmen sighs.

She pulls out her phone, and as she searches for something, I have the distinct feeling I've been called to the principal's office.

"Apparently, you didn't exactly sell it to Tío Gael and Tía Ximena," Carmen says, "because people in the family chat are debating whether you two are even going to make it to the event as a couple."

"*No*," April gasps, leaning over the table like she's watching a telenovela. "What did they say?"

"They said, and I quote," Carmen says, glancing at her phone, "'The boys didn't really seem like they were on the same page. They were very tense. Pobrecitos, maybe they were uncomfortable with all the attention.'"

"Well, we *were* uncomfortable," I say.

"Hey, speak for yourself, okay? I was totally in my element," Felix interjects from the hammock. My eyes slide over to his, and the second we make eye contact, he grins. I frown back.

"You can't make faces like that at your boyfriend around other people," April says, pointing at my sour expression.

"I didn't!" I say staring daggers at Felix when he looks like he's about to disagree. "We talked more, and we have our story straight now. Promise."

Sure, the suit fitting got off to a rocky start, and in retrospect, Tío Gael and Tía Ximena witnessed some not-so-great moments that could have gone smoother. But the conversation Felix and I had in the fitting room felt like it took us out of awkward stranger territory and into something a little more comfortable. Friendly, even. Still, Carmen doesn't look convinced.

"Okay, you can have your story straight on paper," she says. "But seeming like a real couple takes a lot more than that. People are going to notice if you don't seem relaxed around each other."

"Yeah, you have to factor body language into it," April adds, glancing back and forth between me and Felix. "You can't stand ten feet apart all the time and expect it to come across all lovey-dovey."

"Nobody is even here right now. I'm not going to sit on his lap for no reason," I say, not even thinking before the words slip out.

"I mean, I wouldn't complain if you did," Felix shoots back with another easy smile.

"Jesus Christ," I groan, burying my face in my hands. I hate it here. I hate all of them.

"Wait, I might have an idea," April says suddenly, and I look up at her through my fingers. "Don't say no right away."

"Oh, you're off to a terrific start."

"Cami's party is tomorrow night. Her parents are out of town, remember?" April asks, and I already don't like where this is going. "You and Felix can come and test drive your relationship around other people, low-pressure."

I blink at her. "How on earth is that low-pressure?"

"Because this party isn't about you. Plus, people are going to be drunk and distracted. It's a way easier audience than your family."

"She's got a point," Carmen pipes up. "This sounds like it might be helpful."

And I hate to admit it, but I kind of agree. April mentioned Bryce, Savannah, and Jaz were going to the party, and they'd be a pretty decent focus group. I'm not as close with the three of them as I am with April, so I only feel a little bit guilty about the prospect of lying to them to save myself from future, more catastrophic embarrassment at the hands of my family.

I glance at Felix, who's been suspiciously quiet since April brought up the party. "What do you think about all this?"

"I'm down for whatever. I do better in groups anyways," Felix replies, finally sounding serious. "I think they're right. If we want to sell this, we're probably going to need a little more practice."

I chew my lip for a second. I honestly did think Felix and I could get by without getting more involved in each other's lives than strictly necessary, but I guess the bar was higher than I realized.

"Okay," I sigh, and April and Felix perk up. "What's our game plan?"

Within the next hour, roles are decided, outfits are planned, and lies are re-rehearsed. Carmen valiantly offers to be our designated driver, and we decide to pick up Felix at 9:00 p.m. April assures me approximately forty-five times that the party is going to be "very chill" and "no big deal."

It's all totally fine and normal until we're standing in front of Cami's house and I can't for the life of me remember why I agreed to this in the first place. I shift my weight from one foot to the other as muffled rap music and laughter seep out from under the front door. Felix peers down at me, a little crease appearing between his eyebrows.

"We really don't have to do this if you don't want to," he says. It's supposed to come off as supportive, but it makes me want to strangle him.

"Yes, we do," I sigh.

"And it's going to be fine," April says, patting my back. She's got her braids half up in a claw clip, and the bright yellow matching set she's wearing is as sunny as her disposition. She's been in a remarkably chipper mood all day, and I question for the hundredth time how I ended up with an extrovert for a best friend.

"Who's going to believe I secretly started dating a guy and never mentioned it even once?" I ask.

"Everyone!" April replies. "Jaz was seeing some guy for two whole months last summer and only told me about it the other day. Plus, you've always been private about that kind of stuff. This is all practice, remember? Just try to have fun."

"Easier said than done," I mumble.

"I think we can manage," Felix says, flashing me a reassuring smile. I nod, trying to calm my nerves.

But the second we step inside, whatever confidence I had goes out the window. It's loud and crowded, and the air is thick with music, smoke, and chatter. There are people packed into every corner, half of whom I'm not even sure I recognize from school.

"This is 'chill'?" I ask, turning to April.

"To me? Absolutely," she replies over the music. "Come on, they said they were somewhere in the back."

I follow her as she weaves expertly between people, but I can't ignore how many faces turn to look us up and down as we do. I feel a pang of anxiety in my chest, worried that everyone can somehow sense I'm not supposed to be here. I wonder for a second if our friends might feel the same, but push it down immediately. Instead, I remind myself it isn't totally unbelievable that I might have started dating someone and hadn't had the chance to mention it yet. I haven't seen them since school let out. Everything is going to be fine.

Suddenly, there's a tug at the hem of my shirt, and I look down to see Felix's hand holding onto me tightly.

"Don't want to get lost," he says with a lopsided smile, and it's ridiculous, but it's weirdly grounding at the same time. I don't feel quite as shaky as we make our way to the back of the house.

"Hey, over here!" someone calls out, and I follow April as she makes a beeline for the kitchen.

I spot Bryce first, since he's a head taller than everyone else and twice as loud. He's gotten a haircut since the last time I saw him, swapping his usual twist out for a close-cropped fade, and the brightly patterned Hawaiian shirt he has on stands out like a beacon against the other bodies crowding the room.

He gives April a quick squeeze once she reaches him, but when his eyes land on me, he practically jumps across the room to pull me into a bear hug. It effectively squashes all the rest of my nervousness out of my system, along with all the oxygen in my lungs.

"I didn't think you were coming to this!" he says with a grin.

"Neither did I," I wheeze, grateful the music isn't as loud back here so we don't have to shout to hear each other. "This is Felix, by the way."

Bryce greets him by pulling him into a bear hug too. When Felix is finally relinquished, he looks a little dazed. I stifle a laugh as Jaz peeks around Bryce's shoulder. She's dressed in her regular uniform of all-black everything, and her tan arms are slung around both Savannah and April's shoulders, stacks of rings and silver bracelets glinting in the low light.

"Dude, good to see you! Y'all want beer?"

Felix and I both nod and as Jaz fishes two PBRs out of the fridge, Felix takes a second to connect names to faces.

"Okay so, Bryce, Jaz," he says, nodding to each as he goes, "and you're—?"

"Savannah," she says, tucking a strand of her white-blonde hair behind her ear. Her makeup is done immaculately as ever: baby blue smokey eyes matching her nails, crop top, and plaid miniskirt perfectly. But her put-together look is really an illusion, and I realize she's somehow 200 percent drunker than anyone else right as she blurts out, "Please tell me you're into girls."

The way Jaz slaps her arm and cackles tells me this isn't the first time she's asked straight up like that. To his credit, Felix looks totally unphased, taking a long sip from his can before he replies.

"Nope," Felix says, popping the *p*. "I'm as gay as they come. Plus, I'm dating him."

All eyes follow Felix's finger, which is pointing directly at my face. A beat passes, and then everyone starts talking at once.

"Shut UP!"

"When did this happen?"

"No fuckin' way."

I glance at Felix, trying not to glare while also conveying, *you really couldn't have found a more subtle way to drop that information?* Felix smiles back, totally unfazed. Maybe I will strangle him after all.

"Um, can we do one question at a time?" I ask, and Jaz is the first one to pull it together enough to comply.

"How did you two meet?"

"We're childhood best friends," Felix says, and he's such a ham, he pauses to give the chorus of "awwws" time to settle before he continues. "We haven't seen each other in a couple years, but we reconnected a few weeks ago."

"Wait, so we were still in school when this happened? Dude, why didn't you say anything?" Bryce asks, jostling me with an elbow to the ribs.

"It was still really new," I say, surprised by how easily the lie rolls off my tongue. "I didn't want to jinx it."

"Awww, you were worried about messing things up?" Felix asks, tone sweet and teasing, and I resist the urge to frown at him. "Don't worry, you couldn't have chased me off if you tried."

"I can't believe you actually have a boyfriend," Savannah says into her Solo cup.

"Hey, what's that supposed to mean?" I ask, and April laughs at my sour expression.

"Don't be offended, it's not like that. You're adorable. We all know this," Jaz reassures me. "You're in your own head a lot. I feel like you never notice when guys are flirting with you."

"I have no idea what you're talking about," I reply before I realize I'm proving their point.

"Oh, this is unreal," Felix says, sounding a little pained for some reason.

"That sophomore in your art class was pining over you all year, and you didn't pick up on it at all. You're clueless," April points out, laughing when my mouth drops open. She's right, I didn't pick up on that. *Shit.* "Oh, you sweet, oblivious angel. I still haven't forgotten about the guy at the record store either. He was actively, blatantly hitting on you, and you totally ignored him."

Savannah gasps. "Hello, what guy?"

"There was no guy!" I say, but nobody is buying it. "It wasn't even a thing."

"It absolutely sounds like a thing, but hey, lucky me that you didn't notice," Felix says, leaning into me in a way that makes my heart lurch. He's got his arm looped behind my back and braced against the kitchen counter, and it makes me feel like I'm on fire. "Still, I can't believe you got propositioned and never told me."

I sigh, looking up at him. "The only person who's propositioned me lately is you."

"Good," Felix says, looking genuinely delighted.

"Oh, gross," Jaz says. "You two really are cute together."

And shit, my heart jumps again, but this time it lodges itself in my throat. *This is fake*, I remind myself. *This is extremely fake and we are not cute at all.*

Thankfully, as April predicted, the attention doesn't linger on us or our relationship for too long. One impossibly loud song shifts to the next as Savannah tells us about her latest painfully awkward hookup, where she ended up spending half her night comforting the guy about his ex. Jaz complains about her summer job at the coffee shop by her house, which is how I learn that Felix works as a barista part-time during the school year.

The only time Felix moves away from me is when he grabs us

our second and third drinks, but other than that, he's glued to my side. He's still hovering next to me, watching with amusement as Bryce and Jaz debate the proper watch order of the Star Wars movies when I feel his arm slip around my shoulder. I freeze, not sure if I want to lean into his touch or push him off me.

"What are you doing?" I say, as low as I can while still being able to be heard over the music.

"We're supposed to practice acting like a normal couple, and this is how normal couples act," Felix says, finishing off his second beer. "What's not normal, by the way, is looking like you want to jump off a cliff every time I touch you."

"Well, you make me nervous," I mumble, and Felix pauses.

"Oh, really?" he asks with a grin, pulling me a little closer. "How so?"

"Because of *that*," I say, glaring up at him. "Whatever you're doing right now, cut it out."

"I can't stop being hilarious and adorable. I was born this way."

"Don't you dare bring Lady Gaga into this."

Savannah, who Jaz has forcibly switched to water, bounces up to us and grabs Felix's free arm. "Wait, you should come to this concert we're going to in a few weeks."

April gasps, and oh god, she's breaking out the puppy dog eyes already. "Please, please, please come with us."

"Oh yeah? What's the band?" Felix asks.

"It's an up-and-coming country artist. They're playing at this little venue on the East Side," I say, heart flip-flopping in my chest as Felix tips his head closer to mine so he can hear better. "If you say no, April will cry. It's part of her crusade for the perfect summer."

"Don't call it a crusade!" April says, words slurring a bit. "It sounds colonization . . . colonizy . . . shit, I can't talk."

"Colonization-y?" I offer and she nods, still pouting. "Okay, a campaign, then. I didn't say it was a bad thing, by the way."

"You think it's stupid," she says, and I shake my head.

"I don't. Promise."

"Well, you can laugh about it now, but it won't be funny when all of us are on opposite sides of the country for college," April says sternly, and I pause, drink lifted halfway to my mouth. "I don't want everyone to disappear on me the second we graduate."

For a beat, I'm not sure what to say. April and I have had dozens of conversations about our summer plans, but she's never gotten this serious about it before. I knew she wanted to make sure we all spent as much time together as possible, but it never occurred to me that she was seriously this worried our friend group was going to fall apart. She has to know we'd never let that happen, right?

"April, come on," I say gently, lowering my drink. "We're not going to disappear on you."

"Yeah, but everyone says that," she sighs, "which is exactly why we have to make the most of our time while we're all together in one place."

"We will! And we love the campaign," Bryce says, because

nobody is immune to an April pout. "It's sweet that you want to make sure we stick together. Campaign away."

"Yeah, April. Don't sweat it. I'll be there," Felix says, but April still looks sullen.

"You better be," she says to Felix, and then turns to me, poking a finger into my chest. "And we're supposed to be best friends forever. Don't forget about me now that you have a boyfriend."

"That's not going to happen," I reply automatically, because it's not even a question.

The song playing in the background fades out and into something that makes April and Savannah scream at each other in glee, and they pull each other away from the group to dance. My buzzed brain is still struggling to catch up with the conversation, though.

April is my best friend and my favorite person in the world, so letting someone else distract me from our friendship feels absurd. She knows that Felix and I aren't dating for real, so I doubt what she said had much to do with him. There has to be more going on with her than meets the eye, but I can't seem to make sense of it with the music and chatter crowding my ears.

These thoughts are best saved for sober Joaquin anyway, and by the time I finish my third beer, my worries shift into a pleasant, fuzzy calm I can feel in the tips of my fingers. I wasn't planning on drinking too much tonight, worried I might say something that would blow my cover with Felix. But as the night wears on, I find myself relaxing, not worrying about how we're coming off or who's looking at us. I let myself get swept up in the music and the rapid-fire conversations between my friends, and Felix's arm stays around my shoulders, equal parts reassuring and electrifying.

When the girls pull Bryce onto the dance floor and Felix and I are left on our own, it takes me a second to realize that we technically don't need to keep standing so close.

"Are you going to keep leaning on me all night?" I say, more teasing than serious as I glance up at Felix. He smiles lazily back at me.

"Now that you mention it, I think I will," he replies, pulling me in even closer, which I didn't think was possible.

He's turned toward me a little, so we're no longer standing side by side, but we're not quite chest-to-chest either. Even though my limbs feel all light and fuzzy from the beer, the contact still feels magnetic. And maybe it's the alcohol, or maybe it's the smug look on Felix's face, but I get an idea. I take my arm and slowly, deliberately loop it around his waist, tugging him a little bit closer.

"Suit yourself," I say, and exactly like I'd hoped, the confident smile on Felix's face falters.

"Shit, we should get drunk more often," he says, sounding a little dazed, and I stifle a laugh.

"I'm not drunk. I'm just buzzed."

"Everyone says that when they're drunk," he points out, still leaning into me. "But you're having fun, right?"

I find myself nodding before I fully think through my answer. But I am having fun, and I'm pretty sure I would be even if I hadn't had a single drink. I was so nervous about feeling awkward or out of place, but now that I'm here, I haven't really felt that at all.

"It's funny how much everyone has to say to each other even though they do this every weekend," I say, eyes scanning the party as I fiddle with the hem of Felix's shirt. "I didn't realize how much I've missed out on by not coming to stuff like this."

"I'm sure your friends would be happy if you hung out with them more often. I can tell they care about you a lot," Felix says, and when I look up at him again, the sincerity on his face catches me a little off guard. "People like having you around, Jay."

It's such a simple statement, one that shouldn't knock the wind out of me, but it does anyway. And Felix is looking at me with this expression I've never seen on him before, or maybe one that I saw a long time ago. My head feels too light, and I can feel how warm his waist is under my hand, and I'm suddenly afraid again that I might say something stupid.

But the spell is broken when Bryce starts shimmying in our direction, silently begging us to come dance with him. Felix pulls away, and I momentarily mourn the loss of the warmth before he reaches out a hand.

"Come on, I'm not half bad," he says. I shake my head, heart still jackhammering in my chest, and laugh as he whirls away to dance with Bryce.

I end up bopping along to the music anyway as the party thins out a bit, some people leaving early, others drifting off to quieter corners of the house. After a handful of songs, the girls make their way back over to me, and Felix and Bryce follow suit. Bryce has Felix in a near choke hold, and Felix is laughing his head off, dimples flashing. *Cute*, I think, and my heart does another traitorous flip.

"Ask him what you asked me," Felix says to Bryce. "I want to see the face he makes."

"I was saying your birthday is coming up. What's the plan?" Bryce asks, and I feel like I just got hit in the head with a brick. Felix and April, who've both had one too many drinks, start giggling uncontrollably. "Wait, what? Loaded question?"

"My dad is throwing me the world's most dramatic birthday slash coming-out party in the world," I say, and Bryce's eyes light up. "Think quince meets Pride but it's all against my will."

"That's so camp," Savannah says. I guess she's not wrong.

"Why weren't we invited?" Bryce asks as Felix wriggles out of his grip. He slides over to me, standing behind me and resting his chin on my shoulder.

The contact makes me feel a little delirious, so I blurt out, "You want to come?"

"We absolutely do—what the hell," Jaz says, and my other friends nod emphatically.

Maybe I could blame it on the alcohol, or the high from Felix leaning on me and the music vibrating up through the soles of my shoes, but I want to invite them. I can't really think of a good reason not to, not when I feel all light and buzzy and happy. April looks at me with those puppy dog eyes again, and I can't resist.

"Okay, yeah. You're officially invited," I say, and my friends' smiles light up the whole room.

After my fourth beer, the rest of the night is a little bit of a blur, but it's blurry in a good way. I don't remember texting Carmen to pick us up, but I do remember climbing into the back seat of her car, laughing as she complains that we smell like a frat house.

My limbs feel heavy as the night air floats through the windows, cooling my skin where Felix and April are pressed up against my sides, but I feel warmed from the inside out. I'm pretty sure when I wake up tomorrow morning, I'm still going to be glad I invited my friends to the queerceañera.

After a few minutes, I feel Felix's hair tickle my neck, and then the full weight of his head falls onto my shoulder. My heart hiccups in my chest, but I don't push him off. It's the alcohol that's making me soft. It has to be.

Carmen catches my eye in the rearview mirror.

"So, not a bad night?" she asks quietly.

"No," I say honestly. "Not bad at all."

Chapter Twelve

I WAKE UP the morning after the party with a raging hangover and an idiotic text from Felix on my phone. are we gonna do a photoshoot? because i really want to do a photoshoot.

I'd rather not, I reply, feeling groggy. My eyes start to slide shut, but the screen lights up again a few seconds later.

i feel like we could pull this off tho, Felix texts, along with a brightly saturated photograph from some stranger's quince. A girl in a voluminous red dress and her chambelán are strutting through the jungle together, and what must be a photoshopped tiger lies dramatically in the foreground. It's heinous.

I'm going to break up with you, I send, to which he replies :/

I toss my phone aside and rub the sleep from my eyes. My head is killing me and my throat feels like I swallowed sand, but it's probably nothing that Tylenol and a gallon of water can't fix. What I am worried about is the memories from the party that are slowly starting to flash through my head.

I was drunk, I can admit that now. But I didn't act that embarrassing, right? I was a little chattier than usual with Bryce, Jaz, and Savannah, but that's not necessarily a bad thing. And I remember inviting them to the queerceañera, but when I replay the exchange in my head, the dread I'm expecting to hit me doesn't come. I had fun last night, and they genuinely seemed excited about my party, so I don't think I'd mind having them around even if it does end up being a shit show.

But as I continue to backtrack through my memories of the night, they snag on Felix's arm around my shoulders and the way I pulled him into me when I was three beers in. My face heats up, and I shove my face into my pillow and groan. Why the hell did I think that was a good idea? Felix teasing me is one thing. That's just what he's like. But teasing him back, flirting with him even, is unforgivably stupid. He's going to be insufferable about this, I'm sure of it.

My phone buzzes again, and this time, it keeps on buzzing. I flip it over and, speak of the devil, it's an incoming call from Felix. Taking a deep, steadying breath, I hit accept and hold the phone up to my ear.

"Heeey, how's the best boyfriend in the whole world?" he says. His voice sounds pinched and weird.

"What's wrong with you?" I ask, and I hear him let out a pained laugh.

"Ouch, and here I was thinking we made such good progress last night."

See? Insufferable, exactly like I thought. "I'm hanging up."

"Hold on, I called for a good reason," he says quickly. "Remember how our little deal is supposed to be mutually beneficial?"

"Um, sure?" I reply. It takes a second for my muddied thoughts to drift to Felix's family and how they've been worried about him since his breakup. "Why do you ask?"

"Well, my parents are coming to town tomorrow to visit," he says. "They're going to be at the barbecue your mom is hosting, and I know you're invited."

I have to think about it for a second, but he's right. I guess I was invited. Mom texted me about it a while back, before the queerceañera and all the chaos that's come with it. It's the type of thing she always invites me to, and I always say I'll try to make it knowing full well I won't actually go.

But now that Felix and I are fake-together and testing the waters, maybe this is a good opportunity to keep warming Mom up to me being openly gay. This wasn't exactly how I was planning to spend my weekend, but Felix is right, this little charade was supposed to benefit both of us. If we can kill two birds with one stone in an afternoon, I'm all for it.

"So you want us to go to the barbecue and prove that you're doing fine?" I ask, and Felix *mm-hmm*s on the other end of the line. "Yeah, okay, I can do that."

"Wow, you really are the best boyfriend in the world," he sighs.

"I know," I reply and hit end call. A second later, I get a text with one sad, solitary :(in response.

As the day wears on and my hangover subsides, I realize I'm not as nervous about the barbecue as I thought I would be. After the party, I feel way better about me and Felix being able to sell our relationship in front of other people, and with any luck, we'll be able to put Mom and his parents at ease in one go.

When I text Mom to let her know I'm going, she seems pretty excited.

That's wonderful, hijo! she replies. Josh and I are happy to have you, and Olivia and Aaron are going to be over the moon.

I chew my lip, rereading the text with a mix of affection and guilt. Mom's stepkids are totally sweet, both in middle school and overflowing with energy. I babysat them a few times in the fall, but the less time I spend with Mom, the less I see them by extension. Maybe this will be a good chance to reconnect with them too.

Do you want me to bring anything? I type back, and her response comes right away.

No, but it's sweet of you to offer. We'll have more than enough to go around.

The exchange eases the tiny bit of apprehension I was feeling about the barbecue, but later that night, I realize I've made one fatal mistake in agreeing to these plans. Dad's car is in the shop, and April has guitar lessons tomorrow. Barring me paying a ridiculous amount of money for an Uber, Carmen is my only option for a ride.

When I bring it up, Carmen acts like it's no problem at all. It shouldn't be, because it's not like she's going to stay or even say hi. She'll just drop me off and drive away, no problem. So on Sunday, when we pull up behind the string of cars parked along the street, I'm planning on jumping out and letting her get on with her day. But of course, it doesn't work out like that.

Mom happens to be standing in the front yard talking to Olivia and Aaron, who wave wildly when they see me through the passenger-side window. Mom turns to look, and I can pinpoint the exact moment she sees my sister. She shoos the kids toward the backyard and starts to make her way toward the car.

"Ah," I say, because there are no words to express how awkward I know this interaction is going to be.

Carmen sighs as she rolls down the window. Mom ducks down a little to look into the car, squinting against the sun.

"Carmen, it's good to see you," she says, and the softness in her voice is both really sweet and a little sad. "I didn't know you were coming too."

"I'm not," Carmen says quickly, leaning over the center console. "I mean, I can't stay. I have a thing."

I glance over at her, but her expression is impassive. I know for a fact that she doesn't have a thing, but she's planning to crawl back into bed and binge *Real Housewives* for the rest of the day. But I'm not going to blow her cover.

"Oh, okay," Mom says, shifting from one foot to the other on the soft grass. "You know you're always welcome to come when we have get-togethers like this. You can join us whenever you want."

"I know," Carmen says, inflection perfectly neutral.

I wait for a beat, wondering if she's going to say something else, but I'm met with silence. Mom offers a weak smile, and I get the feeling that she wants to extend the conversation but doesn't know what to say. It's all painfully awkward and a little too sad for me to stomach for much longer, so I decide to put us all out of our misery and start unbuckling my seat belt.

"Thanks for the ride," I say to Carmen, and she gives me a relieved nod as I get out of the car. Carmen drives off, and when I turn to Mom, I catch the tail end of a frown on her face before she puts a hand on my shoulder.

"I'm so glad you could make it," she says, smiling at me like the exchange with Carmen was completely normal. She guides me toward the backyard, where music and the sound of meat sizzling drift over the wooden fence. "Josh is finishing up the food. Help yourself to any appetizers you want in the meantime."

"I'll probably grab something later," I say. As we push through the gate, the smell of charcoal, beer, and lime hit me in full force. "I should find Felix first."

"He's probably busy with his parents," Mom says offhandedly, looking out over the party.

"Yeah, but he really wanted me to say hi to them. You know, now that we're dating," I say. Mom's lips purse the tiniest bit, but I can't tell if it's a reaction to me and Felix, or Olivia nearly knocking down both Josh and the grill with an errant soccer ball.

"Right, that makes sense," she replies. I try to read her expression, but it's obvious that she's having a silent parenting conversation with Josh. She tries to wave at Olivia and catch her attention and then sighs. "Sorry, Joaquin, excuse me for a minute. I need to take care of this."

Mom leaves me to my own devices, and I push down the uneasiness prickling in my chest and take stock of the party instead. There are plenty of familiar faces, including some of my dad's old friends. I catch the eye of one of them, who offers a wave as I scan the crowd. My eyes eventually land on Felix, who immediately makes a beeline for me. It's over a hundred degrees outside, but even so, he looks unnaturally flushed.

"Oh, thank god you came," he says, breathless and a little wild-eyed. He's wearing a modern guayabera with a contrasting collar, and I'd be way more distracted by how good he looks in it if he didn't look unhinged.

"I told you I would," I say as he drags me to the perimeter of the yard where we can get a little privacy.

"I know, and that's great, because now it's time to show everyone how happy and well-adjusted I am," he says.

I eyeball him. "Well-adjusted might be a bit of a stretch."

"Cards on the table? I'm a little frazzled," Felix says, and damn if it isn't at least a little bit endearing. "I've already been cross-examined by, like, twelve people about my breakup."

"Well, you're in luck since the best boyfriend in the world is here to save you," I deadpan, and Felix snorts, some of the tension leaving his shoulders.

"My parents are over there," he says, nodding to the opposite side of the yard. I recognize his mom's dimpled smile and dad's ginger hair right away.

"Okay, let's do this," I say. "What's our move?"

"This," he says, grabbing my hand. When he weaves his fingers between mine, I stiffen.

Felix laughs, his nerves apparently forgotten in favor of torturing me. He rubs my thumb in a way that makes me shiver. "I still make you nervous, huh?"

"Nope, not even a little bit," I lie.

I try to compose myself as Felix leads me over to his parents, but any worries I had disappear when they see me. Both their faces light up when they see me, and Felix sighs with relief at that reaction alone.

"Oh man, it's been ages!" his dad says, clapping a hand on my shoulder.

"Hey, Mr. and Mrs. Campbell-Garcia," I say, smiling at each of them in turn. "It's really good to see you again."

"Please, use our first names. You're basically an adult now anyway," Ian says, and next to him, Teresa nods.

"Gosh, you're so grown up," she adds with a smile. "And so cute. Though I guess I shouldn't be too surprised. Felix did go on and on about how handsome you are now."

"*Mom*," Felix says, and oh my god, I think he's blushing. Maybe I'm going to have fun today after all. "Maybe you don't say anything else, okay?"

"Don't listen to him. Tell me everything," I whisper to Teresa, who giggles and slaps my arm playfully. Felix looks like he wants to melt into the ground and disappear, and his dad is getting a real kick out of it.

"Good man, keeping my son on his toes," Ian booms, turning to clap a hand on Felix's back. "See, this is exactly what you need in a partner."

"Someone who drives me crazy?" Felix asks thinly.

"No, someone you can have fun with," Ian replies. "If they also drive you crazy, it's a bonus. I've been married to your mother for twenty years. It sure as hell has worked out for us."

"Jokes aside, I've got to say we were so happy to hear you two got together," Teresa chimes in. "You were always so sweet with each other as kids. Who would've thought you could make it work all these years later?"

"I don't think either of us expected it, but I think that's why we work," I say, trying to ride the line between telling the truth and selling our story. "We've both let each other show up exactly as we are, and it turns out we like each other now as much as we did back then."

"You don't know how good that is to hear," Ian says, and the fondness on both his and Teresa's faces makes my heart clench.

It's obvious how much they adore and worry over Felix, and I'm really glad I've been able to put their minds at ease. Technically, I'm just holding up my end of the bargain, but at this point, it hardly feels like a favor at all. I'm just happy they're happy.

"You're very lucky, sweetie," Teresa says, putting a hand on Felix's shoulder. "This kind of connection doesn't come around every day."

Felix's hand tightens around mine, and he glances over at me with a soft smile. "Don't worry, I know."

I'm still trying to read Felix's expression when an older couple approaches us, a man and a woman I vaguely remember meeting as a kid.

"Ah, so this is the mysterious boyfriend we've been hearing rumors about?" asks the man.

"This is him, in the flesh," Felix says, beaming at the couple. "Jay, this is Maria and Benito Fernández, my parents' old college friends."

"Oh, you're Rocio's son!" Maria says, turning to me. "She must be so thrilled you two got together, since your families are so close and all."

"Absolutely," Felix replies. God, I wish the answer was that straightforward.

"I have to be honest—we were so surprised to hear you and Caleb split up," Benito says, and I can feel Felix's hand tense up in mine. Benito leans over to me and tosses me a conspiratorial wink. "You weren't the other woman, were you?"

"Oh, no, definitely not," I say, but I get this feeling in the pit of my stomach at the way he worded it that's making it hard for me to keep it together. "Felix and I have known each other our whole lives. Things just moved quickly when we reconnected, that's all."

"Plus, the great thing about being gay is that neither of us is a woman," Felix adds, matching Benito's joking tone in a way that diffuses whatever tension was lingering in the air.

Benito laughs, and when Felix's parents join in, I have to assume they didn't pick up on how odd his comment was. To an outsider, the whole thing might have looked like a friendly exchange, but I know Felix. I could tell he was annoyed too, except instead of getting flustered or outwardly angry, he managed to redirect the comment better than I ever could. In a moment of bravery, I rub my thumb over Felix's, mirroring the way he did it to me before. Felix gives my hand a quick squeeze, a smile playing on his lips.

"If you don't mind me prying, what happened with you and Caleb?" Maria says, and Teresa tuts at her.

"Don't put the poor boy on the spot like that," she says, echoing my thoughts.

"Sorry, I'm so curious!" Maria replies, stirring the fast-melting frozen margarita in her hand. "He didn't break your heart, did he?"

Ian frowns, but before he can step in, Felix shakes his head and says, "Nah, nothing like that. He was great and all, but I never really felt like I could fully relax and be myself around him. I guess I wanted to be with someone who made me feel like the best version of myself."

"Well, it's good you have that now," Maria says, motioning to me. Felix tugs me a little closer, and I let him.

"Yeah, yeah it is."

Felix's parents and the Fernándezes get pulled into another conversation, and the second they're out of earshot, Felix turns his attention to me.

"I'm so sorry about that," he says, voice low. I almost expect him to pull his hand away, but it stays firmly in mine. "The 'other woman' thing was so gross. I hate when people project heteronormative bullshit onto me."

"Hey, it's not your fault," I say, and the worried crease between Felix's brows softens. "I'm kind of surprised your parents didn't say something."

Felix shrugs. "They don't always pick up on stuff like that. Sometimes microaggressions fly right over their heads, but when I explain it to them later, it'll click for them. I've gotten good at redirecting weird conversations like that on my own."

"You handled it way better than I would have. Thanks for having my back," I say, and Felix smiles in response. "On the plus side, your answers during the breakup interrogation sounded great. Very well-adjusted."

"Thank god for that," he says with a little laugh. "It's hard to put it into words, but that was the truth. Breakups are never really cut-and-dried."

"I guess I wouldn't know."

"Wait, are you saying you've never dated?" Felix says, peering down at me. "No wonder your friends were having a field day on Friday. Why not?"

I'd love to look him in the eye and say, *because of you, stupid.* But instead, I shrug. "I guess I've never met the right person."

"Well," Felix says, squeezing my hand again, "lucky me."

And right when I'm thoroughly distracted, Mom manages to sneak up behind me.

"Joaquin, could I borrow you for a minute?" she asks, placing a hand on my shoulder. "I could use your help setting up."

Felix gives me a reassuring nod, and I try not to get too disappointed when his fingers slip from mine. Instead, I follow Mom as she leads me through the backyard and past the sliding doors at the back of the house into her kitchen. Dishes heaping with food crowd the island.

"All the food is done. All I need is an extra set of hands to bring it all out back," she says, scooping up a plate of corn on the cob and an armful of condiments while I grab a salad bowl and follow her back outside. "I saw you talking to Teresa and Ian. How did that go?"

"Really great," I reply honestly, placing the salad on a picnic table Mom had set up on the patio. "They're so sweet. I miss them a lot. And I like seeing Felix get embarrassed by them, so it's a win-win."

Mom laughs as we head back to the kitchen and grab more

food. "They're good parents, and they raised a good son. Felix has a bright future ahead of him."

"Yeah, for sure," I say, but the words fall flat.

It's a simple compliment, and one that's true and deserved. It really shouldn't make me jealous, but I have to wonder if Mom is proud enough to brag about me too.

As we head outside again, Mom glances over at me. "I'm really glad you came today. I know you don't always like being around so many people at once."

"I guess, but this is nice," I say, trying to rally and push whatever negative thoughts I had out of my head. "I don't know if April is finally getting to me, but catching up with people like this is fun. I got to see Bryce, Jaz, and Savannah the other night, and it got me thinking that I want to hang out with them more often too."

"That's really good to hear," Mom says, putting the last few plates down on the table and stepping back. When she turns to look at me, her smile is genuine and warm. "It's good to see you coming out of your shell, cariño."

I pause, the pet name catching me off guard. "Cariño" is one of those sweet little terms of endearment that Mom used to sprinkle into every conversation with me and Carmen when we were little, but it's been a while since I heard her use it with me, and I don't think I realized how much I missed it until now.

"Thanks, Mom," I say, smiling back.

A hand reaches out to steady the last plate I'm setting down on the table, and I turn to see Felix has joined us on the patio. Josh trails behind him, balancing a tray of steaming hot burgers and kebabs while Olivia and Aaron cling to his legs.

"Joaquin, it's so great to see you!" Josh says, setting down the food and giving my hand a quick squeeze. His blue polo is smudged with charcoal, and he's got a slight sunburn on the tips of his ears, but he seems totally in his element. "I just mentioned to your mom the other day that it's been way too long since you stopped by. We miss seeing your face around these parts."

"Yeah, you have to come over more," Aaron says, relinquishing Josh to pull on my arm. "I'm stuck on a shrine in *Breath of the Wild* and I know you'd be able to beat it."

"Oh, so that's the only reason you want me around?" I ask with a laugh.

"No way, you're so much more fun to hang out with than Felix," Olivia whines. Next to me, Felix scoffs, but she ignores him. "He only ever talks about boring stuff with Dad."

Josh lets out a good-natured laugh. "It's not boring; we're just talking about work."

"Boooring," Olivia sing-songs and Aaron nods emphatically, tugging on my arm again.

Josh works in IT, so I can only imagine how mind-numbing the dinner table conversations have been since Felix came to stay with them. I turn to Felix, who's making a show of looking very hurt and offended.

"Have you tried telling them that puzzle metaphor about coding? I think it made you sound really cool," I say, and I'm not surprised when Felix reaches out to hold my free hand, weaving his fingers between mine.

"I tried," he replies with a smile. "Guess they're not as easily impressed as you."

Much to Olivia's dismay, Josh and Felix launch into a discussion about Felix's coding program as the other partygoers grab food and drinks and mill around us. About 95 percent of the conversation goes over my head, but it's oddly charming how animated Felix is getting over it. I find myself smiling as I listen, but Mom keeps sending furtive glances my way, and it's kind of distracting. I only realize why when she leans over a few minutes later.

"Joaquin," she says under her breath, looking pointedly at Felix and my hands, which are still intertwined. "Not in front of the kids."

Suddenly, it feels like all the air has been squeezed out of my lungs. The hum of the party is a hundred miles away, and I can feel the smile drop off my face as the meaning of her words hits me in full force.

I thought that everything was going perfectly today. Felix and I finally hit our stride, his parents were thrilled with me, and Josh and the kids were welcoming me with open arms. Everything was going off without a hitch, and there I was, foolishly thinking that Mom and I were finally getting along. It felt so normal between us. I really thought that me and Felix being here together wasn't weird after all. I thought she actually liked the idea of us being together. But she's still uncomfortable with me being out, and I feel so, so stupid for hoping it would turn out any other way.

I want to say something to her or go back to ten seconds ago when I didn't feel like there was a giant, gaping hole in my chest. But I can't do either, so instead, I find myself loosening my grip on Felix's hand. And Felix, too distracted by the parallel conversation he's having to see what's going on, lets me go.

"So what about you, Joaquin?" Josh asks, pulling me out of my spiraling thoughts. "Has Felix gotten you interested in tech now too?"

"Oh, uh, not quite. I'm still focusing on my art."

"And I'm really glad he is," Felix adds proudly, and it would be sweet if I didn't feel like the floor had just vanished from under my feet. "He's gonna make a career of it."

"I didn't know you'd made up your mind about that already," Mom says, and her voice sounds chipper, but her smile isn't reaching her eyes. "That's a big commitment. Are you sure you've thought this through?"

"I have. I've been doing art for most of my life. I can't imagine doing anything else," I say automatically. I'm not sure I can manage to say anything more cohesive right now, not when I'm so distracted. I'm not sure how to feel when Felix jumps in to back me up.

"Any career choice is a big commitment at our age. And personally, I think everyone should pursue what they're most passionate about," Felix says evenly. "I support him no matter what."

"Well, that's nice, isn't it?" Mom says with a smile I'm not sure I believe is genuine.

The conversation drifts back to Felix, back to his 4.0 GPA and the bright future Mom is so proud of, but I'm still frozen in place. My stomach is in knots, and I can't figure out where we're supposed to go from here. I thought for sure that Mom wouldn't be so uptight about me being gay if I had Felix by my side, but what if all of this is pointless? What if no matter how hard I try, she doesn't budge?

"—a plate?" Felix asks, and I snap back to the present moment.

"Sorry, what?"

"I was asking if you wanted to grab some food," Felix says, looking down at me with worry etched across his face. When I don't answer right away, he slips his hand into mine again. It sends a hot flash of guilt up my spine, but before I can think to pull away, he turns to Mom and Josh. "On second thought, could you excuse us for a minute?"

Felix doesn't wait for their response. He tugs me off the patio and past the grill, marching by the other guests until we're standing in the cool shade at the side of the house, far from any prying eyes.

"Okay," he says, turning to look at me. "What's wrong?"

"Nothing," I say, finally pulling my hand free from his. Felix's frown deepens. "I'm tired, that's all."

"Don't do that."

"Do what?"

"Lie to me. I think you're forgetting that I know you," he says, taking a step closer. "That thing you were doing back there? Going totally quiet and zoning out? I know that's what you do when something really gets under your skin."

"Okay fine, I'm upset. Do you want a prize?"

"No, I want you to tell me what's wrong so I can help make things better."

"Can you just—" I almost say *stop*, but that would be another lie. I don't want him to stop, because it's nice that he cares. But I don't know how I can unpack what happened with my mom a second ago, not when it's so fresh. Instead, I say, "Give me a second to breathe."

And to Felix's credit, he does. He slips his hands into his pockets and walks over to stand next to me. We both lean against the cool siding of the house shoulder to shoulder while I suck in deep breaths of hot, suffocating summer air and push them out through my nose. A long minute passes before Felix speaks up again.

"Is it Josh and the kids?" he asks quietly. "Because they really love you. They talk about you all the time."

"Sort of, but that's not exactly it," I hedge. I still don't want to talk about the comment Mom made, but her stepfamily and the weirdness with Carmen are also weighing on me in their own way. That feels like a safer but no less real topic to distract Felix with for now. "Josh and the kids are really sweet, but it's a little odd seeing Mom with her new family when things with me, Carmen, and her are . . . weird."

Felix nods, letting the words hang in the air for a second. The music and chatter of the barbecue thrum in the background.

"Carmen and your mom aren't talking, right?" he asks. "I picked up on it, but I didn't want to meddle."

I shake my head. "It's not meddling. But no, not since the beginning of the year. The divorce wasn't even the breaking point, oddly enough. I think a lot of stuff came to the surface over time that they weren't addressing before."

"I guess that makes sense," Felix says, and I glance over at him.

"You're not surprised they aren't talking?"

"No, not really," he replies. "Your mom is . . . a very particular person. And Carmen has always known what she's about. If something isn't sitting right with her, I'm not surprised she spoke up and set a boundary like that."

"Neither am I. Like, I get it, and I really can't fault her for it."

"But it's putting a strain on your relationship with your mom too?" Felix asks, and I nod. "Okay, yeah, I think I get it."

"Carmen dropped me off earlier, and I could tell Mom wanted her to stay so bad. But they never talk. And with Mom and the queerceañera, I'm worried we might be heading in the same direction—that it's our own breaking point."

"Stuff like that takes time," Felix says, and the gentleness in his voice makes my heart clench. "I know it's easier said than done, but sometimes, you have to be patient with people and hope they come around eventually."

And he doesn't even know it, but I think Felix just said exactly what I needed to hear. I don't have the answers for how to get on the same page with Mom, and neither does Carmen. But maybe I need to keep pressing ahead regardless.

I hear a champagne bottle pop from the backyard, probably to make a fresh batch of mimosas, and a chorus of laughs follows soon after. I take another deep breath and let it out with a sigh.

"I really don't want to go back in there," I murmur.

"Okay, then don't."

I turn to look at Felix again, raising a brow at him. "You trying to get rid of me?"

"Geez, don't make it sound so awful," he says with a light laugh. "You did a great job with my parents today, and if you're feeling wiped, you shouldn't force yourself to stay."

"I don't know," I say, worry spiking again at the thought of leaving things on such a sour note.

"Jay, look at me," Felix says, leaning over to press his shoulder into mine. When I do look up at him, my pulse slows, and my anxiety starts to quiet itself again. "We have time to make things work with your mom. I promise."

I nod, eyes still locked with his. I have to wonder whether he'd still be this confident if he knew the whole story, but I want to believe that he's right, that we'll figure this out together and it'll be all right in the end. Felix only looks away when there's a rustle behind me, and I turn to see Mom approaching us.

"Everything okay, you two?"

"Jay isn't feeling great," Felix says. "I'm going to take him home."

Mom's brows pinch together, and she reaches a hand out to touch my cheek, then my forehead. "You're not sick, are you? No fever?"

"No, nothing like that," I say, taking a step back. "Just feeling tired."

Mom drops her hand, and she looks at me for a beat longer than I expect. "All of a sudden?"

"Guess it just hit me all at once," I murmur, hoping the lie isn't too obvious. Mom pauses again, glancing at Felix and back at me.

"Okay," she says quietly. "Will you text me later tonight? Let me know if you're feeling better?"

"I promise I'll be fine."

Felix and I push away from the side of the house and start to make our way toward the backyard, but Mom speaks up again.

"Joaquin?" she calls, voice tight. Her expression is unreadable when I turn to look at her over my shoulder. "I'll see you again soon, right? The kids . . . well, we all miss you around here."

"Yeah, I'm sure you will," I reply without thinking about it much. For a second, I feel like Mom is going to say something else, though I can't imagine what. But then she nods, and we head back to the party.

As convenient as it would be to borrow from Felix's heritage and pull off an Irish goodbye, I can't bring myself to leave without making my rounds and wishing people well. Somewhere between Josh and the kids giving me three tight hugs and Ian and Teresa offering sweet goodbyes, Felix takes my hand in his again. This time, I don't pull away, and the contact doesn't put me on edge. If anything it feels grounding, and as Felix walks me to his car, I repeat what he said inside my head. We still have time to make things work.

Chapter Thirteen

AFTER EVERYTHING THAT happened at the barbecue, I figured that talking to Felix was going to be a little weird. Having him walk me back from an emotional ledge wasn't exactly part of our agreement. It was raw and vulnerable in ways I'm not used to, and every time I think about the quiet conversation we had at the side of my mom's house, it feels like I'm pressing into a fresh bruise.

But instead of making things awkward, I think our talk broke down an invisible wall between us. Felix texts me on and off over the next few days, and when he offers to bring me lunch after a marathon painting session, spending time with him feels surprisingly normal.

He convinces me to try a new boba place with him a few days later, and when I let it slip that April and I skateboard, he makes me promise to teach him how before summer is over. Felix cheerfully tags along on odd errands I have to run, and I end up picking him up from his coding boot camp more often than not. It's never really about the things we're doing so much as the conversations we have while doing them. Slowly, the collage of seventeen-year-old Felix comes together, and I like the person he's become—much more than is strictly necessary.

I have to keep reminding myself that we're spending time together for a reason, to make our relationship seem real. But the more we hang out, the more the line blurs between our real connection and our fake one. It's especially hard to remember when Felix boldly makes comments that could technically be platonic, but never really sound like it. We're in the painting accessories aisle at the art supply store when he does it again.

"Not to brag, but I've been told I have a great face," he says, waggling a chunky synthetic brush at me. "One of these days you're gonna have to paint me."

I pluck the brush from his hand and put it back in the container it came from. "I can't tell if you're kidding."

"I'm not! I would be a great model," he says, framing his face in his hands. "Look at the material."

I'm feeling a bit indulgent, so I do look, taking in his features with a bit more reverence than I usually allow myself. I look at the scar on his chin from when he crashed his bike in my driveway as a kid, the slight sunburn on the bridge of his nose. I take in the shape of his jaw, his cupid's bow, the way his bottom eyelashes are almost as long as the ones on top. It is a great face, but I shake my head.

"You make a good case, but your request is denied. I hate painting people I know in real life."

"Why's that?"

I shrug. "It's hard to put into words. I guess it feels too intimate."

"We're way past that. I'm dead serious right now," he declares, planting his hands on my shoulders so I can't look away. His brows are screwed together, and I'm pretty curious about what he's going to say next as he sucks in a deep breath. "Jay, paint me like one of your French girls."

I burst out laughing, loud enough that it would be embarrassing if Felix weren't the one who caused it. He laughs along with me at his own stupid joke, but somewhere in the middle of it all, his expression softens.

"I really missed your laugh," he says, and it's so direct and honest I'm not sure how to respond. All I can think is that if I was ever worried we'd have an issue with chemistry, that fear is now long gone.

My train of thought is cut off when my phone buzzes in my back pocket. Felix looks away, and whatever moment we were having fizzles out as I turn my attention to the text I just got. When I see it's from Mom, I kind of don't know what to expect.

We've been texting back and forth about the queerceañera, but it's been hard to nail down specific plans with her. She seemed happy when I told her that my friends were coming, asking for updates on everyone's college searches and summer plans. But then when I asked her about being part of the opening procession alongside my dad, she wouldn't really give me a straight answer. Our latest exchange is about whether I'm going to hold a Mass before the event. She didn't seem happy when I hinted it probably wasn't in the cards, and now the newest message at the top of my notifications confirms it.

You haven't stopped going to church, have you? Felix comes with us every Sunday.

It's all I can do to not bang my head into the nearest wall. It would be bad enough on its own to keep tiptoeing around this issue with her, but using Felix to nudge me in the "right" direction feels like a particularly low blow. And speak of the devil, Felix, who's wandered further down the aisle, peers over at me.

"You okay? You look kind of stressed."

"Yeah, sorry," I reply, shaking my head. "Queerceañera planning stuff, the usual."

"Anything I can do to help?" he asks. My knee-jerk reaction is to think, *stop being so goddamn perfect*, and I instantly feel bad about how bitter that sounds.

"Nothing you need to worry about," I say instead, and Felix smiles.

"All right, whatever you say," he says, dropping the paintbrush he was playing with back in its little cubby hole. "It's getting kind of late though. I have to get an assignment done for the coding boot camp, but I'll meet you at the dance studio for our lesson later?"

"Right, 7:00 p.m. sharp," I say. Honestly, I had been looking forward to the dance lesson April had arranged with her family friend. Not because I thought I was going to be any good, but more as an excuse to hang out with Felix a little bit more. But now, there's a weird feeling in the pit of my stomach that makes me worry I won't be able to look him in the eye.

Felix and I walk out to the parking lot together and get into our cars, but as he drives away, I don't pull out of my spot quite yet. Instead, I take out my phone again and FaceTime April.

When the call connects, she's in her bedroom, nestled into a mountain of plushies at her headboard. It looks like she hasn't gotten out of her pajamas even though it's three in the afternoon, but she has a sheet mask on that would make me laugh any other day.

"You look terrifying," I say succinctly.

"Thanks so much. Nice to see you too," she says but pauses when she sees I'm not exactly in a joking mood. "Hey, what's wrong?"

"Things with my mom are weird," I sigh. "I don't know how to talk to her, not since that comment she made to me at the barbecue. She's answering my texts about the queerceañera, which is definitely something. But her responses all feel kind of weighty."

It doesn't take long to fill her in on Mom's attempts to connect with me after my awkward, rushed exit from her party, and how despite her best efforts, the conversations have still fallen flat. When I tell her about the latest text about church and Felix, she frowns.

"Oh, that's not very subtle."

"Right? And directing it toward me is one thing, but how am I supposed to read that and not feel jealous of Felix too? I don't want to resent him, and when it's just the two of us, it barely even crosses my mind," I say, brushing my hair off my face. It's about a thousand degrees inside my car without the AC on, and my frustration only adds to how suffocated I feel. "But it's hard not to feel like a disappointment when, at least by my mom's standards, Felix always does everything right and I do everything wrong."

"Have you talked to Felix about any of this? Maybe not the jealousy part, but about your mom?"

"Not since this whole charade started, and even then I didn't get into a ton of detail about my relationship with my mom. That's the thing—Felix and I have all these little blind spots that I'm not sure how or when we're going to fill in for each other," I say. "Like, Felix doesn't ever talk about his move across the state, and I never really told him outright that he helped me realize I was gay. There's so much that's left unsaid with us; it still feels weird."

"Well, maybe you can talk about that at your dance lesson later," April says, and I tip my head back until it thumps against my headrest.

"God, that was supposed to be fun. Now I feel like every time I'm in the same room with him, I want to explode. Like, in a bad way but also a good way," I say with a groan. "At the store a minute ago, he said he missed my laugh."

April sits up so fast that her face mask slips. "He *what?*"

"Your face is falling off," I point out, and she quickly slides it back into place.

"Who cares about that? Spill."

"I laughed. He said he missed it. I died inside," I recite, monotone. "Today is giving me whiplash. Actually, scratch that. Felix's entire existence is giving me whiplash."

"Okay, easy fix. You can talk to him about your worries at the dance lesson *and* kiss him."

I give April the best withering stare I can manage, but she looks delighted. "You and Carmen are going to kill me with all your matchmaking. You know that, right?"

"Hold your complaints until after it's over," she says as I start my car and the AC finally roars to life. "Maybe this really will give you a chance to talk things through."

Amrita, the Wards' family friend, has cleared her schedule to coach us for the evening, so Felix and I have the entire studio to ourselves. Felix gets there early, and I show up right as the sun dips below the horizon, pink and orange sky reflecting off the floor-to-ceiling mirrors in the studio. He's got the longer pieces of his hair pulled back into a small bun, and I'm a little distracted by how good it looks.

We put some soft, classical music on the record player and jump right into it. Amrita has the two of us start off side by side, saying it may be easier for us to nail down the basics on our own before we start to practice together. She kicks it off by detailing the proper posture and how to hold our upper bodies. Then she explains the footwork, which looks deceptively simple but feels clumsy when I try it myself. Somehow, Felix's movement are way more graceful than mine.

"You're weirdly good at this," I point out when Amrita takes a few steps back to watch us from a distance.

"If I didn't know any better," he says sweetly, "I'd think you were flirting with me."

"Good thing you know better," I tease, and Felix wrinkles his nose.

I'm not the only one who notices the disparity in our skill set, because Amrita adds, "He's right, you know. I don't say this often, but you're a natural."

"I kind of know how to dance the waltz already," Felix admits, and I almost trip over my own feet. This is definitely the first I'm hearing of it. "If you take a dance class at my school, you get to opt out of PE. Figured it would be more fun than playing dodgeball in the gym every Thursday."

"Why didn't you tell me?" I ask, and Felix glances at me sheepishly.

"I'm a little rusty, plus I've never danced with you before."

"It's good you came in," Amrita agrees. "No matter how experienced you are, finding your footing with a new partner always takes a little time."

The more we practice, the clearer it is that the only one who's struggling to find their footing is me. I can't seem to loosen up, and compared with Felix, I look incredibly stiff. If it were anyone else, none of this would bother me at all. But the whole reason I asked Felix here in the first place was because I thought we could find some common ground, not so I could feel inadequate in new and creative ways. Eventually, Amrita agrees it's time to switch gears.

"Maybe it'll help if you two dance together," she says, which sounds like code for *this really isn't working.* "Let me check if I can find some slower music in the back."

"We can try it out on our own in the meantime," Felix suggests, turning to me. "Practice makes perfect, right?"

"Forget perfect," I mumble as Amrita leaves us to our own devices. "I'd go for passable at this point. Mediocre, even."

"What did I tell you about raising your expectations?" he asks, stepping up to me so we're toe to toe. When I reach up to put my hand on his shoulder, something about it doesn't look right, and Felix taps my wrist. "You're following, so it's your left hand that goes on my shoulder, not the right."

"Why do you assume you're going to lead?" I ask, and it comes across more pouty than I mean it to. I know I'm being difficult, but I can't help it.

"Do you want to lead?" Felix asks, holding back a smile.

I frown at him for a second. "No, I don't know what I'm doing."

He laughs one of those big laughs of his, and I try to smack his arm for teasing me, but he catches my hand before I can manage.

"Promise I won't abuse my power," he says. "A good lead is supposed to make everything feel effortless."

And to his credit, it really does. I figured dancing with another person would end up confusing me even more, but Felix's confident motions make it easier for me to find my rhythm. I'm able to relax a bit, to the point where I'm suddenly aware of how close we are to each other. All my attention goes to the warmth of his hand in mine, and the comforting weight where the other is resting on my waist. When I finally look up from my feet to his face, the smile that spreads across it makes my heart skip a beat.

It's moments like this that make me question why I even feel insecure in the first place. Felix has never put me down for falling behind or sucking at something. He never makes anything feel like a competition—it's my mom that does it for us. But for whatever reason, I've been resenting him for it all this time.

"You okay?" he asks right when I realize I've been quiet for a bit too long. He slows his pace a bit, scrutinizing my expression. "I was just joking around y'know. If you really want to lead we can swap places."

"No, it's not that," I say quickly, but the concerned look on his face doesn't budge. I sigh. "My mom said something to me earlier that got under my skin. She's . . . I don't know. We don't need to get into it."

"We don't need to," he says carefully, "but we can if you want."

I nod, and Felix lets the wheels in my head turn as we find our rhythm and sync up with the music again. I'm not sure how to broach this whole topic, mostly because I'm not sure if Felix even knows how much my mom compares the two of us, let alone how much it bothers me. As one song melts into the next, I steel myself and finally speak up.

"Has she said anything to you?" I ask. "About the whole queer-ceañera thing or about us."

"Not really," he replies. "She's been pretty quiet on my end, but I'm guessing she hasn't been with you?"

I nod, and a crease appears between Felix's brows. "I feel like I can't do anything right. And she brings you up a lot, and I can't help but feel like it's her way of guilt-tripping me."

"What did she say to you?" he asks, hand tightening around mine a fraction. He's not looking at me like I'm crazy or insecure like I thought he might. Instead, he looks worried. Protective, even.

So I don't feel weird about opening up to him and venting about the texts my mom has sent in the last two weeks and how they've made me feel. And even though I was planning to keep it to myself, I tell him what really happened at the barbecue too. Felix listens patiently, and by the time I'm done, my chest feels a little less tight.

"Sometimes I feel like I'm being overly sensitive, or reading too much into things," I say. "But the little comments really build up."

"You're not being too sensitive and you're not imagining things, Jay," he says earnestly. "I really thought the whole double standard thing would ease up if she saw us both excited about the same thing."

"I know. I did too, but it's not your fault she doesn't criticize you. Come to think of it, I'm really glad she doesn't," I say, speaking aloud something I've barely started to process on my own. "But especially when it comes to my sexuality, it's hard to see her be all supportive with someone else but not her own son."

Felix is quiet for a beat. When he speaks again, his voice sounds different. "I'm not sure if this will help, but your mom really isn't as cool with me being gay as you think."

I blink up at him. "What do you mean?"

"She just expresses it differently. I think she feels entitled to be more vocal with you because she's your mom," he says. "With me, I'll mention my breakup or the dating scene back home, and she totally freezes up. I can tell she's uncomfortable even if she doesn't put it into words. And I'm not saying all this to be like, 'oh, I have it so hard.' I don't want you to feel like she's singling you out."

The thought that Felix would be trying to hijack the conversation hadn't even crossed my mind, because everything he said made perfect sense. There's something really insidious about the type of homophobia that lives in the silences and awkward pauses of conversations, where it's not what someone says, but what they don't say. This whole time, I thought Felix had it so easy. And even worse, I was punishing him for it.

"I honestly had no idea," I say. "I guess I hadn't thought about it from your perspective. I figured by the way she brags about you all the time that things were easier between you two."

"I don't blame you," he says, shaking his head a bit. "But I think her going on and on about my accomplishments doesn't have much to do with me at all. At the end of the day, I don't really feel like I can take what she says at face value. That hurts, y'know?"

I can see on his face how much of an emotional toll this has been taking on him. I wonder if he's talked to anyone else about this, but I also wonder if anyone else could understand other than me. All of a sudden, the jealousy I've felt toward him feels beyond ridiculous.

"Do your parents know about any of this?"

"I haven't mentioned it," Felix replies with a small shrug. "Like I said, they're not the best at picking up on that stuff on their own. And I was worried that if I told them, they wouldn't want me to stay with her for the summer and then I wouldn't be able to go to my program. Not an ideal trade-off, but I'd rather be here than not."

"I'm really sorry," I say, but it doesn't feel like enough. I give his hand a quick squeeze, and Felix's eyes finally refocus on my face. His mouth quirks up into a sad little smile that makes my heart constrict.

"Don't be," he says, brushing his thumb across mine. "Like I said, I know it's been way worse for you. But I want you to know that you're not alone."

And just like that, the pressure in my chest turns into something new, something I haven't felt in ages. It's a dull, pleasant ache that I've only ever felt once before, with this exact same boy a whole lifetime ago. Suddenly, the room feels a little too warm. We're standing too close, and the eye contact between us is too charged.

"Wow, look at that difference!" Amrita says, reentering the room holding a stack of records, and I thank every star in the sky that she snapped me out of whatever was going on in my head.

The rest of the dance lesson passes without incident, and the next time Felix slides his hand into mine, it doesn't feel like the floor is falling out from under me. But I can't deny that something shifted between us, and I can't decide what scares me more—that Felix might have felt it too, or that it was all in my head.

Chapter Fourteen

WE'RE ABOUT TWO weeks out from the big event, and things are finally starting to come together. Carmen finds an amazing little venue downtown that has a last-minute opening, and it feels way more my style than a typical quince hall. The renovated warehouse space is pretty small, but it's got whitewashed brick and massive windows that make it feel cozy instead of cramped. Dad and I have nailed down the menu, and April signs on to be the DJ for the evening, which helps me cross another thing off my list.

Some things have been less exciting to finalize than others, namely tallying up the RSVPs. The vast majority of my mom's side of my family isn't coming. I didn't expect them to, since most of them are pretty religious. The sting of rejection still gets to me, just a little.

But there are plenty of other things for me to worry about

instead, most notably the task of convincing everyone that Felix and I are a happy couple the day of. And sure, maybe I'm also still thinking about the little moment we had during our dance lesson. Maybe I keep asking myself if the crush I had on Felix as a kid is back again with a vengeance, and maybe I'm starting to lose sleep over it. That's why, when I come downstairs on a Wednesday morning and Felix is loitering in the kitchen with Dad, I'm not 100 percent sure if he's real or if I'm sleepwalking.

"What are you doing in my house?" I ask groggily.

Felix looks up from where he's leaning heavily on the kitchen island. "Just making sure this counter isn't going anywhere."

I sigh as Dad cackles like it's the best joke he's heard in his life. "You're the corniest person I've ever met."

"And you love it," Felix counters. I hate that he's not wrong. "You left your longboard in my car. I stopped by to drop it off."

"I'm the one who's holding him hostage," Dad adds jovially, pointing at the notepad between them on the counter. "I was talking about the guest list and got carried away. You know, a lot of people are dying to meet Felix."

"That's great, because everyone *is* going to meet him. You know, at the event," I say pointedly, but the words go in one ear and other the other.

"But it would be such a shame if they only had that one day to see you two being so cute together, don't you think?"

"We are pretty cute," Felix concedes.

"Plus, we have to do something to celebrate your birthday," Dad says. "Not the queerceañera, but the actual day of. Why don't we invite the family out to dinner?"

"I don't know . . ."

"Tía Fernanda said she would love to come though," he says, and god, of course he's already brought this up without checking with me first. I don't want to be mad, especially when I know he's coming from a good place, but still.

"Dad, you're supposed to ask me about stuff like this first, remember?"

"Yes, yes, I know. But I wanted to get an idea of whether or not she would be free," he says, and I can already tell shooting this idea down will be near impossible. "Think about it, chaparro. This way, you won't have to share the spotlight on your special day. All eyes will be on you."

"Fantastic," I reply thinly, and Felix tries to hide a laugh by pretending to cough.

I'd be lying if I said that Dad's pushiness about putting me in the spotlight hasn't been getting under my skin, and a big part of me doesn't want to put our fake relationship under a microscope any more than we have to. But as Felix says goodbye to Dad, the gears in my head start turning. The more time Felix and I spend together, the more I wonder if everything between us is going to end the second the queerceañera is over.

If I'm being honest with myself, which I've tried so hard not to do, I know I don't want things to go back to the way they were before. The idea of Felix becoming a stranger to me again is out of the question, and I want to figure out who we are to each other outside of this lie we've built about us. Maybe having him meet my family, getting all that pressure out of the way, will help us get there a little sooner.

"I'm guessing family meet and greet is a no-go?" Felix asks as I walk him out to his car. "I feel like a migraine is a great excuse. People never ask questions when you say you have a migraine."

"I don't know. . . . It might be good for us," I say, and he looks over at me like I've grown a second head.

"Who are you and what have you done with my boyfriend?" he says, smile spreading across his face. I get a little thrill out of the fact that he doesn't say *fake boyfriend*, so I don't correct him.

"I'm thinking we can treat it as a sort of dress rehearsal. If they see us together ahead of time, it'll take the pressure off us to act a certain way at the queerceañera. Might as well get the first impressions over with, right?"

"Wow, already trying to get rid of me, huh?" Felix says, but the delivery falls flat, and I'm not 100 percent sure if he's joking or if he thinks I'm taking a step back from him for real. Before I have the chance to press him on it, he adds, "Sounds like your family is kind of massive, but your dad made it sound like it would be pretty chill."

"I'm starting to realize that everyone in my life has a very different definition of chill than I do," I tease, and he bumps his shoulder against mine in response.

"What can I say? I'm here to spice up your life."

"And you're definitely succeeding," I reply, and it wins me back the smile he dropped a minute earlier.

Predictably, the combination birthday dinner plus mini-reunion that Dad organizes is far from tame. He pulls some strings so we score a private room at an experimental Asian-fusion restaurant downtown, and I can already tell Felix and his adventurous palate is going to have a field day when I check the menu. About twenty people are coming in total—most of Dad's side of the family in Austin, plus April and Ryan for general moral support.

It feels like a decent group for me and Felix to practice with. A handful of my cousins who I haven't seen in a while will be there, and I know they'll be particularly interested in my newly active dating life. But as I turn it over in my head, I'm surprised that Mom comes to mind as someone who could be there too. She's been hovering on the outskirts of the queerceañera planning process for a bit, and I wonder if spending time with me and Felix together in a bigger group would help make things a little less awkward.

After the idea has pestered me for a couple of days, I text Felix asking him what he thinks. I'm a little surprised that he doesn't hesitate at all before saying yes.

i don't think there's anything wrong with giving her a chance, his response reads. if you want her to be there, you should invite her. i've got your back either way :)

I read and reread his text, not even bothering to push down the butterflies that come up when my eyes scan the last line. But Felix isn't the only one I need to run this by, and I'm not sure how well received it'll be. Dad and Carmen are watching *The Great British Bake Off* in the living room when I decide to stop worrying and spit it out already.

"Can I talk to y'all about something?" I ask, and both of their heads perk up from where they're slumped into the sofa. "Would it be totally weird if I invited Mom to my birthday dinner?"

Twin looks of surprise pass across Dad and Carmen's faces as the episode plays on in the background. Dad is the one who rallies first, reaching for the remote to turn down the volume.

"I don't think it would be weird," Dad says, but the words come out slow, a bit hesitant. "What made you think about it?"

"If she does come to the queerceañera, this might be a good test run. She hasn't spent a lot of time with me and Felix as a couple. I don't think she knows how happy I've been. I thought letting her see us together might help her understand."

Dad nods, and a little bit of my nervousness dissipates. "I have no problem with it if that's what you're asking. It's your birthday, so it's completely your choice."

My eyes slip over to Carmen, whose expression is carefully

neutral in a way that feels worse than if she were making a big fuss about it. She's always been eerily diplomatic about me having my own relationship with Mom, and it seems like this is no exception.

"I agree with Dad," she says, and I resist the urge to frown a little. "If you want her there, she should be there. Don't worry about me."

"You sure?" I ask, wishing I could turn the sibling telepathy beam on her for once and know what she's really thinking.

"I'm sure."

"Okay."

"Okay," Carmen says, resolute. "You want to watch the rest of this episode with us? It's vegan week and everyone is about two seconds away from fully losing their minds."

Carmen makes room for me on the couch, and whatever concerns I had before fade away as we cringe over fallen cakes and inedible pastries.

The next morning, when I text Mom asking if she'd like to come to dinner with us, I don't have to wait long before I receive a response: I would love to come. It makes me a little nervous, but I don't feel like I'm walking a tightrope like I did when I agreed to grab lunch with her a few weeks ago. All I can do is hope that this dinner will be good for all of us.

Chapter Fifteen

THE MORNING OF my birthday, I wake up to a flood of "happy birthday" and "can't wait to see you tonight" texts, including one from Felix. I'm kind of amazed that I'm not freaking out about dinner. I am a tiny bit nervous, since Felix is the first boyfriend, fake or not, who I'll be introducing to my extended family. But Felix and I have spent a lot more time together since his not-so-great boyfriend debut with Tío Gael and Tía Ximena, so I have faith we'll be fine.

Late in the afternoon, Carmen and I pick up April, who immediately claims the aux, and then stop to scoop up two of our cousins. Valentina and Elisa are Tío Gael and Tía Ximena's daughters, and even though they're coming to dinner too, the kids always drive separately for "maximum chisme distribution" as Carmen puts it. Our older cousins have all moved away or are off working their first jobs after college, so now that it's down to a few of us left in Austin, it feels even more important to uphold the tradition.

The sun is hanging low in the sky as the girls scoot into the car. Valentina, who's a year older than me and heading to UT Austin in the fall, gives me a little fist bump as she slides onto the seat next to me. Elisa, the baby of the family at barely sixteen years old, practically jumps over her to pull me into a haphazard hug.

"I'm literally so mad at you, by the way," she says as we hit the road.

"Oh yeah? What did I do this time?"

"You got a boyfriend and didn't tell us!" she says, and next to her, Valentina nods.

"She's right. We had to find out from our parents," Valentina adds. "That's pretty embarrassing. They're the most boring people we know."

"Okay, okay, but I'm telling you now. Some people believe in privacy, you know. I don't understand why everyone wants to know things the second they happen."

Valentina says, "Because we love you," at the same time that Elisa says, "Because we're nosy," and we all burst out laughing.

"If it makes you feel any better, he hid it from me too. I only found out when we started planning the queerceañera," Carmen says, and when I catch her eye in the rearview mirror, she winks. It's technically true, but it still freaks me out how good she is at lying sometimes.

April switches to a new song, something synth-y that I don't recognize but Elisa clearly does. She rockets out of her seat, ignoring Carmen when she tells her to buckle her seat belt.

"Your taste in music is perfect, I'm obsessed," Elisa crows around April's headrest. "You're the one who's DJing the queer-ceañera, right?"

"Yep. I can make you a playlist with similar stuff if you want," April offers proudly, and Elisa's eyes shine like she's just won the lottery.

"You're literally the best. You're my favorite now since Joaquin is on my shit list," Elisa says, ignoring me when I start to protest. "Do you have a secret boyfriend too? Or maybe a girlfriend? You're obviously way too cool to be straight."

"I'm not really interested in dating," April says with a laugh, and Elisa balks at her.

"Oh my god, please swap lives with me. My stupid dad says I can't date until I graduate high school, because he's a control freak and he hates me and wants me to die alone."

"You're not going to die alone. You're literally twelve," Carmen calls back from the driver's seat.

"I AM NOT!" Elisa shrieks, and Valentina and I quietly die of laughter as she slumps back into her seat. "This family is a nightmare. I can't wait to go to college so I can do whatever I want."

"I can't wait to go to college either," Valentina says, "but mostly because I want to get away from you and finally have some peace and quiet in my life."

I laugh again as Elisa tries to pinch Valentina. I make a mental note to start hanging out with her more often. I knew I liked her for a reason.

The car is overflowing with music and laughter for the rest of the drive, and I'm almost sad to get out when we finally find parking downtown. As we walk up to the restaurant, I see Felix is fashionably early like he always is, standing out in front and chatting away with one of the valet drivers. He's got a Cuban collar shirt on with one too many buttons undone to not be distracting, and his hair is pushed back from his face.

"Wow, look at that guy," Elisa whispers, elbowing me while we're still a dozen feet away. "Do you think he's here alone?"

"Not quite," I say as Felix catches my eye and waves.

"Wait, *that's* your boyfriend?"

"That's him," I reply, pride swelling in my chest.

I introduce him to the girls as we head inside. The restaurant feels intense and intimate, full of luxurious black-and-red furniture. The hostess guides us to the very back, where they have our private room set aside. A long banquette table stretches the length of the space, set with intricate place mats and orchid centerpieces.

Everyone is trying to figure out where to sit, but I can't stop looking at Felix in the dim, shadowy lighting. He catches me staring, and because I'm feeling bold after that whole exchange outside, I don't look away.

"I like your hair like that," I say.

"Noted," he replies with a smile.

Dad shows up not too long after us, and Tío Gael and Tía Ximena follow on his heels. They seem a bit more at ease with Felix than they were at the tailor shop. Tía Ximena smiles and gives him a kiss on the cheek, but then Tío Gael still pulls Felix's hand into another long, pointed handshake, and then leans over to me.

"He's not giving you any trouble, is he?" Tío Gael asks in a stage whisper.

"Only every day of my life," I reply, and Felix stiffens next to me.

"He's joking, I swear," he says quickly, and the genuinely frightened expression on his face makes all three of us laugh. If I had known the key to them accepting Felix was making him squirm, I would've joined in on day one.

Tía Kristina, who's really my dad's cousin and not my aunt, arrives soon after, her black, chin-length bob gleaming in the low light. Felix perks right up when he sees her. She's by far the biggest gossip in the family, and I texted him an advanced warning to keep an eye out for her at dinner. He doesn't look the least bit surprised when she sets her handbag down on the seat across from us. When she catches both of us eyeballing her, she gives me a little wink.

"I *have* to sit by you two. We have so much to catch up on," she says with a deceptively sweet smile.

Tía Fernanda floats into the room next, and the smell of jasmine and honey wafts in with her. Her dress is a neon enough yellow that it seems to brighten up the whole room, and her finger-waves are wrapped up in a matching scarf. She makes a beeline for me and Felix the second she sees us. When Felix gets up to greet her, she plants a gentle kiss on his cheek before taking his hands in hers.

"What's your star sign, darling?"

"Oh, I don't know," Felix says, equal parts confused and delighted. "I was born April 30, if that helps?"

Tía Fernanda gasps. "A Taurus! That's lovely, really. Joaquin is a Cancer, so you two are very compatible, astrologically speaking."

"I've known that for years, but I'm glad to hear the stars agree," Felix says, smiling back at her, and she sighs happily.

"You have such wonderful energy," she says, and then turns to me, theatrical faux seriousness coloring her expression. "Joaquin, I need you to know I'm very angry with you for hiding your relationship from me."

"Elisa already did this bit with me earlier," I reply.

"Oh, darn it," she says, finally releasing Felix's hands and leaning over to give me a kiss on the cheek too. "I am a little surprised though, the last time we talked, you told me you weren't seeing anyone."

"I guess I was feeling a little shy about it. First real relationship and all," I say, words rolling off my tongue without a second thought. I don't like lying to her, but this feels like it's as close to the truth as I can get for now. If Felix and I were dating for real, I probably would have kept it quiet for that exact reason.

"I completely understand," she says, patting my cheek with her hand. "And hey, I guess you didn't need to download Grindr after all!"

Felix turns to me, eyes wide. "Sorry, what's this about?"

"Nothing," I wheeze.

"It sounds like something to me."

"Don't ask," I say, and between the confused look on his face and Tía Fernanda's sheepish expression, I can't stop laughing.

My shoulders are still shaking when I feel a tap on my arm and turn to see that Mom has snuck in without me realizing it.

"Hey," I say, still mid-grin from Tía Fernanda's antics. Mom leans in to plant a kiss on my cheek. "I'm glad you made it."

"Me too, hijo," she says, returning my smile.

She looks over my shoulder, and I see her eyes soften even more when she sees Carmen. It's the same look she had on her face when she saw Carmen had driven me to the barbecue, and my heart twinges a little as Carmen and Ryan walk over now, caught between feeling hopeful and nervous. Carmen accepts a kiss on the cheek from Mom, and then Ryan extends a hand.

"Mom, you know Ryan," Carmen says. Her tone is polite, and she seems calm enough, but I know my sister. "Polite" always feels like a red flag with her, and her being so reserved is a dead give-away that she feels uncomfortable.

"It's good to see you," Mom says, shaking Ryan's hand, and then looking back to Carmen. "Both of you. I'm glad I could catch you again while you're home for the summer."

"Right," Carmen says. "I'm only here until August."

"I'm sure your father is happy about that. Are you working at all?"

"No, I'm studying. Getting some requirements out of the way so I can focus on my major when I head back in the fall."

"Oh, I thought you might be trying to save up money for the semester," Mom says, and I have to hide a flinch.

It would have been an innocent enough statement if she'd said it to anyone else, but this is exactly the type of thing Mom and Carmen have butted heads about in the past. I know it's going to strike a nerve before Carmen even says a word.

"I have some money saved up already. Besides, I'll have time to focus on finances after I graduate," she says, a biting edge to her tone that wasn't there before. "My studies are what's most important to me right now."

"I didn't mean—" Mom starts, and then seems to think better of her approach and backtracks a little. "I just didn't know that's how you were spending your time. I'm sorry."

"Fine," Carmen says, and the conversation slides to an uncomfortable stop as a frown plays on Carmen's lips.

They both look like they want to say more, but neither seems like they're able to tackle the barrier that's up between them. After an awkward pause, Mom looks back at me.

"Here, before I forget," she says, holding out a small bag stuffed to the brim with tissue paper.

I've never really been big on getting gifts, and when Dad invited everyone to the dinner tonight, I asked him to specify that nobody should feel obligated to get me anything for my birthday. Felix already pestered me about it, because he's a pain in the ass. After the fourth text begging for me to make an exception, I threatened that if he tried to buy me something, I'd tell his parents about all the "late night study sessions" he went to last year that were really house parties. He shut up real quick after that. Still, it would feel rude not to accept a gift now, especially from Mom.

"You really didn't need to get me anything," I say, opening the bag anyway.

"I know, but I wanted to give you something small anyways," she says, watching hopefully as I dig into the gift. When I pull out an array of paintbrushes, I have a really hard time keeping the surprise off my face. My eyes flick to Carmen, and she seems as shocked as I am. "I thought of it after the barbecue, since you mentioned you were still considering art school."

And honestly, I'm a little bit speechless. After the barbecue, I wasn't sure if Mom would come around to the idea of me going to art school, but I'd been holding onto hope that she might be excited for me anyway. And now, after months of dancing around each other, I feel seen by her. It's not lost on me that she says "still considering" art school, even though I said I was sure of my decision. But she's actually trying. She showed up tonight *and* brought a gift that has to do with the thing I'm passionate about, and it finally feels like a step in the right direction.

I turn the paintbrushes over in my hands, tracing the tiny, familiar label on the handles. "How did you know this is the brand I use?"

"I might have had a little help," she says, glancing at Felix.

And, oh, of course he would have had some hand in this. But that also means that she asked him for help, because she wanted to make sure she got this right. Another wave of warmth washes over me at that realization, and I smile at her in earnest.

"This is really thoughtful, Mom. Thank you," I say, putting the gift bag under my chair.

As Mom circles the table to say a quick hello to Dad, I turn my attention to Felix. He holds both hands up in front of him, the picture of innocence.

"You said *I* couldn't get you anything," he says. "You didn't say I couldn't help someone else pick out a gift."

"One of these days, I really am going to strangle you," I reply lightly, and he smiles like I've given him the best compliment in the world.

Slowly but surely, everyone settles around the table, and as the appetizers are brought out, they get to know Felix. The "how did you two get together" questions come up quickly, and since we have practice now, we're able to navigate them pretty easily. I'm not surprised that most of the questions come from Elisa, since it's more about her having an intense fascination with dating in general than it is about us specifically. But as the waiters take away our empty dishes and put new ones in their place, Tía Kristina turns her attention to us.

"So, have you two talked about how you're going to survive long-distance?" she asks, and I stop poking at the pink mousse in front of me to glance at Felix. She must see us hesitate, because she adds, "When the summer ends, Felix will be back home, no?"

It's not like I hadn't thought about it before, Felix heading home at the end of the summer is kind of a given. But honestly, the thought hadn't occurred to me since we'd started spending more time together. Now the idea that I may not know when I'll see Felix again after August is way scarier.

"We haven't talked about it much, but I don't think it'll be a problem," Felix says, and he sounds so confident that I almost believe him.

Tía Kristina doesn't seem quite as convinced. "Oh, really? What makes you so sure?"

"Well, Carmen and Ryan are long-distance," I jump in. "She complains about it sometimes, but they seem to have a pretty good system, so they don't feel the distance as much. Lots of quick calls and check-ins, lots of talking about their feelings. I'm sure she can give us some tips."

"Exactly," Felix says, giving my elbow a reassuring nudge. "It's nothing we can't handle."

"That's really sweet," Valentina says. "I hate when people say long-distance never works. If two people care about each other enough, then they'll make it work."

Next to her, Elisa puts her chopsticks down and leans across the table with the most serious expression I've ever seen.

"Are you two in love?" she asks, and I almost choke on my drink. Felix starts laughing, and before he's able to compose himself, Valentina slaps Elisa on the arm.

"You can't ask people that point-blank, stupid. For all you know, they haven't even talked about it with each other. They only started dating a few weeks ago," she says, and then turns to me and Felix. "Well, but I guess you have known each other for a while, right?"

I nod, passing my mousse to Felix, since I'm not feeling confident about the pink hue. He gratefully accepts it without comment.

"Pretty much for our entire lives," I say. "I don't ever remember not knowing him."

"Then how did you know you wanted to be more than friends now?" Valentina asks, and Felix's hand stills on the plate between us, his fingers warm against mine. "Was there a specific moment?"

I'm not entirely sure how to respond, partly because I'm not sure if I can nail down an exact moment, and partly because I'm afraid any answer I come up with would be way too honest. Thankfully, Felix speaks up before I'm forced to formulate a cohesive answer.

"Sounds cheesy, but I pretty much knew the second I saw him again," he says, catching my eye and giving me a little smile that makes my heart constrict. "As soon as we reconnected, I knew that was it for me."

Valentina, Elisa, and Tía Kristina positively melt at that, and I have to wonder if he only said what they wanted to hear, or if his answer had some truth to it after all.

From across the table, I catch Mom's eye. An expression passes over her face that I'm not sure I can place. It's got a touch of the subtle, barely noticeable discomfort that I'm always hyperaware of, but there's something else too, something softer that I don't expect. I didn't realize she was listening in on the conversation, and I feel a little embarrassed because of how sappy it was. But for once, I don't feel like shrinking away from her gaze or correcting anything that Felix said. I'm not exactly sure what to make of that shift inside myself, but then Elisa pipes up with another question, and my attention is brought back to her over-eager needling.

By the time the second course is replaced with the third, any residual nervousness I'm feeling is long gone. Felix handles all the attention like a pro, and I get to sit back and watch as everyone realizes that he's not just cute but charming too. Even Carmen, who's sitting with Ryan and April at the opposite end of the table, looks impressed.

Felix does his best to keep up with the lively conversation bouncing around the room as everyone switches back and forth between English and Spanish, but every once in a while, he asks me to translate or explain why everyone is laughing. Then he starts leaning over to whisper inside jokes and stupid little observations in my ear.

Eventually, he wraps his arm around the back of my chair and leaves it there, leaning into me in a way that makes my stomach do somersaults. Even in a room full of people, it feels like he and I are a unit. It gives me a boost of confidence, enough that I find myself talking more than I usually do at family functions like this. I'm not really thinking about how I'm coming across or what Mom is thinking about us from where she's sitting in the corner, and it feels good.

Being with Felix like this makes me feel like I can do anything. There's a warmth radiating from deep in my stomach that makes me feel invincible, and I find myself wishing I could always feel like this. I could tell myself this is fine, that whatever Felix and I are doing now is enough for me. But it's not enough, at least not anymore. It hits me all at once how much I want this, how much I want *him*, for real.

Felix catches my eye again and, like he can hear my thoughts, smiles one of those private little smiles that burns me up inside. He tips his head toward me, close enough that I can feel his hair tickle my cheek.

"This is really nice," he whispers, quieter than he needs to.

I pull back and hold his gaze for a second, but all I can do is nod back at him, because I don't trust myself to speak without blurting out exactly how I'm feeling. I want to ask him if he feels the same way I do, or if he's still playing pretend.

The last time I thought I knew what he wanted, back when we were kids, it blew up in my face. Maybe that's what I'm doing all over again, assigning more meaning to our friendship than it actually has. I was heartbroken back then, and I'm not sure I can go through that with him again.

Felix turns his attention back to the jokes flying around the table, and the heat in my chest is still there, but now there's a weighty, familiar dread sitting behind my ribs too.

Chapter Sixteen

AFTER DINNER, MOST of us don't want the night to end quite yet, but a few folks say goodbye out by the valet. Tía Fernanda is one of them, giving me a kiss on the cheek as she explains she has to get back home to Luna and her twelve-step skin-care routine. I'm not surprised that Mom looks like she's getting ready to leave too, giving my dad a quick hug and then scanning the group until she spots me and Carmen. She makes her way over to us, giving us both a peck on the cheek.

"Thank you for inviting me," she says and looks over at Carmen, who's halfway listening in another conversation with Felix and Ryan. "You said you're here until August?"

"Huh? Oh, yeah, end of the month," she says over her shoulder.

"I would love to see you again while you're here," Mom says, fiddling with the strap of her purse on her shoulder. Carmen nods in a way that doesn't feel like a real affirmation.

"Sure," she murmurs back, even though I know she doesn't really mean it. When Felix elbows her and pulls her attention away, I almost feel relieved.

"Thank you for coming," I say quickly, turning back to Mom. "And for the gift. It really means a lot to me."

Mom's eyes soften when she turns back to me. "I'm glad, hijo. If you paint something using them, you'll have to send me a picture, okay?"

"Yeah, absolutely," I reply, and she returns my smile, smoothing a hand across my back, warm and familiar and grounding. "I am going to yell at Felix for helping you pick them out, though."

Mom chuckles, and it surprises me a little. Things have been so weird with us lately, it feels like it's been a while since I heard her genuinely laugh at anything. It's nice.

"Don't be too hard on Felix," she says. "He obviously cares about you a lot."

And that really does throw me off. I think it's the first time she's acknowledged me and Felix as anything other than friends. Maybe inviting her to this dinner really did make it easier for her to accept us as a couple. Maybe I am getting through to her.

When my thoughts drift to the queerceañera, I don't think it's a terrible time to bring it up.

"Hey, Mom?"

"Hmm?" she hums, a little distracted as the valet pulls up with her car.

"I can . . . I can count on you to come to the queerceañera, right?" I ask, and she pauses at the edge of the curb. My throat tightens, but if I don't ask now, I'm afraid I'll never really know what she's thinking. "I know the party is a little bit out there, and you weren't really sure about it. But everyone is working so hard on it, and I think it's going to be nice. I'd like it if . . . I mean, I do want you there."

Mom's eyes search my face, and for a beat, I'm afraid she's going to say no. But then she reaches her hand out again and squeezes my shoulder.

"If this is what you want, then I'll support you," she says, and I feel like I can breathe again.

"So you'll come? For sure, then?"

"I'll be there, cariño," she replies, and I smile as she gives my shoulder another squeeze.

I wave as she drives off, and it feels like a huge weight has been lifted off me. I kind of can't believe that I'm finally making progress with Mom. Still, when I rejoin the group, I don't miss the way Carmen's eyes linger on Mom's car as she drives away.

The rest of us walk down to the waterfront in little groups, our overlapping conversations and snippets of laughter drifting through the warm night air. Carmen is hand in hand with Ryan, April is arm in arm with Valetina and Elisa, and I find myself wishing that the night would never end. I feel a little drunk on everyone's company, and the smile Felix is wearing tells me that he feels the same.

At first, when his knuckles brush mine, I think it must be an accident. We're walking side by side after all, it's bound to happen. But then he does it again, sending a pleasant shock up my arm. The third time, I'm positive he's doing it on purpose, and the butterflies in my stomach are going insane. When I don't pull away, he slips his hand into mine.

"We sold our relationship pretty well back there. I don't think we need to do PDA," I say under my breath.

"I know," he replies, and my heart lurches. And even though it's pointless, I lace my fingers with his anyway.

A comfortable silence falls between us as we walk along the river. The sun set while we were at dinner, and the temperature has thankfully dipped a little in its absence. City lights shimmer on the surface of the water, and a few bats whiz overhead in the darkness. Felix and I have drifted far away from the rest of the group now, but I don't mind. There's something magnetic in the air, and I don't want to waste it.

"This makes me feel like a kid again," Felix finally says, sliding his thumb against mine. "We were always like this before, huh?"

"We really were. Though I'd argue you were way more touchy-feely than I was."

"Let's call it a tie," he says with a little laugh. "I do miss how things used to be, though. It's like, when you're a kid, you're affectionate with no pretense at all. It's the most honest thing in the world. It kinda reminds me of when we went to pick berries that last summer I was in Austin. Do you remember that?"

My breath catches in my throat, because there's no way that's a random, innocent question. I remember our parents had hauled us out to a berry farm on a rare, cooler day in May. Felix and I ran off together like we always did, hiding out in the apple orchard nearby. The trees were mid-bloom, and we sat together and talked for almost an hour as the flower petals rained down all around us. Then his hand was in mine, and we were nose to nose, and between a tangle of branches, we shared our first kiss. Felix moved away a month later before I ever had the chance to ask him what it meant.

"I remember," I say quietly. "But I wasn't sure you did."

"Oh, come on," he says like he can't believe I'd ever think that. When he sees I'm serious, he stops walking, and the intensity in his eyes catches me off guard. "I never forgot that day. I never forgot about any of it."

My heart swells, but there's that feeling behind my ribs again too, and all the doubt that comes with it. I want to trust him—I really do. But all I can think about is how the last time I felt like this about him, it all fell apart, and I never figured out why.

"Sometimes, I feel like I know you so well I can read your mind," I say, looking up at him. "But other times I have no idea what's going on in your head."

"What do you mean?"

"Why did you stop picking up?" I say before I can stop myself. Felix still hasn't let go of my hand. "After you moved, why did you ignore my calls? I know it's stupid that I'm still hung up on it, but I keep wondering what I did wrong."

"You didn't do anything wrong," he says, fingers tightening around mine. "You didn't, I swear."

"Then what happened?"

"I liked you, that's what happened," he answers, words coming out in a desperate rush. "I liked you so much, Jay. I thought the feelings would fade when I moved, but they didn't, and it fucked me up. I wasn't making friends at my new school, I felt depressed all the time. I missed you like crazy, and talking to you on the phone just made it worse."

His words hang in the air between us, and I feel like I'm frozen in place. All this time, I thought the only explanation for why he had disappeared was that I didn't matter to him as much as he mattered to me. I can't comprehend the fact I had it all backward.

"I thought you got tired of me or that you regretted what happened between us," I say numbly. "I never knew any of that."

"You couldn't have, and that's my fault. I'm so sorry," he says, and some of the tension that's been eating away at me for years finally releases. "I wanted to make it up to you somehow when I came back to town. But when I showed up to lunch with your mom, I could tell you didn't want to have anything to do with me.

And I didn't blame you, because what I did was stupid and immature. I thought ending things cold turkey would make it easier to move on."

"Did it?" I ask. "Make it easier, I mean."

"No, it didn't," Felix says. There's this look in his eye like he wants to say more but doesn't know how. He leans forward, and my pulse races. "Jay, I—"

"Where have you two been hiding?" April says, coming around a bend in the walkway. Then her brows shoot up, eyes dropping to where Felix's hand is resting in mine. "Shit, oh god, I'm sorry. I was going to ask if you wanted to ride back with me and Carmen."

It feels a little like I was woken up from some strange dream, and I'm too stunned to respond. What were Felix and I doing a second ago? What was about to happen?

"It's okay," Felix says when I hesitate. I turn back to him, and that urgent, searching look I saw before is gone. "Go with them, I'll see you tomorrow."

"Yeah, see you tomorrow."

Felix squeezes my hand one last time, and then lets me go.

When April and I rejoin the main group, we say goodbye to everyone in a flurry of hugs and cheek kisses. My head is spinning from everything Felix said, and the hand that held his is burning. I feel like I need to reframe everything I've thought about Felix in the last six years, but I don't even know where to start.

April and Carmen know better than to ask me anything while we're still around my family, so they wait until we're walking to the parking garage, and then they pounce.

"You have to tell us what happened," April demands, tugging on my wrist. "I'm the worst friend in the world for interrupting, and you can totally yell at me about it later, but right now I need details."

"But if you two were making out or something, you can keep that to yourself," Carmen adds, but I'm not really listening.

"He apologized," I murmur, still in a daze, and they both turn to me. "He apologized for ghosting me. I can't believe it."

"Well, that's kind of major," Carmen says. "Did he explain why he did it?"

I fill them in as we walk up the steep incline of the parking garage, voice echoing off the concrete walls. I tell them about his reference to our first kiss, about how he didn't want things to end between us, and how that made it hard for him to move on. I tell them about the apology and the look on his face before April interrupted us.

"I mean, what he did *was* immature, but we were kids," I say once I'm finished. "I thought he was toying with me this whole time, but he's not the guy I made him out to be."

Both of the girls have odd looks on their faces, but April is the one who speaks up first. "Dude, he's literally in love with you."

"Please don't mess with me right now," I say, heart in my throat.

I don't want to get my hopes up and then feel crushed when things don't work out. "We just became friends again, and things with his ex still seem complicated. I'm not sure if that's where his head is at."

"Well, *I'm* sure. Look," Carmen says, pulling something up on her phone. "Does this look platonic to you?"

Lit up on the screen is a candid photo of me and Felix at dinner. I'm in the middle of laughing at a joke, probably something Elisa said, but that's not the important part. It's the look on Felix's face that steals all the air out of my lungs. His arm is draped over the back of my chair, and his chin is tilted toward me. That lopsided smile I love is starting to spread across his face, and his eyes are so soft it makes my heart ache. He's looking at me like I'm the only person in the room, like I'm the only person in the whole universe.

"You're a stalker," I say to Carmen, even though I'm dying a little inside. "This was half a second out of almost three hours we were at dinner. It doesn't prove anything."

"And the entire conversation you two had by the water, that felt platonic to you?" April presses. Turning to Carmen, she adds, "They were holding hands."

"One hand," I correct automatically, and they both roll their eyes. "What if he was acting for the fake dating bit?"

"You two were completely alone."

I pause. "Okay, good point."

"My god, the Twitter gays would eat this up," April says.

"Please don't publicize my idiocy on the god-forsaken bird app," I sigh. We reach the top floor of the parking garage, and the city skyline rises up around us, lights twinkling against the navy-blue sky. "I get what you're saying. I really want to believe he likes me, but how can I know for sure?"

"You're never going to know," Carmen replies gently. "Not with Felix, not with anyone you like. Being honest about your feelings is almost always going to be a bit of a gamble. But you two have a real shot, and if you know how you feel, I think it's worth taking that chance on him."

I take a deep breath, the warm summer air filling my lungs. "I wouldn't even know where to start."

"You're already going to be 'together' at the queerceañera," April points out. "It would be crazy romantic to tell him then. Like, romcom-level romantic. You could show him how you really feel about him with some big gesture or something."

As I look out at the city lights, I'm surprised that I don't hate the idea. It's not something I would normally consider, but this entire situation is far from normal. The girls exchange a look as I mull it over.

"Oh, I want to enable this so badly," Carmen says, "Are you really considering it?"

"I'm not *not* considering it," I hedge, but an idea is already starting to solidify.

I think back to the conversation Felix and I had at the art

supply store when he begged me to paint him. I've never been one for big speeches or pouring my heart out in words, but putting my feelings down on canvas? That's something I could do.

The next morning, I'm lying in bed when I see Carmen has texted me the photo she snapped of me and Felix at dinner. Y'all really do make a cute couple, she sent in the message under the picture, just sayinggg.

I tap on the photo to bring it into full view, and seeing the look on Felix's face again makes me want to shove my face into my pillow and scream. I can't stop thinking about his hand in mine, the feeling of having him there next to me at dinner.

It's not a surefire thing that Felix feels the same way, or that he's over his ex, or that the timing of this is right for either of us. But I can't ignore the way I feel about him. I keep trying to convince myself that Felix is less important to me than he really is, and I don't want to do that anymore. He feels like home to me, and for once in my life, I don't want to overthink it.

So when I catch myself wishing I could post the photo of me and Felix at dinner like I would with a real boyfriend, I don't second-guess myself like I normally do. I open Instagram and post it.

Since Felix, April, and I have plans to look at flower arrangements at a nursery and I wasted a good chunk of the morning in bed, I get ready for the day in record time. I'm always excited to see

Felix, but this feels different. We're finally on the same page after six whole years of misunderstandings and heartache. And at the end of all this, we might be a real, genuine couple.

April picks me up, windows rolled down and music blasting, and the entire ride there, I feel invincible. But when we pull up to my mom's house to pick Felix up, there's a shiny black Jeep parked in the driveway that I don't recognize. And there's a guy leaning against it talking to Felix who I don't recognize either.

We get out of the car, and I can see that he's tall, even taller than Felix. He's got cropped, bleach-blond hair and a face you would see on the cover of college catalog, and the way he's smiling at Felix turns my insides to jelly in the worst way possible.

"Do we have a stranger-danger situation on our hands?" April asks as we walk up to the pair.

"Not quite," Felix laughs. He turns to the guy next to him, adding, "This is April, and this is Joaquin."

Not Jay. Not "my boyfriend." Just Joaquin. Then Felix puts a hand on the other guy's bicep, and I realize who's standing in front of me.

"Guys, meet Caleb."

Chapter Seventeen

WELL, SHIT.

"I'm on a pre-college road trip with my friends," Caleb says like that's a totally normal and casual thing to do. "I decided to stop over in Austin for a bit, check out Felix's old stomping grounds. It was kind of a spur-of-the-moment thing."

"Very on-brand for you," Felix says, and I feel something twist uncomfortably in my chest. "We're supposed to go pick out flowers in a few minutes, though. I don't want to abandon these guys."

"That sounds cool. Mind if I tag along?" Caleb asks without sparing me or April a second glance. "I'd love to catch up with you, plus I've been cooped up in this car for the last four hours. Gotta stretch my legs."

"Oh, sure. I don't mind," Felix says, looking at me. "Do you?"

I try to read Felix's face to see if he wants me to intervene, but I can't read his expression, and I don't want to be rude. I suck it up and slap on my best fake smile.

"Not at all," I reply.

In the end, we decide to take one car to the nursery, and Caleb heroically offers to take us in his Jeep.

"I got it detailed for this trip," he says. "It'd be a shame if I didn't get to show it off."

As he hops into the driver's seat, April shoots me a *this guy is such a tool* look that I deeply appreciate.

Caleb and Felix chat away in the front as I try to squash down my jealousy. I know Felix has history with him, that's how exes work. But it was way easier to ignore when the ex in question wasn't right in front of me. And after everything I've heard about the loose ends of their breakup, it's really hard for me to believe that Caleb "spontaneously" decided to stop by on a whim.

April fishes her phone out of her pocket and starts typing furiously. A second later, my phone buzzes in my hand.

Is this guy his ex???

Yep! I reply. Kill me :)

April texts back instantly. I say this in the harshest way possible . . . he's a major flop.

Thank you so much.

"Felix was filling me in on this whole coming out party you're doing. It sounds pretty fun," Caleb says, eyes connecting with mine in the rearview mirror. "So Felix is like your chaperone?"

"He's my date," I say, but Caleb keeps on talking like he didn't even hear me.

"Well, my parents always kind of knew I was queer, so I never officially came out."

"They've been allies for, like, a million years," Felix says over his shoulder. "Caleb literally has baby pictures at a Pride parade. It's hilarious."

"That kind of support is a real privilege," April chimes in, fixing Caleb with a pointed stare in the rearview mirror.

"Oh, totally. No denying it," he says, but also doesn't elaborate.

As we pull into the nursery parking lot, there's this bitterness gnawing away at me that I don't want to feel. I know that everyone's coming out journey is difficult in its own way. And if I weren't already feeling insecure about it or if the queerceañera weren't happening in the first place, then maybe it wouldn't get under my skin. But that is where my head is at, and I'm too tired to fight it.

We head inside the massive greenhouse that takes up the bulk of the property. The humidity is next-level, and it feels like the summer heat is amplified by the tall, arching glass walls. The place is jam-packed with hanging baskets, palms, and rows of succulents and seasonal flowers.

Felix goes off to find our florist, leaving me, Caleb, and April loitering near the entrance. And, to my immense displeasure, Caleb turns to me the second Felix is out of earshot.

"You know, Felix is so laid back, I'm a little surprised you've been able to drag him to do stuff like this."

"I wouldn't call it dragging. It was his idea to get involved in the first place," I say, trying and failing not to sound annoyed. "Felix is a great guy like that."

"Oh, he's the best," Caleb says with a smile that's way more patronizing than it is genuine. "It's been crazy hearing how much goes into the whole thing. Every time he updates me on it, I'm like, woah, you're really going above and beyond."

All of a sudden, the floor feels like it's dropped out from under me. "You two have been talking?"

"Yeah, we've been texting most days since he left," Caleb says, pulling the leaf off a philodendron vine trailing down from the ceiling. His eyes slide over to me. "Did he not mention that?"

I want to say something back, anything that will get rid of this awful hollow feeling in my stomach, but I'm frozen in place. April must pick up on it, because she quickly tries to change the subject.

"So, have you been around town much, or did you just get in?" April asks Caleb.

"We drove around a little bit, but I'm not sure if Austin is really my scene," Caleb muses as Felix rejoins the group, seemingly with no luck finding our florist. "I figured by the way people rave about it that it was going to be all cool and edgy or whatever, but it feels a bit overrated. No offense."

"None taken. Folks who were born and raised here have a way of keeping things authentic," April says with a Nobel Peace Prize–worthy smile. Her tactfulness never ceases to amaze me. "Maybe you can check out the live music scene while you're here. There's this hole in the wall on the East Side that brings in small country acts on Friday nights, it's really fun. We're going to a concert there with Felix and some of our other friends in a few days."

"Ahh, so that's what you've been up to the past few weeks," Caleb jokes to Felix, jostling his hip. "Isn't that a little too 'yeehaw' for your taste? I really can't imagine you at a place like that."

"I mean, I can," I say. When Caleb raises a brow at me, I add, "I know what he likes. We did grow up together after all."

"That's funny, he didn't mention you much," Caleb says.

He says it innocently enough, but it feels like he's looking down his nose at me. I mean, he literally is, because he's freakishly tall. But he's being condescending too, and I hate that.

"I totally have mentioned him," Felix interjects, but Caleb shrugs it off.

"Guess I forgot. Maybe it wasn't that important."

"Or maybe you don't know Felix as well as you think you do," I reply.

The second it comes out of my mouth, I realize how passive-aggressive I sound. Actually, scratch that, straight-up aggressive. April is giving me a look that says she's both impressed and a little concerned, so I know for sure that I crossed a line.

"I'm, uh, going to text the florist and see where they're at," I say, stepping aside to pull out my phone. And as if I'm not embarrassed enough as it is, Felix decides to follow me.

"Hey, are you okay?" he asks, voice low enough that Caleb can't hear us from where he's poking around the Venus flytraps. "If you're mad about our conversation last night, I really am sorry."

"What? No, that's not it at all," I say quickly. "Last night was good—*really* good. What you said meant a lot to me. I'm a bit off today, I guess."

Felix's worried expression softens a bit. "I feel like you just said 'it's not you, it's me' but with more words."

I let out a huff of air that's halfway between a sigh and a laugh. "I guess I did."

"As long as we're okay, that's all I care about," he says. "But it would mean a lot to me if you made Caleb feel welcome while he's here."

And god, jealousy rears its ugly head again, lodging itself in my throat as I try to formulate a response. I almost press Felix on why he cares if Caleb feels welcome, especially since he showed up without warning, but it feels unfair of me to ask. Felix is thoughtful almost to a fault. That is, after all, one of the reasons I've had such a hard time deciphering how he actually feels about me. It doesn't feel like the right time to push him, so instead I ask, "How long is that, exactly?"

"Just this week," Felix says, fiddling with the hem of his shirt. "I know we have a bunch of last-minute stuff to handle for the queerceañera, but he and my other friends want me to show them around town this week."

I didn't think it was possible for my heart to sink even deeper into my stomach, but there it is. Maybe Felix doesn't mean it that way, but it feels like a rejection. He has been nothing but helpful and attentive when it came to party-planning so far, which I thought, *hoped*, had something to do with spending time with me. But now, the old fear bubbles up again that maybe this isn't that important to him after all. Maybe *I'm* not that important to him.

"Oh, okay," I manage to say.

"I'm not trying to ditch you, I promise," Felix says quickly. Either I have the worst poker face ever, or he's literally learned how to read my mind. "It'll be one of the last times I get to see everyone before they're off to college. Otherwise, I'd tell them I'm busy. But I don't want to leave you hanging. Maybe we can do something together? Meet the gang?"

I raise an eyebrow at him. "Oh, because I made such a stunning first impression?"

"Ethan and Oscar will love you, I promise," Felix laughs, and some of the pressure in my chest eases up. "Is that a yes?"

It's impossible for me to tell if Felix is telling the truth, if he really wants to spend time with his friends, or if it's an excuse to spend more time with Caleb. But I don't want him to think that I'm some immature, jealous jerk. Maybe I have to accept that Caleb is a part of his life whether I like it or not.

"All right," I say, swallowing my pride. "Yeah, why not?"

Chapter Eighteen

IT'S ABOUT A billion degrees inside the concert venue when April hands me and Savannah two cold sodas, and even though the cool aluminum can feels like a gift from god, I'm still mad at her.

"Oh, stop pouting, drama king," April says, and Jaz snickers next to her while Bryce looks on sympathetically.

"I can't believe you sullied our extremely sacred perfect summer plans by inviting a bunch of people we don't know."

"You didn't even care about the perfect summer plans until I brought this up!" April scoffs, and I frown as I take a sip of my drink. "Besides, if it wasn't this group outing, you would've had to hang out with all of them on your own, and that's way worse."

We're standing near the back of the small venue, near a small bar that houses the concessions and merch. The stage is sheltered under a small overhang, but the back half of the concert hall is open air. There's a little more airflow where we are, but as a crowd starts to gather and conversations and excitement buzz around us, I'm sure we'll all be sweating in no time.

Savannah fans herself, her long, fine hair already sticking on her neck in the merciless humidity. "What's so bad about hanging out with Felix's friends tonight?"

April and I exchange a look, and our friends pause.

"Wait, what was that about?" Jaz asks.

"One of the guys coming, Caleb, is Felix's ex," April blurts out, ignoring my look of betrayal in favor of nursing her soda.

Bryce gasps, hand coming up to cover his mouth like this is truly the most upsetting thing he's ever heard. "Oh my god, *no*."

Jaz leans in with a wicked glint in her eye. "Do we hate him?"

"We're supposed to make him 'feel welcome,'" I reply, making air quotes with my free hand.

"Oh okay, so we totally hate him."

"No, we're going to be super nice for the thirty minutes that we have to chitchat before the headliner comes on," April says, linking arms with Jaz. "Then we can ignore them for two hours straight. And that, my friends, is the beauty of inviting people you barely know to a concert."

"I take back every complaint I made before," I say. "I love you and your evil genius brain."

"You better hold onto that warm fuzzy feeling, because your boyfriend and his crew are here."

I turn to where April is pointing, and sure enough, there's Felix making his way through the crowd, flanked by Caleb and two other guys. Their faces don't really register in my brain, only because Felix is wearing a cutoff tee and the shortest shorts I've ever seen on him, and I'm not entirely sure it's not making me go into cardiac arrest.

"Hi," I say weakly as he meets up with our group.

"Hey, stranger," Felix says. He slips an arm around my waist and plants a small kiss into my curls, and my entire brain short-circuits. *What the actual fuck was that?*

"Okay, introductions," Felix says, like he didn't just ruin my entire life. "This is Joaquin, obviously. Then there's April, Savannah, Jaz, and Bryce."

And of course, Caleb has to speak up first.

"I'm Caleb," he says, and to my friends' credit, they manage very polite smiles in reply. "Sorry for crashing your plans like this."

"You're so full of shit," Felix says with a laugh, and it's like music to my ears. I loop an arm around his waist, pulling him closer. Caleb's eye flick down to my hand placement and back to Felix's face.

"I guess I couldn't resist seeing you," he says, and I'm feeling positively murderous until the guy standing on the other side of us, sporting a dark buzz cut and a deep tan, looks at Caleb and grimaces.

"Cringe," he says succinctly.

"Homophobe," Caleb replies without any real bite.

"Shit, I can't take you guys anywhere. I'm Ethan, by the way," says the other friend. His dark blonde hair is mussed up like it hasn't seen a brush in ages, and he's got an old, holey Metallica shirt on, which strikes me as a kind of funny fashion choice for a country music venue. Ethan points to the buzz-cut guy next. "This is Oscar."

Oscar gives a little wave, the colorful string bracelets around his wrist flashing bright in the sun. "Caleb was kidding, by the way. He antagonizes me as the token straight friend of the group."

"My condolences," I say, and he nods sagely.

"It's a difficult cross to bear, but someone has to carry it," he replies, putting a solemn hand over his heart. Between the dry sense of humor and calling Caleb out, I immediately decide he's my favorite, and apparently, so does Savannah.

"You're all seniors, right?" she asks, and I'm not sure if I've ever seen someone bat their eyelashes in real life, but that's got to be what she's going for. "Or, I guess I should say 'were' seniors."

"Yep, freshly graduated. I'm going to Georgia Tech in the fall," Oscar says, and then points to Ethan. "This one is going to Boston University. Caleb is the only freethinker who decided to take a gap year."

"I want to take some time to rest and refocus on personal development," Caleb says, and I think that even if I didn't hate him, I'd still want to gag hearing him say that with a completely straight face. Personal development, my ass. "Thankfully USC was cool with it, so I'll head there once the year is up."

"Oh, I know someone who did that," Bryce says. "She was doing internships and stuff. Is that what you're gonna do?"

"Not sure. I want to travel abroad, see the real world, and have authentic experiences, you know?" he replies. Gag times two. "I haven't planned out anything specific though. I want to leave my options open."

"This guy thrives on being unpredictable," Felix says, and Caleb grins at him.

"Shut up, you love it," Caleb replies, and that's when I notice he has a nose ring.

I frown as Jaz asks another question about his gap year, and Caleb keeps chatting. Didn't Felix tell me that he got his nose piercing with a friend? Was Caleb the person he was talking about? If Felix is still wearing his, I'm not sure what that means about their relationship, but it doesn't feel good.

"You okay?" Felix asks me quietly, letting the others continue the conversation in the background. "You're kind of zoning out."

"Just trying not to die of heat stroke," I say, since it's the first thing that pops into my head. Felix gives me a little space, pulling back from where he's been pressed to my side, and I immediately mourn the loss of the closeness. Damn him for caring about my needs.

"Let me see if they have some ice for your drink," Felix says, heading over to the concession counter. To my absolute horror,

Caleb has the nerve to follow him. He leans right up against Felix as he talks to the bartender, shoulder to shoulder, and there's no way in hell he's not doing it on purpose.

April notices the way I stare after him, and under her breath whispers, "Woah, if looks could kill."

Bryce ends up joining Felix and Caleb at the counter, and the three of them talk for a while, laughing loudly in a way that would be cute if Caleb weren't part of the equation. Savannah, Jaz, and April keep the conversation flowing with the other guys, but I can't seem to concentrate. All I can think about is stupid Caleb and his stupid gap year and his stupid nose ring.

Felix is still at the counter with Caleb and Bryce by the time the opener comes on. It's an acoustic solo act that sadly doesn't drown out the sound of everyone's voices in the audience, so we haven't reached the point in the evening where April promised I'd be able to sulk in peace. Instead of wallowing, I head over to the bar myself. When I sidle up next to Felix, it looks like he's just snapped out of a dream. Or from my point of view considering Caleb is there, a nightmare.

"Shit, sorry, I completely forgot why I came over here," Felix apologizes, leaning back over the counter to ask for more ice like he had promised.

"We get so wrapped up in our own little world when we're together," Caleb says, glancing at me behind Felix's back. "Guess old habits die hard."

At this point, I'm positive he's trying to get under my skin. Felix asked me to be nice, but I'm not sure I can manage it while looking Caleb in his smug, annoying face.

When Felix turns back with my drink, I pluck it out of his hands and push off the counter.

"Well, don't let me interrupt," I say as sweetly as I can manage, and turn on my heel to return to the other group.

I only get about halfway there before Oscar comes bounding up to me.

"Dude, please tell me Savannah is single," he says without preamble, which is kind of adorable and maybe the only thing he could've said that would pull me out of this Caleb-induced funk.

"She absolutely is single," I reply, and Oscar's face lights up.

"Throw me a bone here. What does she like in a guy?"

I chew the inside of my cheek for a second, mentally reviewing the catalog of boys I've heard her mention over the last three years.

"She tends to go for confident guys, but they end up being kind of shitty to her. She's a real sweetheart and doesn't deserve that. I think she'd appreciate a change of pace, so don't try to be cool or play hard to get. All you have to do is be nice, okay?"

"Hell yeah, nice is my middle name," Oscar says with a grin, giving me a playful punch on the arm. "I knew you were cool from what Felix has told us, but man, you really are the best."

I pause, my drink halfway to my lips. "Felix talks about me?"

"Oh yeah, of course he does," Oscar says easily. I think back to

Caleb's comment in the greenhouse about Felix never mentioning me and feel vindicated. I knew he was full of shit. "Felix kept dropping your name, like 'Jay and I went and did this' and 'Jay told me the funniest thing the other day.' He wasn't subtle about it at all. Ethan and I were really curious because he never talks like that about anyone. And Caleb was . . . well, you know."

"I really don't," I say, feeling lost.

"Caleb can be a little bit overbearing, especially when it comes to Felix," Oscar says slowly, choosing his words carefully. "Don't get me wrong, I love the guy. But he always thinks he knows best. He never really let Felix do what he wanted."

Now that I think about it, this does sound familiar. It echoes what Felix said at the barbecue about their breakup, and how he never really felt like he could relax and be himself with Caleb.

"I honestly didn't even know that Felix was still talking to Caleb," I say, and Oscar frowns.

"Shit, maybe I shouldn't have said anything," he says, rubbing the back of his neck. "But between you and me, I can tell Felix is really happy with you. He seems different, even over text. For what it's worth, I'm rooting for you two."

"Thanks, man," I say, feeling oddly touched. "That's really sweet."

"Told you nice was my middle name," Oscar says, flashing me another smile as he turns to rejoin our little group.

I trail after him with renewed hope and a mountain of new questions swirling around my head. Felix talking about me with his friends isn't nothing, but I'm still not sure if the connection we have holds a candle to whatever he had with Caleb. When I turn my head to look over at them one last time, all I can focus on is the spot where Felix's arm is touching Caleb's, and how badly I wish I were in his place.

April is happily bopping along to the opener as I slip back into our circle of friends, and next to Jaz, Oscar pulls Ethan into an affectionate chokehold.

"What are you boring the girls with now?"

"Details of our great American road trip," Ethan replies, tapping Oscar's wrist until he finally relinquishes him.

"It sounds so wild," Savannah says, turning to Oscar. "Y'all already drove to Florida and looped all the way back along the Gulf?"

"Yeah, we decided we wanted to split the trip in half and come back to Texas in the middle so we could rest a little," Oscar replies. "The second half of the trip is longer. We're driving to San Diego and then riding the Pacific Coast Highway all the way up California."

"Shit, that sounds like it took a lot of work to plan," Jaz says. "And a lot of money."

"We all saved up for a while to be able to afford it. But we wanted this to be special, you know?"

"Right, this is our swan song after all," Ethan says with an exaggerated sniff, and Oscar punches him hard in the arm.

"You've gotta stop calling it that, you freak. It sounds like one of us is dying."

"Well I'm probably never going to see you again after this," Ethan says, dodging as Oscar tries to punch him again. Next to me, April stops swaying along to the music.

"You really suck—you know that?"

"Whatever, man. I'm just being realistic," Ethan says with a shrug. My heart sinks as I glance at April, and the carefree smile she was wearing earlier is long gone. "Everyone says they're going to keep in touch after high school, but that never actually happens."

"I mean, some people do," April says, far more earnest than either of the boys. "My moms are still friends with people they knew in elementary school."

"Eh, but that's one in a million. Gotta keep your expectations low so you don't get hurt."

"Dude, that's really fuckin' dark," Oscar says, shaking his head.

"I'm a realist, what can I say," Ethan replies.

Neither of them seems particularly bothered by the conversation, but what Ethan says leaves a weird, bitter taste in my mouth. But if I think I'm bummed out by it, nothing compares with the crushed look on April's face when I look over at her again.

"Hey," I say, leaning over so she can hear me over the music.

"Don't listen to him. He was running his mouth to be funny. That's not going to be us, okay?"

"But what if it is?" April asks, as serious as she was at the house party. "How can you know for sure?"

And honestly, even though I believe with my whole heart that I'm right, I don't know how to answer her. I wish I could show her how much she means to me, to help her understand that I'm not going anywhere, but I'm coming up blank. The music swells, and Savannah takes the opportunity to grab April's hand and start swaying back and forth. It effectively distracts her from the conversation, and while the whole thing still doesn't sit well with me, I don't want to ruin the show for her by bringing it back up now.

When the opener ends, we all decide to inch closer to the stage, not wanting to linger in the back for too long and miss out on finding good standing room. As we navigate through the crowd, Felix finds me again.

"Having fun?" I ask, wedging myself between him and another concertgoer.

"Not as much as I could have if I'd stuck with you," Felix says with an easy smile, and my pulse quickens a little.

If he had said something like that days ago, I might've taken it at face value and let myself feel excited. But now, I'm starting to question if what I thought was Felix's flirting is really meaningless banter after all.

"What were y'all talking about earlier?" I ask, trying to sound very casual and almost managing it.

"The queerceañera, believe it or not," Felix says. "Caleb told the guys about it the other day, and they're kind of obsessed. They've been asking me about it nonstop. It's happening on their last day in town, and I wanted to ask you if we could invite them. Only if you're cool with it, though."

Ethan and Oscar seem fine enough, and I wouldn't mind them coming even though I barely even know them, but Caleb? I literally can't think of anything I want less than to have him there. But I know that Felix wants to spend time with his friends as much as he can while they're here. I feel like it would be cruel to say no. So even though it feels like torture, I say, "Okay, sure."

Felix notices my hesitation, because of course he does. "I know it might be a little weird to have Caleb there, but I think it would be weirder if I invited everyone else *except* for him. Stuff with him is . . ."

"Complicated?" I offer, and Felix lets out a huff of laughter.

"Yeah, okay, maybe I need to add some new adjectives to my vocabulary. I'm still trying to find my footing with him."

Felix fiddles with the lid of his water bottle, and all I want to do is shake him. I want to ask him what the hell any of that means, where he stands with Caleb, and where he stands with me. Instead, I say the first cohesive thought that pops into my head.

"I didn't know you two were talking," I say, and Felix shoots me a questioning look. "At the greenhouse, Caleb said you two had been texting all summer."

"Just in a group chat with all our friends. We haven't really been talking one on one, it's been pretty surface level," Felix says, and some of the pressure lets up from where it was crushing my lungs a second ago. But Felix's eyes are still searching my face. "Did it bother you when he said that?"

Obviously, the answer is yes, but it feels like such a loaded question, one I can't answer honestly without putting my entire heart on the line. I open my mouth, not sure if I want to deny it or change the subject, but thankfully I don't have to. The bass and drum players for the headliner come onstage, and the crowd roars to life, drowning out whatever words I was about to say.

But then, same as when we were walking by the river, Felix slips his hand into mine and gives it a squeeze. I look up at him and he looks down at me, and I can't for the life of me figure out what he's thinking. When the lead singer comes out, the bodies around us rush forward, and as we're pushed closer to the stage, I lose my grip on Felix's hand. The music starts playing, loud and energetic, and I've never felt more confused in my life.

Chapter Nineteen

I'M IN MY room, approaching hour three of staring at a blank canvas, when I get a text from Felix.

Caleb wants me to show him around today, rain check on the playlist curation?

A sharp splinter of anxiety stabs at my gut. April, Felix, and I were supposed to go over the music for the queerceañera. It didn't need to be a three-person job, but Felix was the one who asked to be included in the first place. And now he's going to hang out with Caleb instead.

Fantastic.

It's np, I reply. You know, like a liar. April and I can finish it today.

Ever since the concert, Caleb has been taking up way more of Felix's time than I thought was even possible. If I'm giving him the benefit of the doubt, it kind of makes sense. Caleb, Oscar, and

Ethan are only in town for a little while, so their time together is limited. But after seeing the way Caleb acts with Felix, it's way harder to squash down my worries.

My phone buzzes again, and it's another text from Felix: miss ur face

I'm not sure what I want to do more, scream into a pillow or block his number. I read the message again, and my stomach has the audacity to get butterflies. If Felix started teaching a master class on sending mixed signals, he'd be a millionaire in no time.

I take a screenshot of Felix's texts and send them to April without a caption. Within seconds, I get an incoming FaceTime call from her. Sighing, I hit accept.

"You're freaking out," April says when the call connects.

"Of course I'm freaking out," I say, sprawling face down on my bed. "My fake boyfriend might be cheating on me with his exboyfriend, except you can't even cheat on someone when you were never really together in the first place."

"He's not cheating on you," April replies, and I bury my face in my comforter. "Felix and Caleb obviously have history, but I saw the way he acted when we were at the show. He obviously cares about you a lot."

"Yeah, but cares about me in what way? How can I know for sure whether he sees me as more of a friend?" I ask, voice muffled by the comforter.

"You won't know for sure until you tell him how you feel," April says gently, and I groan.

This is exactly why this stupid canvas in the corner of my room is still blank. It's extra frustrating because I can picture what I want to paint perfectly. I want it to be the scene at the orchard that Felix and I talked about after dinner. The canvas would be framed by the branches of the apple trees like the viewer is peeking through them. Felix and I would be in the center facing each other, with petals in the foreground concealing parts of our faces as we lean into each other. I can picture the concept so clearly, but I can't seem to get it out of my head and onto the canvas.

I was positive that I wanted to do this after Felix met my family, but now I can't get myself to start it because I'm not sure if I'd just be wasting my time. It feels like the conversation I had with Carmen and April on the roof of that parking garage was a million years ago, even though it's only been a handful of days. Everything that night felt too good to be true, and maybe that's because it was.

"Maybe I should change my name and start a new life far away from Felix," I say popping my head up. On my phone screen, April raises an eyebrow at me. "Do you think the witness protection program would take me?"

"What do you need protection from?"

"The horrors of having romantic feelings for someone," I say, and it makes April laugh so hard I can't help but smile too.

"You're right," she says when she finally catches her breath. "That sounds like a great allocation of taxpayer dollars."

"I mean, I do think it would qualify as an international incident if Felix flakes out on the queerceañera after all."

April tilts her head to the side, peering at me in the viewfinder. "Is that what you're worried about? Felix backing out?"

"Kind of," I murmur, but the way my heart rate spikes reminds me that it's no minor concern. "The main reason I believed that Felix was going to follow through on the fake dating bit is that there was something in it for him too. His parents were all worried about him after his breakup, but what if that doesn't matter anymore? If he and Caleb are on such good terms or if they do get back together, then what's stopping him from leaving me to fend for myself?"

"I don't think he would do that to you," April reassures me, but I can't seem to get out of my head about it.

"I feel like I never really know with him. With a friend like that, no wonder Ethan said all that stuff about friends dropping off the face of the earth," I say. I'm being overdramatic at this point, but April frowns, and I realize my mistake a second too late. She looks like a deer caught in headlights, same as she looked at the concert. I probably should have picked a better time to bring it back up again. But now that I have, I want to get to the bottom of how she's feeling, and I want to help. "Hey, are you still bothered by what he said? I told you, he was being an asshole about it on purpose."

"I know, I know," April sighs. She looks like she wants to say more, but then pauses. "I don't want to hijack your freak-out. Feels a little rude."

"No, please do," I reply honestly. "Even I'm sick of hearing myself talk at this point."

"Okay, it's just . . . do you really think he's wrong?" April asks, picking nervously at the ends of her braids. "People always say they're going to keep in touch, and then they don't."

Okay, so this has been bothering her more than she's let on. I can handle this, though. There's no reason for her to be anxious when we're on the same page.

"I guess, but when we say that to each other, we both genuinely mean it. And besides, we're not like other people," I point out, but April's face falls even more.

"Everyone says that too!" she says. "It's the same thing people say when they get into relationships. They swear they're not going to let their partner take over their life and then poof, they disappear off the face of the earth."

I think back to Cami's party, about April's face when she told me she didn't want me to ditch her now that I had a boyfriend. Since I haven't really dated, fake or otherwise, it hasn't come up before. All this stuff with Felix is new for me, but I guess it's new for our friendship too.

"Are you worried that's going to happen if Felix and I get together?" I ask, and April looks away from the camera, brows furrowing as she thinks.

"I don't know."

"April, come on!" I say, laughing a little without meaning to. "That's ridiculous, I'm not going to—"

"I know it's ridiculous, okay? You don't have to rub it in," she says, and shit, I'm not laughing anymore. I didn't mean for it to sound like I was making fun of her, but that's probably how it came across anyway. Before I can clarify, April presses on. "I'm never going to have a partner that's going to split my attention. I don't have a sister or cousins like you, so my friendships are always going to be my priority. It's kind of hard realizing that might not be the case for other people in my life, and I don't want to get left behind."

My heart sinks as the words tumble out of her mouth, and when she's finished, I'm a little speechless. Not because her fears are so outlandish I can't see where she's coming from, but because I'm an idiot for not speaking to her sooner given how much stress she's been bottling up. Now that we're talking about it, I'm not sure how to help her understand that I'm here for the long haul.

"I'm not going to leave you behind," I say honestly. "Thinking about the future after graduation feels like I'm staring into a black hole, and the only thing that makes me even remotely okay with it is that I know you're going to be there with me. We can't predict the future, but we can figure it out as we go, okay?"

April nods, but her troubled expression doesn't soften much. I want more than anything for her to take what I said to heart, because I meant every word of it. It just doesn't feel like enough.

"I wasn't laughing at you," I say after a pause. "I promise I wasn't."

"I know," April replies, but I don't think she really means it.

We stay on FaceTime a little longer, conversation moving to the unfinished queerceañera playlist and the other last-minute things we need to check off our list. But April stays uncharacteristically quiet, and I can tell her head is a million miles away. I want to find the words to make things right, but apparently, all I'm good at these days is putting my foot in my mouth. By the time we hang up, I feel twice as anxious as I did before she called.

The second I toss my phone aside, I feel the painting in the corner weighing on me too. Everything with Felix is still unresolved too. As much as I want to get out of my head and give him space, I can't seem to let any of my worries go.

I'm about to roll off my bed and grab something to eat as a distraction when my phone screen lights up again. I glance down, wondering if April forgot to ask me something and decided to call me back and groan when I see the notification.

To add insult to injury with the whole Felix situation, the photo of us at dinner is still up on Instagram, racking up likes. I was feeling all brave and confident about our future when I posted it. Taking the photo down now would look sketchy as hell, so now I'm stuck with it immortalized on my page until after my queerceañera is over.

It only takes a few seconds to pull up the photo on my phone. I know soft launching your relationship on social media is bound to garner a decent amount of attention, but even I'm surprised by how many comments the post has gotten. Family members who don't even follow me on Instagram are spamming me with heart eye emojis. I saw this on Facebook! So cute, one comment reads, and all the blood drains out of my face.

I've never had a Facebook account and Carmen deactivated hers ages ago, so there's only one explanation for what happened. I click into my browser and pull Dad's page up, and yep, there it is. Dad posted the photo and tagged me in it. And below it, right under a string of hearts posted by Tía Fernanda, there's a comment from Mom. Some photos can stay private.

I stare at the words for a second, feet rooted to the ground. The comment is so empty out of context, but I know exactly what she's trying to say. It's not just that some photos can stay private. These types of photos should stay private. Me being gay should stay private.

It's a knee-jerk reaction, but I instantly feel ashamed. Then I feel angry at myself for feeling that way. Why should I feel bad when I didn't do anything wrong? Hell, I didn't even repost the photo myself. This isn't my fault. It shouldn't even be my problem in the first place.

And all at once, the frustration that's been simmering inside me all morning, or maybe for weeks, finally boils over. Everyone has been piling all their expectations on me, day in and day out. I keep trying to make everyone happy because I don't want to rock the boat, but really all I'm doing is making myself small. And at the end of the day, I'm exhausted. I don't want to put up with any of it, not anymore.

Dad is stretched out on the couch in the living room, nose buried in some book. I march up to him and put the screen between him and whatever he's reading.

"Did you post this on Facebook?"

Dad squints at the screen. "I did! I love that picture. Very cute."

"You should have asked me first," I say, livid. He seems to finally notice that I'm fuming, because he takes his reading glasses off and stares up at me.

"What's wrong? You two look so happy."

"That's not the point," I shoot back, and his eyes go wide in confusion. "You have no boundaries, Dad. You do whatever you want all the time and expect everyone else to go along with it, and it's exhausting. Not everybody thinks the same way you do. Why don't you get that?"

There's hurt and concern written all over his face, but I don't want to hear whatever he has to say. Instead, I grab the car keys off the side table and make a beeline for the front door.

"Hijo, where are you going?" he calls out as the front door slams behind me.

The entire drive is a blur. My eyes are trained on the road, but my mind is going a mile a minute, and my chest feels like it's on fire. My anger flares when I think about Mom's comment, about all the comments she's made to me in the last couple of months. I can't believe I thought she was making progress, that everything I was doing with Felix was making a dent in her bullheadedness. It's insane how much time I've wasted trying to appeal to her, trying not to step out of line, and it makes me want to scream.

My hands grip the steering wheel so hard that when I finally park and turn off the ignition, my knuckles are aching. I ring the doorbell five times before Mom comes to the door.

"Joaquin, what on earth—"

"Why do you think it's okay to say something like this?" I demand, holding up my phone so she can see the comment she left.

A look of genuine shock passes across her face like she never thought I'd seriously confront her. But then she quickly composes herself, tucking a strand of dark hair behind her ear. "I'm not sure what you're talking about. I didn't mean anything by it."

"Yes, you did. Otherwise, you wouldn't have said anything at all," I say, struggling to keep my voice even. "*Some photos can stay private*. Why does this picture have to stay private, but you post ones exactly like it with Josh all the time? How is this any different?"

"It's not the same thing, hijo," she says like she's explaining it to a child, and it makes my blood boil. "This could make people uncomfortable."

"No, it makes *you* uncomfortable," I fire back.

"That's not true," she insists. "I worry that being so public about your sexuality could make your life harder than it has to be."

"The only person who's making my life harder because of my sexuality is you," I reply. "But instead of talking to me about any of this, you make snide comments about it that make me feel like I'm the problem."

"I just want what's best for my kids."

"No you don't! If did, you would actually support us instead of nitpicking and criticizing everything we care about. Hobbies, career stuff, nothing is good enough for you. This is exactly why Carmen doesn't want to talk to you either."

The last bit slips out before I even think about what I'm saying, and my mom looks like she just got slapped in the face. She opens her mouth, closes it again, and takes a second to breathe.

"Bringing up Carmen like that isn't fair," she says quietly.

"What you're doing to *me* isn't fair. You make me second-guess everything I say and do around you. It's painful. How can you not see that?" I ask. My voice keeps getting louder with every sentence, all my frustration pouring out at once. "I'm not some random person you get to push around. I'm your son."

My voice breaks at the end of the sentence, and it forces me to take a breath. I know I have to stop talking, otherwise I'll tell her that she's been hurting Felix too, and that's not my battle to fight. When I finally speak again, Mom's expression is one I'm not sure I've ever seen before on her, eyes shining with unshed tears.

"This is who I am, and I'm not going to let you or anyone else make me feel ashamed of it anymore," I say evenly, and this time, I really, truly mean it. "If you can't get on board and respect that, then I don't want you at my queerceañera. I'm not sure if I even want to be around you at all."

I turn on my heel and get in the car without looking at her again. There's a bead of sweat trickling down my back, and my hands are shaking, but I did it. I finally told her off, and I can't tell if I feel unstoppable or if I'm ten seconds away from falling apart.

But the adrenaline from the fight dissipates quickly, and I realize it's the latter. I only go a mile or two before I have to pull over, because the tears welling up in my eyes make it hard to see the road.

I don't regret anything I said. It was long overdue, and I think I had to get it all out in the open—not for her sake, but for mine. Even though I'm glad I did, it still feels like someone just punched a hole clean through my chest. It still feels like my entire world is crashing down around me. So I stay on the side of the road, head in my hands until I don't have any more tears left to cry, and then I finally go home.

Chapter Twenty

CARMEN HASN'T TEASED me at all for two whole days, and it's starting to freak me out. I'm aware this might sound nice, healthy even. But the only reason she's holding her tongue is because she saw me right after I got back from having it out with Mom, with puffy red eyes and everything.

She didn't ask me what happened then, and she hasn't asked about it since. Instead, she's being a little too nice, which is somehow worse and way more awkward. She lets me take my shower first with zero complaints. She fills the gas tank without asking me to pay my fair share. She plays her music at a volume that no longer shatters my eardrums from two rooms away. Red flags all around.

Dad follows suit, giving me plenty of space, which I'm kind of grateful for. I've never really yelled at him before, and now I'm not sure how to act around him. I want to apologize for snapping at him, because I know I didn't go about that conversation the right way. But I meant what I said to him about boundaries too, and I want him to take me seriously.

The only person I've talked to about the whole ugly thing is Felix. I got so wrapped up in my own head after having it out with Mom that I forgot to text him for almost twenty-four hours straight. It doesn't sound like much, but we've been talking pretty much nonstop since we exchanged numbers. Eventually, he got my attention by double texting me.

not to go full conspiracy theorist on you, but i'm thinking there's some correlation between your mom stress cleaning the entire house and the fact you haven't texted me all day, he said, then added, no pressure, but i'm here if you want to talk

It was such an endearingly on-brand way to reach out, I didn't even think twice before I clicked into his contact info. The phone rang once, twice, and then the call connected.

"You know, I was starting to think you finally made good on your repeated threats to block my number," he said when he picked up. "Thrilled to be proven wrong."

"If you keep sending me K-pop fan-cams in the middle of the night, then that threat is still on the table. Don't get too complacent."

"Never. But while I'm still on your good side, I'd love to hear what's kept you so quiet the last two days."

So I tell him everything. I tell him about almost biting my

dad's head off, about showing up on my mom's doorstep, and how furious I felt.

"Part of me feels silly that I blew up at her over a Facebook comment, you know? But it wasn't one single comment. It was all the frustration I've been feeling about her for months," I say. "There's this feeling in the pit of my stomach every time she acts like she's okay with my sexuality when she's obviously not, and I'm tired of pretending she's not lying to me. Or lying to herself."

"That's impressive, honestly," Felix says, voice muffled as he passes the phone from one ear to the other. "Following your gut isn't easy, especially when you have someone actively telling you not to."

"Me and my gut have a lot of work to do, that's for sure," I reply, and Felix laughs softly on the other end of the line. "But for a second there, I think she understood what I meant. I feel like I got through to her. It was like I saw her mask drop and she was just . . . confused. Like she didn't even fully realize how much those comments have been bothering me this whole time. And that hurts, but I don't know, I think it's also kind of sad."

"That is sad," Felix says slowly, and I can tell he's processing it on his end too. There's a pause, and when he speaks again, his voice is warm and quiet. "I really hope she does understand, for both of your sakes. And for Carmen too."

Felix listens as I dissect the conversation I had with my mom, letting me think out loud and get all my frustration out. He only interrupts to validate my feelings when I start to backtrack or make some self-deprecating joke, and the more I talk, the lighter I feel.

Eventually, the conversation shifts away from my parents and onto other topics. Felix shares what he's been up to this week, and even though hearing about Caleb stings, it isn't as bad as I'd anticipated. Felix keeps mentioning little things that reminded him of me around Austin, so even though we haven't seen each other in a few days, it seems like he's been thinking of me the whole time anyway.

The conversation stretches on for hours until we both started losing our voices. It's a little after 1:00 a.m. when we both start nodding off and we finally decide to call it a night.

"I'm really glad you called," he says before I hung up. His voice is low and muffled, and I can picture him curled up on his bed, phone wedged between his face and the pillow.

"So am I," I reply, glad he can't see me smiling on the other end of the line.

The call makes me feel a little more sure of my footing with Felix, enough so that I'm able to break through my art block and start his painting. And once I do, I'm reminded of why I always turn to art as a stress reliever. The whole time I'm transferring my sketch over to the canvas and blocking out the underlayer, my brain goes silent in the best way.

It's only when I have to wait for the paint to dry that all the doubts and worries about Caleb and my parents start creeping back and taking up real estate inside my head. I try writing my toast in the meantime to silence them again, but thinking about the queerceañera only makes it worse.

I'm on my bed staring at an empty page in my notebook when I hear a gentle knock at my door. Dad pushes the door open a little, poking his head in tentatively.

"Special delivery, if you want it," he says, holding out a plate of sliced mango sprinkled with Tajín, exactly the way I like it. First, I yell at him, and now I make him come to me with apology fruit. *Man*, I think, *I am such a dick.*

I wave him in and, before I lose my nerve, ask, "Can we talk?"

Dad settles on the edge of my bed, and I move my stuff aside to give him my full attention.

"I'm sorry for yelling at you the other day," I start, and it instantly feels like a weight has lifted off my shoulders. "It was immature, and I could've handled the whole thing better."

"I appreciate that," he replies, reaching out to squeeze my arm. "But I think I owe you an apology too. I should have asked you before sharing that picture. I know I get a little carried away sometimes."

"Maybe a little," I mumble, and he gives me an apologetic smile.

"I know I can't shield you from every disappointment in life, but I've always figured if I could be your biggest and loudest cheerleader, maybe I could make those parts of life a little less difficult. But I see how going overboard can sometimes have the opposite effect. I want to support you, not smother you."

"I get it, I really do. I know it's coming from a good place."

"I'm glad you know that. When I posted that photo, all I was thinking about was you and Felix. I assumed that since you posted it yourself, you wouldn't mind if I shared it too."

When he puts it like that, it makes perfect sense why he did it. If Felix and I had a normal relationship, then my dad posting a photo to show his support would have been really sweet. But Felix and I are anything but normal, and I'm starting to see how keeping that from Dad might not have been the best idea.

"My relationship with Felix is more complicated than you know," I say, but for some reason, he doesn't look surprised.

"Oh, I might know a little," he says, and when I realize what he means, my jaw drops.

"Did Carmen tell you? God, I'm going to kill her."

"Hey, go easy on her. She hinted there was more than met the eye there, but only after I'd already posted the photo," he says. "I'm still not sure exactly what's going on with you and el gringito, but I've known you two for your entire lives. I want to believe it'll all work out eventually."

The too-familiar feeling of uncertainty twists in my gut. "Yeah, I hope so."

"Are you two having issues?" he asks. "Is that why you're feeling so stressed?"

"No. I mean, sort of, but that's a whole other thing," I sigh, leaning back against my pillows. "The reason I flipped out at you the other day wasn't because of him. It was because of Mom."

Dad's face falls a bit, a crease forming between his brows. "She shouldn't have said what she did on that post."

"Yeah, but this time, I finally said something back," I say. Thinking about the conversation brings all the emotions I felt back to the surface, and I realize I'm not sad anymore. I'm exhausted. "I don't know how to move ahead with her. Unless she changes the way she talks around me, I don't think I want to spend time with her. But she's so stubborn. I'm not sure if that'll ever happen."

"I'm so sorry, mijo. I can't pretend to understand where her head is at. I didn't understand it even when I was living with her," he says, voice thick with emotion, and I'm reminded again of how hard it is for him to watch me butt heads with her too. "Remember that I'm happy to step in if you want me to, but I understand if you want to handle this yourself. Either way, I want you to know I'm here for you."

I don't want to get upset, but I feel tears pricking my eyes anyway. It takes me back to what he said to me the night he came up with the idea for my queerceañera. *I can't say for sure if your mom will come around, but if I have to be proud of you for the both of us, then I will.*

"I know it's silly, but I wish I could magically stop caring what she thinks overnight," I say, letting out a shaky breath.

"It's not silly. You care a lot about everything, and you have a big heart, chaparro. You might want to turn it all off sometimes, but it's your superpower. You know what I always say, right?"

"Uh, don't cut peppers and then rub your eyes?"

"Well, yes. But also, you've got a lot to offer," he says, reaching over to pat my knee. "If someone else doesn't see that, even if it's your mom, that doesn't make it any less true."

"I'll try to remember that," I promise, and for the first time in days, I feel like I can breathe again. Dad moves to get up from my bed, but then his eyes land on the painting in the corner, and his face lights up.

"Is this for Felix?" he asks, and I nod.

"I want to give it to him at the queerceañera, and tell him how I really feel about him," I say, still feeling a bit shy about the whole thing. "It might be a disaster, but I think I'm going to go for it anyway."

"Wow, you've got some real game," he says, a little in awe, and I burst out laughing. "I'm serious! And you're a smart guy. It took me until my twenties to realize that you can be scared but still move forward anyways. The fact that you're figuring that out now? Well, I'm really proud of you is all."

Something about that hits me way harder than I expect it to. Not only because he's proud of me, but also because I'm proud of myself too. I've come a really long way since the beginning of the summer. I never thought in a million years that I'd be excited about taking risks and standing up for myself, but I want to keep doing it, even if it's messy. That's how I know I have to put myself out there and tell Felix the truth. There's a chance it'll all go up in smoke, but if there's also a chance we could get a happy ending, then I'm going to take it.

Chapter Twenty-One

THE FINAL DAYS leading up to the queerceañera are a blur. It feels like every hour there's something new that Carmen or Dad needs me to sign off on, and besides that, I'm spending every waking moment reviewing the run of the show so I don't forget the day of. I barely have time to go get a long-overdue haircut and pick up my suit from Tío Gael in the middle of it all.

Between me running around making the final decisions about the event and Felix's newly packed schedule with Caleb, we don't see each other much, but we do text a lot. His constant stream of messages help to keep my jealousy about Caleb mostly at bay, and combined with the pep talk from my dad, I'm able to focus on finishing his painting.

Call it a post-procrastination energy boost or divine inspiration, but it all comes together much faster than I expect it to. The branches around Felix and I take shape quickly, and so do the apple blossoms. Our faces take the longest, and even though I said painting people I know is awkward, I end up finding it oddly therapeutic. Maybe it's because I'm pouring so much of myself into it, or maybe it's because it's Felix, but there's more emotion in this piece than a lot of the stuff I've made before. Putting the finishing touches on it doesn't feel as daunting as I'd thought. Now, I just feel giddy.

Things finally slow down the afternoon before the big day. All the plans are in place, the painting is finished and drying in my room, and the only thing left is to pick up my family from the airport. Tía Regina and Abuelo are flying in together from Puebla and staying at our house, and I've been so busy with everything else I haven't had time to feel nervous about seeing them. But now I'm getting jittery about it, and my fears from the day Carmen and Dad pitched the queerceañera to me bubble up again.

I try to remind myself that Abuelo and Tía Regina both support me, and they wouldn't be traveling here if they didn't. Tía Regina has made that clear, messaging me on WhatsApp every other day leading up to her flight about how excited she is to see me. But Abuelo is nowhere near as vocal, and even though I know he's a man of few words by nature, it still feels a little intimidating to see him for the first time since I came out.

Thankfully, Valentina and Elisa help to drown out the noise inside my head. They didn't want to miss out on the festivities, and after about a hundred begging texts from Elisa, Carmen agreed to have the girls sleep over in her room so we can all get ready in the morning. They get to our place with overnight bags as the sky starts going pink and hazy around the edges. And even though they totally don't need to, both of them insist they want to ride to the airport with us.

"It's part of the experience," Elisa says with a flourish, and I snort as she takes out what has to be the biggest makeup bag in existence from her duffel.

"She's kind of right," Valentina says, and Carmen nods from where she's perched on her bed. "Your quince basically starts tonight, at least in terms of the energy. The party starts as soon as everyone is together, you know?"

In a weird way, it makes sense. There's a certain electricity in the air I can't put my finger on, but it does feel special. All the jumpy excitement ramps up even more when Valentina, Elisa, and I pile into Carmen's car, Dad opting to drive his own so he can spare Abuelo permanent hearing loss from Elisa's music choices on the drive back.

By the time we line up to wait by the baggage claim, I feel like I could vibrate out of my skin. But the second that I see Tía Regina waving wildly at me from the throng of other travelers, my excitement wins out over the nervousness. Abuelo trails behind her as she rushes to greet us.

"Oh my gosh, look at you!" she says, pulling me into a bone-crushing hug. She looks more like she stepped off a runway than a plane, dressed in an effortlessly breezy jumpsuit and heels. Her perfectly highlighted hair hangs in a shiny, straight waterfall down her back. "What happened to the little kid I was expecting to see, huh? You look so grown up."

"I am legally an adult as of last week," I reply, and Tía Regina slaps my arm, and then tugs me back into another hug.

"Nooo, don't say that. You'll always be seven years old inside my head."

"Let the boy breathe," Abuelo says with a chuckle, and Tía Regina finally releases me to say hello to everyone else. Abuelo's mostly gray curls are mussed from the flight, and when he smiles at me, his eyes crinkle at the corners behind his glasses. "It's good to see you. It's been too long."

For a split second, I worry he won't want to hug me, but when he does, the knot of anxiousness tugging at my heartstrings unravels a bit more. There's no hesitation from him, no fresh awkwardness I was so worried would pop up now that I'm out of the closet. Instead, it's warm and familiar and normal in a way I hadn't realized I needed.

"It's really good to see you too," I say, and I'm so glad it's the truth.

Everyone is so busy exchanging hugs and kisses that Tía Regina and Abuelo almost miss their suitcases coming around the baggage carousel. We divvy everyone up between our two cars, and Tía Regina delights Elisa by scream-singing along with her on the ride home. By the time we pull into the driveway, my face already hurts from smiling so hard.

Bags are dropped at the door, and everyone naturally congregates in the kitchen. It's not long before Tío Gael and Tía Ximena show up with Tía Fernanda in tow, and as Valentina and Elisa predicted, it feels like the party has officially started.

"I'm starving," Tía Regina says, riffling through our kitchen cabinets as Tío Gael pulls the good tequila off the shelf. "Where are the snacks? All you have is a bunch of ingredients."

"That's because we actually cook in this house, unlike some people," Dad replies. Tía Regina turns to slap his arm, and I get a sudden, bizarre vision of me and Carmen doing the exact same thing in twenty years.

It's always funny seeing Dad, Tío Gael, Tía Fernanda, and Tía Regina together. They all have the same laugh lines and silver at their temples, subtler versions of the same look Abuelo sports. The four siblings are rarely all in the same place at the same time, but when they are, they're loud enough to shatter the sound barrier. Tía Regina complains loudly until Dad pulls out ingredients to make some finger food, and Tío Gael passes me a half-shot of tequila with a wink. Across the room, Elisa gasps.

"He is *underage!*" she says, and Valentina hides a laugh behind her hand.

"The legal drinking age in Mexico is eighteen," Tío Gael replies. "And it's a special occasion."

"Right, and I've totally never had alcohol before this exact moment," I deadpan, which earns me a belly laugh from the adults in the room and a truly scandalized look from Elisa.

"I'm lucky I've never had to worry about you where drinking is concerned," Dad says as Tío Gael passes another shot to Abuelo, who's listening in with quiet amusement. "Carmen on the other hand . . ."

"Hey, you only had to pick me up drunk from one party in high school!" Carmen squawks. "I'm a very responsible person. You're lucky you have an angel like me for a daughter."

"The hangover you had the next day wasn't very angelic," I point out, and Carmen wraps an arm around my neck like she's going to put me in a chokehold.

Before she has the chance to do any real damage, Dad wipes his hands on a kitchen towel and raises his own shot glass.

"To family, angelic or not, and to Joaquin!"

"To Joaquin!" everyone echoes, and I'm smiling so hard it's hard to take a sip from my glass.

As Carmen and Tía Regina both knock their drinks back in one go, I look around the room. Having all the important people in my life in one place like this feels so special, it gives me an idea. I grab my phone and pull up my text conversation with April, which has been uncharacteristically bare since our tense FaceTime a few days ago.

You're not doing anything tonight, are you? I send, and part of me worries that she might not reply. But thank god, I get a response less than a minute later.

Planning on getting lots of beauty sleep so I can upstage you tomorrow, why??

You should come by my house for some authentic Zoida family chaos

April's response is almost instantaneous. Should've said that sooner, omw!

Ideally, I would have loved to talk to April right when she got to my house. But when she pulls up about fifteen minutes later and pops her head into the kitchen, I barely get the chance to say hello before my family descends on her.

"April! It's good to see you," Dad calls out, and Tío Gael and my tías turn to wave her into the room. Tía Regina has never met April in person, so it takes a second for recognition to dawn on her face.

"This is the famous April? I've heard so much about you!"

"Oh my gosh, hi, I love the sound of that," April says, making a show of flipping her braids over her shoulder. "Yes, it's me, famous as ever."

"You are as cute as a button. No wonder Joaquin chose you as his one solitary girlfriend of his life," she says. Carmen, who's already had another shot of tequila, bursts out laughing as April and I both groan in unison.

"Can you please just delete that from your collective memories?" I ask, and Valentina shoots me a pitying look.

"It's a part of your journey," she says in a put-on, inspirational tone. "You have to embrace it."

"Wow, and here I was thinking we were cool," I tease, and Valentina shrugs.

"That might be the case, but bullying as a love language is always going to remain a constant in this family."

"Truer words have never been spoken," Carmen adds.

I manage to extract myself from the group as Elisa corners April to ask her where she got her outfit and whether she has more music recommendations. At the other end of the kitchen, Dad and Tío Gael are squabbling over what Luis Miguel album they should play next over the kitchen speakers, and Tía Ximena, Tía Fernanda, and Tía Regina are picking over some puff pastry they've just taken out of the oven. Their jokes and laughter fill the space, and even though I'm loving every second of it, I still need a second to myself.

I'm not surprised that Abuelo has the same idea as me, leaning against the far kitchen counter with a glass of tequila, watching everyone else interact with an amused twinkle in his eye. He's more of an observer, like me, and I've always felt at ease with him because of it. Still, I feel a little hesitation as I join him, like I'm still not 100 percent sure of our footing with each other.

"Has everyone exhausted you already?" he asks, a smile playing on his lips as I lean against the counter next to him.

"Not completely," I reply with a laugh. "It's nice having everyone in one place, isn't it?"

"It really is. Seeing the family together like this makes me happy, but it also reminds me of how much we miss out on since we live apart."

"I guess that makes sense," I say, trying to picture it from his perspective. It's not something I usually dwell on a lot, but I guess in a way, it is kind of bittersweet.

"I suppose you're used to it, since this is how it always was for you growing up," Abuelo says. "But watching you and Carmen and the other kids grow up in photos instead of in person is hard. There's just so much you miss."

"If it makes you feel better, I've never felt like you've missed out on the things I really care about," I say, and I mean it. Abuelo flew in for my middle school graduation, he called to congratulate me on every art award I've ever gotten even though I know he hates talking on the phone. "You've always been here for the important stuff."

"I definitely try to. It's important to show up for the people you love in any way you can," he says, and I can't help but think about the queerceañera. I know what he's hinting at, and I almost think he's going to leave it at that. But then, he adds, "Your dad didn't give me any details, but he did say that your mom might not make it tomorrow."

The non-question knocks me off balance a little. There's a

small, hollow feeling behind my sternum about Mom, but it's not as all-consuming as it was days ago, and it feels like a small relief. But I wasn't expecting to talk about this tonight, at least not so directly.

"Oh, yeah. We're not on very good terms right now," I reply, trying to choose my words carefully. "I don't want to go into tomorrow worrying whether someone at the party really supports me or not."

Abuelo nods, taking a slow sip of the tequila in his hand. After a beat, he says, "I understand you may have been nervous about inviting me for the same reason."

"That's not . . . exactly true," I try, but he waves me off.

"It's okay if you were. I'm part of a different generation. We don't always say the right things or appreciate the way the world is changing," he says, and I let out a breath that was trapped in my lungs for far too long. "But Joaquin, I want you to know this. Even though I may not understand everything, I am always going to support you."

And shit, now I feel like I'm going to cry. I can't do that before my queerceañera even starts; it has to be bad luck or something.

"I'm really happy to hear that, Abuelo," I manage to say around the lump in my throat. "And I'm really glad you came."

Abuelo smiles at me, and his eyes crinkle with the exact same crow's feet I see on Dad every day. "So am I."

"Hey, why do you look so serious?" Carmen interjects, sliding up next to me and jamming an elbow into my side, effectively ruining the moment. "Here, open."

She holds the corner of a tostada up to my face and I dutifully let her pop it into my mouth. Carmen pulls me back into the conversation at the center of the room, some dumb debate about which male celebrity is the ultimate DILF, which then prompts a ten-minute Spanglish explanation of what constitutes DILF in the first place. Underneath all the laughter, though, the warmth in my chest from the conversation with my abuelo stays there for the rest of the evening.

We all stay up way too late chatting, even though we have all the time in the world to catch up at the queerceañera itself. The party only breaks up when it gets truly ridiculous that we're all still awake, especially considering we have an early morning and a full day of festivities to look forward to. I walk Tío Gael and Tía Ximena out, and April trails along after me, twirling her car keys around her finger.

"Your family is a true extrovert's paradise," she sighs happily as Tío Gael and Tía Ximena back out of the driveway. "Doing this queerceañera once isn't enough. We need to find new things to celebrate every year so we can keep throwing massive parties like this."

"Sometimes I'm so sure you're the normal, sane one of the two of us, and then you go and say stuff like that," I reply, and April bumps her shoulder against mine, a soft laugh drifting off into the clear night air.

"Seriously, though. I'm going to miss seeing everyone once this is all over."

"That's kind of why I asked you to stop by," I say, and April turns to look at me. "You know the conversation we had the other day about not wanting things to change next year?"

"I'm okay with it, really," she says, but I shake my head.

"I can tell that you're not. I shouldn't have tried to brush it off or make light of it, that was really uncool of me. And I don't want you to feel silly for feeling that way, being freaked out by it is normal. But I thought about it more, and I think I figured out why I'm not worried about us."

April pauses, raising a brow at me. "Okay, spill."

"I think we're going to be fine because you're not just my best friend, you're a part of my family. Blood doesn't mean that someone is going to show up for you the way you want them to, but you always do for me," I say, and April's eyes start to go impossibly wide and watery. "That's why I wanted you here tonight. It doesn't matter if I get into a relationship or if life gets hectic, because I'm always going to lean on my family. And that includes you."

April is fully frozen now, lip trembling in a way I know means she's trying not to cry. "When the hell did you learn how to express your emotions?"

"I dunno, this girl I hang out with is always saying I should tell people how I really feel, so—" The rest of my quip is cut off when April flings her arms around me, squeezing me hard enough that I forget what I was going to say in the first place.

"I love you, and I really needed to hear that. It was, like, the most touching way of saying 'bros before hoes' I could've ever imagined," she laughs. It sounds a little watery, but my eyes are feeling misty too, so who cares.

"Love you too, but that's the grossest, most heteronormative phrase ever."

"It's the thought that counts," she says, squeezing me even tighter. And this time, I think she believes me when I say we'll be okay.

By the time I head back inside, wish everyone else good night, and climb into bed, it's well past midnight. I should be getting some rest, but I don't think the anticipation in my system will let me at this point, so I pull up my texts. There are a handful of messages from family friends and distant relatives saying they're excited about tomorrow. Jaz and Savannah sent outfit options in our group chat, and Bryce has replied to every single one saying they all look great. Eventually, I scroll up to Felix's name, click into our conversation, and type out a message.

Are you asleep?

His response comes almost instantly. not even a little bit, i feel wireddd. are you nervous?

More excited than nervous, I send, biting my lip. Pretty sure I'm going to have the most intense eye bags anyone has ever seen, though.

you're gonna look perfect, Felix replies, and it's the last thing I see as I drift off to sleep.

Chapter Twenty-Two

WHEN MY ALARM goes off the morning of the queerceañera, there's another text from Felix waiting for me on my phone. I jump out of bed and practically trip over myself on the way to my window, pushing the curtains aside to squint into the early morning light. Sure enough, there's Felix in the driveway, perched on the hood of his car with a paper coffee cup in each hand.

Someone is up and making a racket in the bathroom, and I can hear Dad moving around the kitchen, but I manage to sneak out without drawing their attention. The summer air feels bright and clear when I step outside—it's early enough that the sun isn't at its maximum intensity yet, and the sky is still a little orange around the edges. When Felix sees me approaching, his face lights up.

"You're an idiot," I laugh, in lieu of a real greeting, grabbing the cup he's holding out to me. "You really should have slept in."

"I know, I know. But I got all worked up about today, and I figured you might need a second to yourself before things get insane," he replies with one of those genuine, well-meaning smiles that's so charming I'm a little starstruck. I hop up onto the hood of his car so we're sitting shoulder to shoulder. "Not to put you on the spot, but how are you feeling about everything?"

I frown a little, drawing my knees up to my chest and cradling my coffee in both hands. I know that "everything" is code for the fight with my mom, but I'm not exactly sure how I'm feeling.

"I don't know," I reply after a beat. "Since my mom hasn't reached out since the fight, I don't think she's going to show up today."

"And you're okay with that?"

I'm not exactly sure how to answer that. I'd be lying if I said I wasn't disappointed. In a perfect world, the argument with Mom would never have happened in the first place. But given that's not the way things have panned out, I stand by what I said to her during our fight. I don't want her there if it means worrying that she's uncomfortable or doesn't support me fully. If this is the way things have to be, then I think I can accept it, even if it hurts.

"I think I'm as okay as I can be for now," I say. "Does that make sense?"

"That makes perfect sense," Felix replies. "No matter what happens, I'm proud of you for standing up for yourself."

"Thanks," I say, leaning over a bit to bump my shoulder against his, which wins me another smile from him. "I think I'm proud of myself too."

Felix's eyes linger on my face for a second or two longer than they have to, but then he looks away to take a sip of coffee. I don't have the same self-control, because I can't seem to tear my eyes off him. There's a slight breeze ruffling his hair, which still looks a bit damp from his morning shower. He's gotten a bit of a tan in the time we've been together, and it looks good on him.

Maybe it's silly, but I catch myself wishing we could stay like this a little bit longer. Not just sitting on the hood of his car on a perfect summer morning, but all of it. The party-planning, the inside jokes that started overnight, the little secrets we share, the never-ending string of texts. It's been one of the most challenging months of my entire life, sure. But I also got Felix back, even if it was only for a little while.

"There is another reason I'm here," Felix says, pulling me out of my thoughts. The sincerity in his voice catches me a little off guard. "I guess the coffee has a dual purpose."

"Does it?"

Felix nods. "This is also apology coffee, for being MIA the last few days when y'all were wrapping up all the event planning. I feel like I should have helped you out more, especially since things have been tough with your mom."

"I appreciate that," I say carefully. "You couldn't have guessed Caleb was coming to town."

"God no," Felix says with a little huff. "I honestly don't know what I would have said if he had asked me ahead of time."

I peek at him from the corner of my eye, but I can't quite read his expression. "Really?"

"I'm glad I got to see Ethan and Oscar but, well, you know," Felix trails off, and it makes me want to scream, because I don't know. Does he mean that he wishes Caleb hadn't come at all? Or that seeing Caleb again brought old feelings back that he thought were in the past? "But it doesn't change that I'm still here for you, for all of this."

I nod, suddenly fascinated with the dust accumulated on the hood of his car. "I think when he showed up, I almost started to worry that you were going to back out of this whole thing. I was afraid you were going disappear on me."

"I guess I deserve that," Felix says quietly. "But I'm here. For the queerceañera, and for you."

Again, Felix's sincerity catches me off guard. I want to believe him or ask him if he means what I think he means when he says that, but I get tongue-tied instead.

"Right," I say nervously, "gotta fulfill our agreement, right?"

The second the words leave my mouth I realize I've made it sound like this is the end of the line for us. I don't mean it that way at all—just because the lie ends today, it doesn't mean we have to. We don't need excuses to keep seeing each other, and Felix has the rest of the summer in Austin. But I know it didn't come out that way, and when I finally look up at him, I can see it written all over his face.

"That's not all this has been to me," he says, brows drawn together, eyes as intense as I've ever seen them. "You know that, right?"

I'm trying to think of what to say, but a second-story window slides open, and a gasp cuts through my train of thought. I look up, and Carmen is glowering at us like we've committed some unforgivable crime.

"Hey, y'all aren't supposed to see each other before the event!" Carmen calls out, leaning out the window. Felix and I exchange a puzzled look.

"I'm pretty sure that's only a thing at weddings," I call back, still feeling shaky from the moment that Carmen has so inconveniently interrupted.

"Nooo, it's about the anticipation," she whines. Elisa sticks her head through the window and nods furiously like this is common knowledge. "You're going to ruin the drama of it all."

"Oh, I wouldn't want to do that," Felix chuckles, pushing himself off the hood of the car. When he turns to me, I think there's no amount of time I could spend with him that would dull the anticipation I'm feeling. "See you at the venue?"

I nod, heart in my throat. "See you there."

Felix says a quick goodbye, and the girls wave him off as he pulls out of the driveway. But right as I'm about to head inside, another car pulls into the driveway. I'm not surprised when Tía Ximena jumps out of the car with my suit in tow, but then Tía Fernanda and Tía Kristina pop out too.

"Wait, what are all of you doing here?" I ask, as Tía Fernanda loops her arm through mine and Tía Kristina drops a kiss onto my cheek that I'm sure will leave a lipstick mark.

"Well, it would be easy to drop off your suit and get ready for the party at home," Tía Ximena says, hefting the garment bag over her shoulder, "but I figured it would be so much more fun to all get ready together."

"She didn't want Valentina and Elisa to steal all the fun," Tía Kristina stage-whispers with a wink in my direction. Tía Ximena rolls her eyes, but she's fighting back a laugh.

"We all wanted to be part of the fun."

"It's your special day, so we figured you deserved all the love and attention you could get," Tía Fernanda says warmly, jostling my shoulder with her typical infectious joy. "So, what do you say? You have room for a few more people in your entourage?"

I grin at each of them, and my heart feels so full it almost hurts. "Absolutely."

The second we head inside the house, the insanity that Felix so aptly predicted begins. I'm shoved up the stairs and into the shower first, which turns out to be one of the last moments I have to myself all morning. Carmen quickly claims the bathroom as soon as I'm out, and the second I've changed into comfy sweats, all eyes are on me.

"First we'll deal with your hair, and then your face," Tía Regina says matter-of-factly, steering me into Carmen's room where all the women have set up shop to get ready. Elisa is sprawled on the floor rummaging through Tía Kristina's makeup bag, Tía Ximena and Tía Fernanda are steaming my suit, and Valentina is filing her nails on the bed.

"What's wrong with my face?" I ask as I'm deposited in front of the vanity.

"Nothing, nothing," Tía Regina says, pulling out a spray bottle and combing her fingers through my curls. "But a little makeup can go a long way."

"Yeah, we have to cover up the dark circles you have from staying up all night texting your boyyyfriend," Elisa teases, and I bite my lip as the other women *ooo* and *ahhh* so I don't give her the satisfaction of laughing at her jab.

"Oh, that's darling," Tía Kristina says. "Please tell me you really were texting all night."

"I might have been," I hedge, and there's another chorus of *ooos* that makes my cheeks heat up.

"You're all going to embarrass the boy to death before he even gets to the venue," Tía Fernanda tuts. "I have to agree with Regina though, a little bronzer never hurt anyone."

"I guess it can't be any worse than the last time I had my

makeup done. There were cat whiskers drawn on in waterproof eyeliner that didn't budge for three whole days," I say, and Tía Regina stops rewetting my hair to quirk an eyebrow at me in the mirror. "I was eight. Carmen was going through a phase."

"Did someone say my name?" Carmen calls out from the bathroom.

"Only to slander you," I shout back, and Valentina laughs.

"No cat whiskers this time," Valentina assures me. "Elisa has been watching makeup artists on YouTube for as long as she's had access to the internet. She's really good. I could do your nails too if you want?"

"Yeah," I say with a smile. "Why not."

Elisa connects her phone to Carmen's speakers and turns on music, and they all get to work. As Tía Regina works on slicking back my hair and Elisa applies primer and concealer and a dozen other products I can't keep track of, Valentina starts coating my nails with clear, shiny polish and finally asks a question I know has been coming all morning.

"So, are you nervous?"

"Of course he is!" Tía Regina interjects, and Tía Kristina hums in agreement.

"She's right, it's part of the experience. That's what makes it fun."

"I don't know about the fun part, but you're right that I'm nervous," I admit as Elisa pats powder under my eyes. They don't realize that a large part of that has to do with the painting in my bedroom, and the not-quite-boyfriend they were teasing me about. "But it's not a bad nervous. I'm excited too."

"I felt the same way right before my quince. I was so pumped I thought I was going to pass out," Elisa says.

"That's because you forgot to eat breakfast that morning, stupid," Valentina mumbles, and Elisa sticks her tongue out in response. "The scariest part for me was the big entrance, after that it was smooth sailing. But walking in and having everyone staring at me? Yikes."

I tried to picture it, the sea of faces looking at me as I walk into the main hall of the venue, and my stomach turns. Tía Regina sees my frown in the mirror and pats my cheek.

"Don't torture yourself over it now. Remember that everyone is there to celebrate you; that's all that matters," she says, shielding my face as she mists my head with hair spray.

"She's right. We all just want you to have a good time," Tía Fernanda chimes in. "When you walk into that room, you can look around and know that every single person there supports you."

"Yeah, I guess you're right," I say, surprised to find a lump in my throat as I absorb what they said.

It's the type of thing that a month ago, I would have had a hard time wrapping my head around. I would've brushed it off as an exaggeration, as some pleasantry to make me feel better. But now, it's not so hard to believe. All my family and friends came together because they want this to happen and want me to have support.

And without meaning to, my thoughts drift to Mom. There's a little pang in my chest when I think I might look out into the crowd and not see her today or about how she fawned over Carmen as she got ready for her quince. But looking around the room now, with my tías, cousins, and Carmen all fussing over me, it doesn't hurt as much as I thought it would. This is different, but maybe that's okay.

Before I get too lost in thought, Elisa pulls away, finally finished with my makeup.

"We support you, but we're also here to party," she says with a grin, and Valentina rolls her eyes.

"And we're celebrating your coming of age too," Valentina adds. "You know, since you're a real adult now."

"I don't know if I have come of age, whatever that means. I still feel like I don't know anything at all," I reply honestly, and Tía Regina laughs a little as she takes a step back too, admiring her work.

"I think admitting that you don't know anything is a sign of real maturity. Maybe you're not so far off after all," she says, then claps her hands together. "Your hair is officially perfect! Don't you dare touch it, okay?"

Tía Ximena and Tía Fernanda crowd around me as Tía Regina steps aside, and I blink at my reflection in the mirror. She's slicked most of my hair back but left one curl at the front to fall artfully onto my forehead. And whatever Elisa did to my face does look better than the ill-fated makeover Carmen gave me as a kid—my skin looks bronzed and glowy, and she does something to my lashes that make them look a mile longer than they actually are.

"Wow," I murmur as everyone beams at me. "I look . . . good."

"Geez, don't sound so surprised!" Tía Fernanda laughs.

"Yeah, you can't look that bad. We do share the same genes after all," Elisa says proudly, and this time, I don't hold back the laugh that bubbles up from my chest.

Now that I'm presentable, everyone else has to switch gears and finish getting ready themselves, so I get kicked out of Carmen's room and left to my own devices. The house is filled with a flurry of noise and activity—Dad is running between the kitchen and his closet like a chicken with its head cut off, Carmen is on the phone with the florist, and it feels like every particle of oxygen in the house has been infused with perfume and hair spray. The excitement and giddiness in the air is palpable, exactly how I'd remembered.

I finally get a second to myself when I retreat to my bedroom and change into my suit. As I slide on the jacket, an unexpected wave of emotion hits me in the chest. Tío Gael and Tía Ximena managed to capture my idea perfectly. The result is a showstopping floral tux covered in roses. The blues and purples are darker and more subdued than how they appear on the Pride flag, so the pattern is subtle but still eye-catching, exactly how I'd wanted. We paired the suit with a semi-sheer, iridescent white shirt underneath and ditched the tie, because that's what felt most like me.

And that's the thing, I *do* feel like me. I've never worn anything this dramatic in my life, but as I pick up the small silver crown that finishes my outfit and look in the mirror, I love what I see. I thought for sure that when this day came, all I'd want to do is hide under a rock. But I don't hate the idea of being the center of attention, and it feels unexpectedly good to want to be visible like this.

For some reason, I think of Mom again, and it takes me a second to pinpoint why. It's not because I need her approval or want to prove anything to her, at least not anymore. It's more that I'm genuinely happy, and I wish it were enough for her to be happy for me too. It's a vague, dull kind of sadness that I'm not sure how to process. But then there's a knock at the door, and when I answer, Carmen pokes her head in the room. She gives me a once-over, looking impressed until her eyes land on my face.

"You look—"

"If you say constipated, I'm deleting you out of my thank you speech and my life."

Carmen pauses. "I was going to say you look very regal."

"Good save."

"Do you want me to help you with that?" she asks, pointing to the crown that's still in my hands. When I nod, she comes over and nestles it into my curls, producing a bobby pin out of thin air to secure it. "You really do look cool as hell. I mean that from the heart."

"I kind of do, right?" I say, trying to match her energy, but even I can tell that my smile comes off a little fake.

Her eyes meet mine in the mirror, and I already know what she's going to say. "It's Mom, isn't it?"

I don't bother asking how she figured it out without me saying a thing. Knowing her, she might not have even asked Dad for details about my fight with Mom. She could have figured it out through weird sister telepathy. She's right, but I don't want to get emotional. I take a deep breath, trying to clear my head.

"If she doesn't show up, that's on her," I say.

"That's true," Carmen replies. "But it's okay if you're upset about it at the same time."

"I really don't want to be," I say, words almost catching in my throat.

"But are you?" she asks gently, and I hate that the answer is yes. The disappointment I've been pushing down for days threatens to overflow, and I blink hard to keep the tears from stinging my eyes.

"A little," I say around the lump in my throat. "I guess I just wish things were different."

Carmen rests a hand on my shoulder, and all of a sudden, she's the one who looks misty-eyed. I can tell she's searching for something to say to make it right, but she's coming up blank, and I don't blame her. We both stand like that for a beat, sort of at a loss. But then someone honks their horn outside, and the moment passes when Carmen turns to look out the window.

"Crap, April is early," she says, a little panicked. "I'm not even close to being ready. You grab the painting and go on without me, I'll meet y'all at the venue."

I nod, and as she rushes off to get dressed, I'm not sure if the ball of anxiety in my stomach is smaller or bigger than it was before.

Chapter Twenty-Three

CARMEN HAD SHOWN me pictures of the venue before, but when April and I walk into the main hall, I'm kind of blown away. The ceilings are at least twenty feet high, fitted with chandeliers that add a little bit of sophistication to the industrial space. There are little lights strung into the wooden rafters too, casting a warm glow onto the white brick walls.

A handful of round tables are set up on either side of an aisle that cuts through the center of the space. In the end, there's a clear open space that will double as both the main stage and the dance floor. And there's also an old-timey photo booth tucked away on one side of the room, which is a nice bonus on top of the photographer who Carmen hired.

We only have about an hour before people are supposed to start showing up, so the staff are already starting to set the tables with light gray linens and flower arrangements. April gets her laptop hooked up to the soundboard near the dance floor, testing out the equipment she brought from home to make sure it's all set. It's a little funny seeing her in formal wear with chunky headphones around her neck and wires all around her. She ended up rewearing one of her previous homecoming dresses, a ruffly, green dress with flowers embroidered all over, and got a fresh set of goddess braids to match the look. She looks like a little woodland fairy if woodland fairies also listened to nightcore.

I let her do her thing while I find the perfect spot for Felix's painting. I was able to bring one of my more lightweight easels from home, and I prop it up off to the side, draping a spare table-cloth over it until it's ready for the big reveal.

And even though everything is all set, as I watch everyone put the finishing touches on the venue, I feel like I could jump out of my skin at any second. There's a dangerous cocktail of excitement, doubt, and apprehension simmering inside my brain, and it makes me feel a little bit unhinged.

When Dad shows up with the catering staff, I feel like I can relax a little bit. He catches my eye from across the hall and, having not seen my outfit in its full glory yet, practically has a heart attack.

"Dios mío, I wasn't ready for this. The suit looks incredible! Let me take a closer look," he gasps, striding over. He takes in all the little details of the outfit with childlike glee. "You look very sparkly. I think it suits you."

"Thanks, Dad," I say with a smile. One of the caterers starts waving Dad over, and he checks his watch.

"You should probably go to the back soon, no?" he asks. "We don't want anyone to see you in case people start getting here a little early."

"I will in a second, but have you seen Carmen? She said she would meet us here, but I haven't seen her around."

"Well, she left the house before me, so she should be here already," Dad says, perplexed. Then, seeing the concern on my face, he adds, "Don't worry about it. I'll find her."

I try not to worry as I make my way through the back hallway and into the dressing room the venue has set aside for me. I try not to worry when fifteen minutes pass, and Carmen still won't answer my texts. I only let myself fully freak out when April texts me that guests are starting to arrive, but Carmen isn't there to greet them like she said she would.

I know I'm supposed to stay in the back, but if I have to sit around for another second, I think I'm going to lose it. I pop my head out into the hallway that runs around the perimeter of the venue, and the coast looks clear. I figure I can probably sneak around a bit without being seen, as long as I don't get close to the grand entryway at the front of the building.

I can hear soft music and the low hum of conversation filling the main hall as I creep up to one of the smaller side doors. Peeking inside, I see the room is about half-capacity. Jaz and Savannah must've gotten here early, because they're chatting with my cousins as family friends and relatives mingle around their respective tables. But I still can't see Carmen, at least not from this vantage point.

"Joaquin, holy shit!" I hear Bryce say, and I turn to see him hovering near one of the side doors. "You look amazing, god damn. But I thought we still had a few minutes before this started. What are you doing out here?"

"I'm looking for my sister. Have you seen her?"

Bryce squints into the main hall, eyes scanning the room. "No, I don't think so. I was looking for Felix to say hi, but I couldn't find him either."

I didn't think it was possible for my pulse to get any quicker, but now it's pounding in my ears. Felix has to be around here somewhere. He can't flake out on me now. There's literally no way. My suit jacket feels too tight and too hot all of a sudden, and I scramble to think of what to do.

"Can you find April and tell her to meet me out here?" I ask. Bryce, probably seeing the terror splashed across my face, quickly gives me a two-finger salute and heads into the hall.

At this point, I'm teetering on the edge of a nuclear-level freakout. I can't stand still and wait for April, so I head further down the hall, trying to look into the room from a different angle to see if I could find Carmen. One of the side doors is propped open, giving me a clear view of the back of the venue, but she's not there either. *Shit. Shit, shit, shit.*

I'm about to pull away when I recognize a familiar voice, out of sight but close enough that I can hear him. I shift a little, and Caleb's shock of bleached hair comes into view.

"I'd bet you a hundred dollars he says yes," he boasts. Someone a little out of view nudges him lightly with their elbow.

"Oh yeah, big guy? What makes you so sure he wants to get back together with you?" I hear Ethan ask, and I feel the room tilt on its axis.

"It's so obvious," Caleb replies, and I don't need to see his face to imagine the confident smile he's wearing. "You saw the way Felix was acting when we went out. Plus, he dropped everything to hang out with me this week. He definitely still has feelings for me."

I take a step back from the door. I don't want to hear this. I can't hear this, not fifteen minutes before I'm supposed to tell Felix how I really feel about him.

"He dropped *some* things to hang out with *us*," Oscar says, equal parts teasing and pointed. "Dude, I love you, but he's literally dating someone else. Maybe you have to accept that now isn't your time."

"Joaquin isn't a factor in this," Caleb says, and Oscar groans. My mouth feels dry. I want to leave, but I can't seem to pull myself away.

"God, that's bold, even for you," Ethan says with a laugh.

"Felix and I have always been endgame. We shouldn't have broken up in the first place, and Felix knows it," Caleb continues, and he sounds so sure of himself that it starts to mess with my head. "The second this is all over, I'm going to fix things with him. We belong together, y'know?"

Oscar replies with another argument that Caleb will probably ignore, but I can't hear him anymore. I finally manage to take a step back from the door, and then another. Was I right in thinking that things between Felix and Caleb weren't really over after all? Maybe my crush on him has blinded me to the truth, and all the signs I thought I was picking up from him were just wishful thinking. If they were, then what the hell am I supposed to do now?

I'm still mid-spiral when April rounds the corner and practically runs right into me.

"Hey, Bryce said you needed me. What are you—?"

I grab April's hand before she can finish and tug her down the hall, away from Caleb and away from the noise, and back to the dressing room where I can freak out in peace.

"Caleb is going to ask Felix to get back together with him," I say breathlessly once we're inside. "He said Felix still has feelings for him."

"What? How did you even find that out?"

"I overheard him talking to his friends," I say, starting to pace back and forth. "He said I'm not even a factor here. What if I've been kidding myself this whole time?"

"Slow down a sec—"

"What if this was all some pit stop on the way to Felix getting back to his normal life? As in, his normal life without me, where he has a boyfriend who actually has things in common with him?"

"That's it, I'm putting you in time out. Sit," she says, grabbing my shoulders and planting me on the couch across from the door. "Breathe."

"I'm practically hyperventilating. If anything, I'm breathing too much."

"Okay, then breathe less," April says patiently. She kneels in front of me so I can't look away. "I'm going to say something crazy, but I need you to stick with me, okay? So now we know Caleb wants Felix back. Who cares?"

"Who cares?" I echo incredulously. "I care, obviously."

"No, I mean, does it really even matter? Caleb can crush on Felix all he wants. Are you really going to let that stop you from going after him too?"

"Um, maybe?"

"No!" April says, loud enough that it makes me jump a little. "You know how you feel about him, and you know what you want, right?"

"Yes, but—"

"There's no 'but' about it," April says, squeezing my knee. "You know what you want, and you're going to fight for it."

"I do know what I want, but what if that's not enough?" I say, and my heart sinks as I finally put words to all the feelings weighing me down. "What if I put myself out there and end up getting hurt?"

"That's always a risk," April replies gently. "I get the urge to push your wants and needs aside because you're afraid of rocking the boat. But if you wait until the path ahead of you is totally clear, then you're never going to move forward."

"I know you're right, and it all makes sense, but I can't shake the feeling that everything is going to shit," I groan, burying my head in my hands. "I had all these ideas for how today was going to go, and this wasn't part of the plan. I mean, Jesus, Felix isn't even here. What if he doesn't show?"

"Wait, what?"

"He's late. Like, really fucking late," I say miserably. "And to top it all off, Carmen is literally missing."

I hear movement in the hallway outside, and April squeezes my knee again, letting out a sigh of relief. "Well, good news, I think we might have you covered on the last part."

My head snaps up, and thank god, Carmen is framed in the doorway.

Chapter Twenty-Four

MY SISTER IS breathing hard, holding the bottom of her silver, floor-length dress in one hand and her heels and clutch in the other. It looks like she had to sprint to get here in time, and for a solid five seconds, we just stare at each other.

"Where the hell have you been?" I say, and it comes out a lot harsher than I mean it to.

"Okay, I know you're probably pissed, but I promise I have a good reason for being late," Carmen says, still trying to catch her breath. I can't think of a single thing that could be worth causing me this much anxiety, so nothing can prepare me for what she says next. "I went to talk to Mom. I wanted to see if I could convince her to come today."

I feel my mouth go dry. One, because outside of my birthday dinner, Carmen has barely spoken with our mom in months, let alone had some kind of intervention. And two, because Carmen is here alone, and I have to think it's because their conversation didn't go well.

"I'm going to let you two talk," April says, getting to her feet and giving my shoulder a quick squeeze. "I'll stall until you're ready to make your entrance."

I murmur a thank you as she leaves me and Carmen alone in the dressing room. But when my sister crosses the space and sits down next to me, I'm not even sure what to ask her. Apparently, Carmen is thinking the same, because after a beat she says, "I don't know where to start."

"Maybe with the part where you completely disappeared off the face of the earth?" I say, and Carmen sucks in a deep breath.

"I went to Mom's right after you left the house with April," Carmen starts, words coming out in a rush. "I wasn't planning on talking to her at all or getting involved in the fight you had, because I felt like it was your business and not mine. But this morning, I could tell it was bothering you more than you were letting on. And when you said you wished things could be different, I figured I'd at least try to see if they could be."

"Carmen, you didn't need to—"

"I know, I know. But I wanted to," she says firmly, and I sigh.

Of course Carmen would put her personal feelings aside to try to help me. That's exactly the kind of big sister she is. I don't know whether to feel grateful or guilty that she put herself in that position for me. Still, I have a lot of questions about how things played out.

"The last time I talked to Mom, I told her I didn't want her here unless she could accept me as I am," I say. My throat feels tight, a sort of knee-jerk anxious reaction when I think about what Mom could've said to Carmen. "She's obviously not here, so I'm guessing her answer was no."

"I wouldn't put it that way," Carmen says, and I can't really imagine what she means. "I think me showing up was a little bit of a shock, so she was more willing to listen when I tried to explain why we've been frustrated with her these last couple of months. I told her that her opinions are too rigid and that even though she thinks she's pushing us in the right direction, she's been pushing us away instead. She was sort of arguing with me for a bit, and I honestly thought I'd made a mistake trying to reason with her. But then Felix stepped in."

"Wait what?" I say, sitting up straighter on the couch. "Hold on is he here? Please tell me he's here."

"Yes, you didn't get cursed with a runaway chambelán," Carmen reassures me. "When Felix overheard me talking to Mom, he ended up jumping in and trying to explain things from his perspective too. He backed me up a lot."

I let out a long breath as relief washes over me. Felix wasn't late or flaking out on me after all. If anything, it's the opposite. He cared enough that he stayed behind to reason with Mom, which I know must have been hard for him for his own reasons. All my worries about him not caring enough about this, about us, feel silly now.

"It felt like we were getting through to her—like something clicked," Carmen continues. "She admitted that she has stuff to work through on her end so she can show up for us in the way we want her to. It sounded like she wanted to come, but I reminded her about what you said, that if she wasn't 100 percent sure she could be fully supportive, she shouldn't be here at all. That's why she decided to stay behind."

I don't know what to say, but even if I did, the lump in my throat would make it impossible. All I've wanted for months is for Mom to be honest about the way she's treated me. And now, I finally feel like she's taking some responsibility, and I hardly know how to react.

But then Carmen pulls her clutch into her lap and undoes the clasp. She takes out a small, twice-folded piece of paper and holds it out to me.

"She wrote you a letter and asked me to pass it along," Carmen says. When I hesitate, she adds, "You don't have to read it now, if you don't want to."

"No, I . . . I think I want to," I say, taking the piece of paper from her. I've been honest with Mom about how I feel, and it seems like now she wants to do the same. I want to hear what she has to say. With shaky hands, I unfold the note.

Mom's familiar, looping handwriting fills the small page. The letter isn't long, and it only takes me a minute to scan the words she's written. Most of it is confirmation of what Carmen has already shared with me—she didn't realize how much she was pushing me away, and she wants to make things right. But then I reach the last paragraph, and I find myself hanging on every word.

I'm so sorry that I've made you feel like you need to change in order to be good enough for me. Hearing the way Carmen and Felix talk about you made me understand what true, unconditional support looks like. You deserve to be around people who love you exactly as you are, today and every day. I promise to work on myself until you can trust that I'm one of those people too. Until then, keep being yourself, cariño. Now it's my job to catch up.

I swallow thickly, eyes scanning the words again and again. I think Carmen can tell I'm still processing, because she reaches out and puts a hand on my arm.

"I really wanted to make this right for you, and so did Felix. But we still couldn't make it happen. I'm so sorry," Carmen says, voice thick with emotion.

I can count the number of times I've seen Carmen cry on one hand, but now her eyes are filled with unshed tears. And the thing is, her apology doesn't make any sense at all. I'm getting choked up too, but it's not because I'm sad that Mom isn't here. I'm not thinking about winning her acceptance or her permission to be myself.

Tears well up in my eyes because Carmen and Felix went way outside of their comfort zones to do this for me. After everything they've already done to make this day go off without a hitch, they're still going to bat for me in ways I'd never expected. And I've never, ever felt so loved in my life.

"You don't need to apologize, Carmen," I say, putting my hand over hers where it still rests on my arm. "I wish Mom could be here, but I do deserve people who support me fully and love me unconditionally. And I know that I have that with you."

Carmen's lip wobbles dangerously. "You're really okay with this?"

"I really am," I say, and it's the complete, honest truth. "What I'm not okay with is you making me cry right before I even go out there. If I ruin my makeup, Elisa is going to kill me."

Carmen laughs hard at this, tears finally spilling over and rolling down her cheeks, but she doesn't seem to care. She pulls me into a quick, crushing hug, and now the tears I have to blink back in my own eyes are happy ones.

"We should get going, you have a grand entrance to make," Carmen says with a sniffle, and as she pulls back, I get an idea.

"After the fight with Mom, I was only planning on having Dad escort me in," I say. "But I want you to be a part of it too."

Carmen takes a deep, steadying breath and nods. "Let's do it."

※ ※ ※

By the time Carmen and I dry our eyes, we're running a few minutes late to start the procession. Carmen stays behind to quickly touch up her makeup while I hustle toward the grand entrance, and there are a hundred half-baked thoughts bouncing around my head as I rush down the hallway. I have to somehow explain all this to my dad, and I have to find Felix and thank him for trying to help me.

It turns out I don't have to look very hard, because when I careen around the corner, I practically take Felix out in the process.

"God damn, way to make an entrance," Felix wheezes, hooking his arm around my waist to keep me from falling over. Then, something in his expression shifts, and his ears go a little pink. "Holy shit. You look incredible."

It takes everything in me not to melt at the way he's looking me up and down. Well, that and the fact he looks really, *really* good himself. He's got his hair pushed back the way I like it, and the royal blue suit he's wearing is definitely his color. It complements mine exactly like Tío Gael promised it would, so we look like a perfect pair.

"You know," I say, hyperaware of the fact he hasn't taken his hand off my waist, "a wise man once said we clean up pretty nice."

"And I stand by that. It was a great idea to keep your outfit a surprise," Felix says, grinning at me. After his reaction, I couldn't agree more.

Seconds later, Dad emerges from the main hall, where I can hear the din of the partygoers mellow into a low hum. April is announcing our entrance, and as Felix and I untangle ourselves from each other, the nerves hit me all at once. This is happening, right now, no more delays.

"¿Todos listos?" Dad asks, straightening his tie. Right on time, Carmen rounds the corner.

"Now we are," she says, a little breathless.

I turn to Dad, who looks almost as relieved as I was to see Carmen made it after all.

"I know it's a little outside of tradition, but I want Carmen to be part of the procession too. You willing to share the spotlight?"

"Screw tradition," Dad says with a fierce smile. "For you, mijo, I'll do anything."

Dad extends an arm with a flourish, and Carmen rests her hand in the loop of his elbow. They turn to the doors in unison, and I seriously feel like my heart is going to burst out of my chest. Every other version of my queerceañera I'd been imagining can't compare with this.

Felix and I move off to the side so we won't be in full view of everyone in the main hall, and Dad and Carmen push the doors open. April cues up the music as they head in together, and oh god, it's finally starting. All of a sudden, I feel like I've forgotten everything I'm supposed to do. I can't remember the order of events. I can't even remember my own name. But then Felix slips his hand into mine and gives it a squeeze, and it snaps me out of my nervous daze.

"I take it Carmen explained everything?" Felix asks quietly, searching my face, and I realize my eyes must still be a little red. "You, okay?"

"I'm okay—more than okay," I whisper back, tearing my eyes off the long, terrifying aisle we're about to walk down to look at his face. It feels like he's the only thing keeping me rooted in the moment. "I'm all right with Mom not being here. The fact that you and Carmen even tried to talk to her at all means the world to me. Thank you, Felix. I mean it."

A little tension goes out of Felix's shoulders, and he squeezes my hand again. "I tried my best. I wanted today to be perfect for you."

My heart swells, and I have so much I want to say to him it's overwhelming. But when this is all over, I can tell him how much this has meant to me. Right now, I want to give him shit for almost ditching me.

"Oh, you wanted today to be perfect?" I say, and his brows draw together. "So perfect that you got here an hour late?"

"Shut up. I might not have thought that part through," he concedes, holding back a laugh.

"Here I was thinking you had finally decided to cut and run."

"Wouldn't dream of it," Felix says, pulling my hand through the crook of his arm so we're ready to make our grand entrance. "No more surprises, I promise."

Felix smiles at me, and for a second, everything slows down.

I recognize the way he's looking at me, because it's the same look he's wearing in the photo Carmen took of us at dinner. He's looking at me like I hung the moon and stars in the sky myself, and it's hard to imagine a world where he's not the person by my side in moments like these. It feels so obvious now that the silver lining I was looking for was him all along.

"Hey, Felix?" I ask as the music in the main hall shifts. It's our cue to head in, and as we walk to the doors, he leans down a bit so he can hear me better. "Would you mind if I had one more big surprise up my sleeve?"

Felix pulls back to look at me, and he's got this glint in his eye that I can't get enough of. It's the one that drew me in when we were kids and the one that's made me fall for him all over again six years later.

"I'm down for anything as long as we're in it together," he replies with a grin. And with my arm in his and my heart on fire, we step into the spotlight.

Chapter Twenty-Five

I THOUGHT I would get tunnel vision as Felix and I made our grand entrance, but it's pretty much the opposite. I'm incredibly aware that everyone is looking at us, and if I wasn't clinging to Felix's sleeve, I know my hands would be shaking. But this is a once-in-a-lifetime moment, and I want to enjoy it, even if I'm scared shitless.

I force myself to hold my chin up and take a look around. I make eye contact with April's moms on one side of the room, sitting at a table with my tías from Mexico. Bryce, Savannah, and Jaz give me thumbs-ups from one table over, and Ryan and Abuelo look on further down the line, eyes shining with pride. When I look back up front, I catch April grinning at me from the DJ booth.

By the time Felix and I make it up front, my nerves have calmed a bit, and I'm feeling pretty good. I didn't trip and fall on my face, which feels like a major accomplishment. Felix puts his hand over mine one last time before stepping back, leaving me front and center at the mic stand. My hand goes to my breast pocket, and—

"I forgot my speech," I say into the microphone, stunned at my own stupidity.

Between my mild freak-out and the tearful conversation I had with Carmen, I forgot the note cards with my toast in the dressing room. And it's so ridiculously on-brand for my life at this point that I don't panic, I start laughing instead. The tension in my shoulders finally releases, and a few people in the audience chuckle as well.

Maybe it's the adrenaline that's dulling my sense of embarrassment, but I'm not that fazed. I know who I want to thank, and it took me so long to write my toast that I think I have most of it memorized anyway. I straighten my suit, square my shoulders, and regroup.

"You know what? I'm just going to wing it," I say, taking a deep breath. "When y'all got your invites to this, I'm guessing you might have been a little surprised that I agreed to any of this in the first place. And honestly, there were so many times when I wanted to back out and give up on the whole thing. Without my three biggest cheerleaders, I don't know if we could have pulled this off."

"I owe all this to my dad, Carmen, and April, our amazing DJ for the evening," I say, taking a second to look at each of them in turn. "I can say for certain that I wouldn't be standing up here if it wasn't for you three. You all push me to be a better person every single day. You also push me to the edge of my sanity half the time, but we don't need to talk about that."

Another wave of laughter ripples through the audience. I need that moment of levity, because I know it'll be hard for me to push through this next part without getting emotional.

"I also want to thank all of you for showing up for me today, not only to support me as a friend or a relative but also as a queer person trying to find their place in the world. Coming out has been such a blessing, but it's also been one of the most vulnerable and nerve-wracking experiences of my life.

"It hasn't been easy to stand in my identity, and I'm realizing it's not something you do once, but something you have to learn to do over and over again. And for a long time, I thought I would have to fight that battle on my own. I couldn't imagine a world where people would stand by me as a gay, Mexican teen living in Texas. That's why this matters so much to me. You showing up today means it's not me against the world like I'd thought, and I'm going to cherish that forever."

I take another deep breath, and I don't think it's my imagination that I see a few misty eyes out in the crowd. I need a few more seconds to compose myself so I can blink back the tears filling my own eyes and brace myself for what's coming next. My nerves are gone, and I feel oddly confident.

"Last but certainly not least, I want to give a special thanks to my chambelán," I say, still speaking out to the audience. "A lot of you know that Felix and I spent a good amount of time together as kids, and then a lot of time apart as teens. When we reconnected, I realized that there are some things that never really changed.

"You were always annoyingly handsome, and clearly that's still true," I say, turning to Felix. He's biting his lip to keep from smiling too big, and it makes my heart flip-flop in my chest. "I always thought of you as my knight in shining armor, and I still feel like you'd take a bullet for me. I mean, you agreed to meet my entire extended family, and that's basically the same thing, right?"

Another laugh bubbles up from the crowd, but at this point, everything else is fading to the background. It's just me and him now.

"But there is one thing above all else that I'm glad stayed the same, and that's the way I feel about you," I say, stepping away from the mic.

When I lift the cloth covering the painting, it feels like everything goes quiet. All of my doubts and fears melt away, and my eyes are locked on Felix's stunned face. His eyes are tracing every brushstroke, and I can't tell if it's the lights or some unspoken emotion that are making them shine.

"You had my whole heart in that apple orchard. You had it after you moved, even after years went by. And you still have it now," I say as Felix turns to look at me again.

"Is this for real?" Felix asks, and the softness in his expression takes my breath away. He steps toward me, searching my face the same way he did when we walked by the river. "Please tell me this is for real."

I smile, reaching up to touch his cheek. "I mean every word."

Felix's hands come up to cradle my face, and between one heartbeat and the next, he leans down to press his lips against mine. And somehow, even though I've been thinking about this kiss for what feels like ages, it's even better than I'd imagined. It holds every ounce of fondness and adoration I've held for Felix since we were kids, and by the time we pull away, my heart is so full it feels like it's going to burst out of my chest again. When I look into his eyes, I know now that I have him again, there's no way I'm ever going to let him go.

Chapter Twenty-Six

I WISH I could remember what happened after that moment, but honestly, I think I blacked out. I vaguely recall Dad grabbing the mic to say a quick thank you to everyone for coming, but the only thing I can really focus on is Felix's hand in mine, anchoring me to the stage.

When the waiters start to bring the food out, the focus shifts away from us standing up front, and I finally get my bearings again. Felix and I are supposed to join the guests and sit down for dinner, but I'm dying to talk to him in private. As great as it was to confess my feelings, there's a hell of a lot more I want to set straight. It seems like his head is in the same place, because we both turn to each other at the same time.

"Can we talk in private?" Felix asks, face flushed. "Or maybe kiss more? Either would be good. Or both."

"Let's go with both," I say, squeezing his hand. The only issue is that I seriously doubt anybody is going to let us sneak off for too long. My eyes scan the room and land on the photo booth on the far wall. "I have an idea."

Before anyone can stop us, I pull Felix along the side of the room, and we scoot into the photo booth together. I don't even have time to think of what to say next before he pulls me in for another kiss. His hands are warm on either side of my face, and I can feel him smile against my lips.

"That was the most romantic thing that's ever happened to me in my life," Felix says when he pulls back.

"I literally felt like I was going to pass out the entire time," I reply breathlessly. "I had no idea how you were going to react."

Felix blinks at me. "You're kidding, right? I've been flirting with you nonstop for a month. How did you not pick up on this?"

A little voice comes over the speaker in the photo booth, and I realize it must start automatically.

"You're impossible to read!" I say, poking him in the chest. *Three, two, one, snap.* "How was I supposed to tell you were flirting for real when we were literally putting on an act? Also, Caleb being all possessive and weird threw me for a loop. It seemed like things between you two were unfinished."

"It wasn't weird with Caleb because things were unfinished with him. It was weird because things were unfinished with you," Felix says, fingers tracing along the edge of my jaw. "He kind of guilt-tripped me to spend time with him this week. I knew he was still hung up on me after the breakup, and I was already feeling bad about moving on from him so fast, so I felt like I couldn't say no."

Three, two, one, snap.

I pull back, searching Felix's face. "When you say you moved on from him fast, how fast are we talking?"

"I already told you, as soon as we reconnected," he said with a shrug, and I think back to Valentina questioning him at our family dinner. "When I saw you at lunch, I knew I was screwed."

"At lunch?" I repeat. "You've really liked me this whole time?"

"Pretty much," he says, and it's so ridiculous that I burst out laughing. *Three, two, one, snap.* "You said it yourself. Those feelings never went away completely. I saw you sitting at that table and it all came rushing back."

"Well, now I feel stupid that it took me so long to figure it out."

"It only took you six years," he teases, pulling me in again. "But I'm not complaining. It was worth the wait."

Our noses bump against each other as he pulls me in for another kiss. *Three, two, one, snap.*

As much as I want to hide in the photo booth and keep making out with Felix, we both agree that it might be bad form to hide from my guests for the entire night. We reluctantly hop out and rejoin the party, but not before grabbing the photos we took first.

"These turned out pretty cute," I say, and Felix leans down to take a look, resting his chin on my shoulder.

In the first frame, we're arguing, both of us looking flustered. In the next, he's holding my face in his hands, deep in conversation, and in the one after that, we're laughing our asses off. The last frame shows us both smiling into a kiss, and we look really ridiculously happy.

"I'm saving this forever," he says, beaming at his copy as we walk over to our table.

It takes a second for us to find our place cards, but even then, we don't get the chance to sit down. Ryan intercepts us first, putting one hand on Felix's shoulder and one hand on mind.

"My dudes," he says very seriously. "That was romantic as hell. I almost cried."

"I *did* cry," Valentina chimes in from one table over. "I'm never going to emotionally recover from this."

Next to her, Elisa nods emphatically. "My standards are officially too high. I'm not going to be able to date, like, a normal person now and it's all your fault."

Tía Kristina approaches Felix with a glint in her eye that tells me she wants to get the scoop on the whole thing directly from the source. "You looked so shocked. Did you have any idea he was going to say all that?"

"No, I really didn't! It was a total surprise," Felix says proudly, wrapping an arm around my waist. I can already tell his ego is going to grow five sizes by the end of the night from all this attention, but I don't mind.

Suddenly, Carmen materializes next to me. "What are y'all doing? We're going to wrap up dinner soon, you should get ready for the waltz."

"We haven't eaten yet," Felix points out. "Or sat down."

"Then congrats, you're having an authentic quince experience," Carmen replies with a smile. But before she disappears on me again, I pull her aside, leaving Felix to his adoring fans.

"I wanted to thank you again for everything you did with Mom," I say, rubbing the back of my neck. "I know that must have been really difficult for you. And I don't know what this means for you and Mom's relationship, but I hope she apologized to you too."

"She did, and I really do think she meant it," Carmen says with a small smile. "It's on her to follow through on what she said, but I think if she does, I'd be open to spending time with her before I head back to college."

Just like that, the last of the weight pressing down on me lifts. "I'm really glad to hear that. Everything you've done for me this past month, with Felix and with the queerceañera, has been amazing. I guess I wanted to say I appreciate it a lot. And I appreciate you."

"I appreciate you too, but you being all sincere twice in one day is kind of giving me the creeps," she says with a laugh. "I'll always be on your side, okay? If she doesn't stay true to her word, I'll give her hell."

"Oh, I believe you," I say, and Carmen sneaks in a quick hug before returning me back to Felix.

As we head to the dance floor, April catches my eye and points to me and Felix, drawing little hearts in the air with her hands that I can only assume is her way of saying *I'm so happy for you* and *we need to talk about this later.* I give her a thumbs-up as the soft dinner music that's floating through the speakers slows and she queues up the song we had practiced back at Amrita's dance studio. Felix turns to me and holds out a hand.

"May I have this dance?"

"If you tried to get out of this now, I'd kill you," I say with a smile, and he grins back at me.

"I'll take that as a yes."

He takes my left hand in his right, but before he guides it to his shoulder, he dips his head and presses a kiss to my knuckles. And god, the way my heart somersaults is almost painful.

"I'm not sure I'm ever going to get used to this," I say as we get into position.

"You better; you're stuck with me now," Felix replies, giving my hand a squeeze as the music starts. "Don't look at your feet, okay? Look at me instead. I'm prettier than the floor anyways."

"You can't say stuff like that or I'm going to mess up," I mumble, feeling my face heat up. But he's right, looking into his eyes is making it easier for me to follow his lead through the steps of the dance. But the way he's looking back at me is so intense, it brings a fresh question to mind. "Do you think people are going to notice we're different now? Like, real dating instead of fake dating?"

Felix chews his lip, mulling it over for a second as I step forward and he steps back, perfectly in sync.

"I don't think we were particularly subtle before. I mean, I was kind of all over you at your birthday dinner."

"Hmm, true. Now that I know you were crushing on me, you were laying it on kind of thick," I tease, and Felix's jaw actually drops.

"Shut up, I was pining!"

"You know, Carmen and April clocked you that night. They were totally convinced you were into me."

"Well, I'm glad someone noticed, because you sure as hell didn't," Felix pouts, and it's so cute that I burst out laughing.

I'm totally distracted, so when Felix steps forward, I forget to step back, and he bumps into me hard enough that I almost fall over. We grab onto each other to steady ourselves, and then we're both laughing. I'm sure we look ridiculous to everyone watching, but I can't bring myself to care.

Once we manage to pull ourselves together and sync up with the music again, the rest of the waltz goes off without a hitch. It's still a relief when it's over though, and I let out a sigh of relief when the music finally tapers off into something more upbeat.

Felix and I stay on the dance floor as it opens up to everyone, mingling a little as April expertly blends one song into the next. By the time my friends make their way over, the dance floor is packed, and the party is well underway.

"You guys are so cute it's kind of gross," Jaz says, pulling me into a hug as Bryce squeezes the life out of Felix like he's his own personal squeaky toy.

"This entire night has called me single in seventeen different languages," Savannah says with a melodramatic sigh, looping her arm through mine and leaning her head onto my shoulder. "I'm going to have to live through your love vicariously."

Felix wiggles a brow at her. "Orrr you could go talk to Oscar instead. You know he's here tonight, right?"

"Ugh, you are such a menace," Savannah whines, ears going pink as Jaz waves April over from the DJ booth.

"See, I've been saying this about Felix from day one and nobody believed me," I say. Felix replies by sticking his tongue out as April bounces over.

"Talk fast, because I only have two minutes until the next song starts," she says breathlessly, "I refuse to put this playlist on shuffle until at least 10:00 p.m. It's against my code of ethics as a DJ."

"Stop, you're killing it," Jaz says, leaning in so April can hear her over the music. "Don't forget us when you're famous."

"VIP passes to Coachella for life, I swear," April says, pressing a hand to her heart.

"I think we need to go next year, you know, to scope it out for you in advance," Bryce says.

"Once we're in college, we can visit each other and catch music festivals in one go," Savannah says, and April nods excitedly. "Lolla, Boston Calling—"

"And Gov Ball in New York," Jaz adds, elbowing me. "The second you get accepted to Pratt, we're buying plane tickets. We'll sleep on your dorm room floor if we have to."

A month ago, I probably would've thought making plans like these was overly optimistic. But I can picture it so clearly, all of us finding time for one another a year from now, so it doesn't feel ridiculous to nod along. I want to show up for them the same way they showed up for me tonight.

"I'll mark my calendar," I reply. Then, catching April's eye, I add, "Let's not wait to make memories later though, okay? We still have the rest of the summer ahead of us."

April's smile widens as Savannah and Jaz throw their arms around my neck, and I'm pretty sure they're going to suffocate me before the night is over, but I don't mind one bit.

Felix and I spend most of the party alternating between getting dragged back to the dance floor by our friends and fielding questions and compliments from family. And just as Carmen warned us, we don't ever get the chance to sit down and eat uninterrupted.

But I do spend about half of the queerceañera with Felix's lips on mine instead, so I can't really complain.

By the end of the night, my voice is gone, my feet are killing me, and my face is numb from smiling so much. As the catering staff starts packing up and the crowd thins out a bit, I finally get to catch up with Dad. He's waving off one of the waiters when I sidle up next to him, and his arm goes around my shoulders automatically.

"Man, what a night, huh?" he says with a grin. Like most of the other guests, his tie and jacket are long gone, and his sleeves are pushed up to his elbows.

"Understatement of the century," I reply with a laugh. "This whole thing was nothing like I pictured it. I didn't think hosting a queerceañera was going to be like this."

"Like what?"

"Easy," I say without thinking, and then frown a little. "I mean, getting here was hard. You know that. But now that it's happening, it's like—"

"It was meant to be?" he finishes.

"Something like that," I reply, leaning against him. Despite all my doubts and fears about this whole thing, my queerceañera feels like a success. Not because everything went perfectly, not even close, but because I put myself out there and I don't have any regrets. "I didn't realize how badly I needed this, to feel connected to everyone. Thank you, Dad."

"Any time, hijo."

I pull back and frown at him. "Hold on, not any time. Give me at least five years before you throw another party like this."

"No promises," he says with a laugh, and I shake my head in disbelief. But after tonight, making more time to celebrate myself with the people I love doesn't sound like the worst idea in the world.

Epilogue

IT'S ONE OF those summer evenings where everything feels like it's moving in slow motion. The birds have quieted down, and even the cicadas are more subdued than usual. The August heat is no joke, but a breeze is pressing its way up from the south, guiding pink and purple clouds across the dimming sky.

Heat radiates up from the concrete of our driveway, so even in a tank and shorts, it feels like I'm melting. Felix has his hair tied back, and it's finally long enough now that almost all of it is off his neck. He's holding onto both my hands for dear life, one foot on my skateboard and the other planted firmly on the ground.

"I regret adding this to the summer bucket list," he says for the fourth time.

"If I had to watch every single TWICE music video for you, I think you can handle this."

"Hey, don't pretend you didn't love their choreo."

"I did, and my point still stands," I say, but the pout on Felix's face doesn't budge. I sigh, squeezing his hands. "If you fall, I'll catch you. Promise."

"Cute, but what if I fall backward?"

"April will catch you."

"No promises, big guy," she says from where she's stretched out in the grass, soaking up the last rays of sun with Carmen.

Dad is grilling something with Ryan out back that smells amazing. Most of our evenings lately have been like this, but Carmen and I have also grabbed dinner at Mom's place twice now. It was Mom's idea after reflecting on what Carmen and Felix talked to her about on the morning of my queerceañera. We agreed to see her on the condition that she'll keep working on the way she communicates with us, and we get to be honest about how she's making us feel in return.

So far, it still feels a bit tentative and awkward, but it also feels like it's working. It's a totally different vibe from these backyard cookouts with Dad, but at least it's not tense because things are being left unsaid. In a weird way, the awkwardness feels nice. It feels like progress.

All in all, the last two months have flown by. April has kept all of us busy, even inviting Valentina and Elisa to tag along with our friend group to drive-in movies, museum exhibits, and more concerts than I can count. It wasn't a mad dash to cross things off an anxiety-induced bucket list, and I couldn't have pictured a better summer if I'd tried.

Felix is heading back home in two short weeks, but we've been making the most of our time together, so his departure doesn't feel as daunting as I thought it would. We've already agreed to visit each other as much as our classes and our gas money will allow, and we're going to call each other every night, even if it's only for five minutes. That part was an expert tip from Carmen and Ryan, who will be back to long-distance in a few weeks too. Felix has promised that he's not going to let a single one of my calls go to voice mail, and I believe him.

"I think this is definitive proof that you're the athletic one out of the two of us," Felix says, still clinging to my hands.

"That's very funny coming from a covert ballroom dancing expert."

"Anyone can be coordinated on land," he says, clearly stalling. "This is a death machine. This is gravity-defying."

I give him a pointed look, and he sighs, finally sucking it up and trying to stand on the board with both feet. He seems like he's okay, but as soon as I try to give him a little momentum to roll down the driveway, his legs turn to jelly. He pitches backward to try to correct his balance, and as he tumbles off, he takes me down with him.

"Damn," Felix wheezes, looking up at me from where he's sprawled on the sidewalk. "Did you just fall for me?"

I really don't want to laugh, but I can't hold it in. It's exactly the kind of horrible joke that would have made me want to roll my eyes three months ago. Now, it makes me want to kiss him. I lean over to press my lips against one of his dimples.

"You're so lucky you're hot, otherwise you'd never be able to get away with making such god-awful jokes."

Felix faux-gasps. "You think I'm hot?"

"Totally. But you're still the corniest person I've ever met."

"And you still love it," he says, scrunching his nose.

"I really do," I say, leaning in for another kiss, this time on his lips.

In two weeks, Felix will be back home, and summer will be over. But this time, childhood memories aren't the only thing I'll have left. Now I have new memories with Felix: belly laughs and long conversations, and sunrise coffee runs and art museum dates. I have the photo booth strip from my queerceañera pinned to my easel, and he'll have his copy tucked in his wallet. I'm not sad about the summer ending, because this time, I know it won't be our last.

Acknowledgments

TWO UNEXPECTED, MONUMENTAL things happened over the course of writing this book. First, I came out to my family. And second, I started making art again.

The first bit is kind of a long story, and since you literally just finished reading a whole entire novel, I'll spare you the details. But this book helped me navigate coming out on paper at the same time that I was trying to do it in real life, and I never would have worked up the courage to put myself out there if Joaquin hadn't done it first.

And then, he got me to draw again. Writing about Joaquin's love for art made me want to return to a hobby that I'd abandoned years ago. Now it's impossible to imagine what my days would look like if I didn't have that outlet and source of joy.

So I guess my first thank you goes to Joaquin. Writing his story helped me write my own story. Maybe that's a little corny, but, hey, this is a rom-com. What did you expect?

Many more thanks are in order, starting with my amazing agent, Mary Moore. Thank you for having my back and being my rock through the whirlwind of the last three years.

To my editor, Carolina Ortiz. I'm forever grateful for the incredible opportunity to work together. You helped bring the best out of this story and out of me as a writer, and this novel shines because of it. Thank you for helping me write a book that I'll always cherish.

Thank you to everyone at HarperTeen who helped make this book the best it could be: Rye White, Gweneth Morton, Meghan E. Pettit, Allison C. Brown, Shannon Cox, John Sellers, Kim Craskey, and Vivian Lee. And a big thank you to Julia E. Feingold, Alison Donalty, and Nicole Medina for the magical, swoon-worthy cover.

Thank you to the family members who accepted me when I was finally ready to open up. And to the friends who supported me through it all: Jenna, my favorite fake girlfriend and fellow rom-com scholar. Chai, who understands me and my books in a way that makes me want to cry if I think about it too hard. And Charisse, who loves love so much that it changed my life.

To Gege Akutami, who has caused me irreparable brain damage in the two years that I wrote and edited this book. Thank you for inspiring me to put my characters in increasingly ridiculous, emotionally distressing situations, much to the chagrin of my readers.

Thank you to the small army of strange and wonderful people who follow me online for my art. It's so weird that I get to give you all a shoutout in the acknowledgments for this novel when at its inception, I hadn't picked up a sketchbook in five years. Here's to hoping I don't get suspended on Twitter before this goes to print.

And to anyone who struggled to finish this book because it hit too close to home, because you're feeling the same pain that Joaquin felt. Even if you're alone right now, I promise there are people on this planet who were born to love you exactly as you are. Please stick around so that you can meet them one day.